ADVANCE PRAISE FOR **FOUR EQUATIONS**

"...The plot is very believable, as are the characters. Brennan is a likeable protagonist, and Elize is engaging. The "villains" are well portrayed and suitably reptilian (and if I may say so, typically Swiss!). And of, course, the story ends nicely, with cosmic (or more accurately, legal) justice tidying things up. FOUR EQUATIONS IS A GOOD READ."

-Jim Napier
Mystery and Crime Fiction Reviewer and Creator of
the award-winning website, deadlydiversions.com
Regular Contributor to *The Ottawa Review of Book*

"...A gripping tale, told with élan and touching on a little-remembered facet of the Holocaust, namely the incredible challenges Jews, who had fled and survived persecution, had to face when trying to recover their money from those to whom they had entrusted it for safekeeping. I couldn't put it down – read it cover to cover in one sitting!"

-Harley Mintz,
Former Vice Chair Deloitte, Canada

"Four Equations is an exciting thriller with an uncommon blend of financial intrigue, little known Holocaust truths, and family revelations spanning two generations. The author weaves a tale brought to life presumably from his own extraordinary experiences... a compelling realistic thriller that is a pleasure to read. Not to be missed."

-Mark Medicoff
Adjunct Professor of Communication
Champlain College of Vermont, Burlington
Lecturer at John Molson School of Business
Concordia University, Montreal

FOUR EQUATIONS

TO: Julie & John,

How is the Body? (yours I mean)
Enjoy the read.

Robert Landori

June 21/16

A NOVEL
BY
ROBERT LANDORI

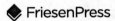 FriesenPress

Suite 300 - 990 Fort St

Victoria, BC, Canada, V8V 3K2

www.friesenpress.com

ISBN

978-1-4602-6624-3 (Hardcover)

978-1-4602-6625-0 (Paperback)

978-1-4602-6626-7 (eBook)

1. Fiction, Historical

Distributed to the trade by The Ingram Book Company

To: the memory of the 600,000 Hungarian
Jews who perished in the Holocaust

CAST OF MAIN CHARACTERS

Jack Brennan	A Cayman Islands Bankruptcy Trustee
Elize Haemmerle	Brennan's friend
George Brennan	US Treasury Secretary and Jack's uncle
Dr. Peter Gombos	A Hungarian Nobel Laureate
Dr. Hans Arbenz	Gombos's friend
Dr. Helmut Studer	The *Pro Nobis* Foundation's Managing Director
Enrico Moretti	A Swiss Banker
Jacques Odier	Another Swiss Banker
Hans-Ruedi Schmidt	Executive VP of Moretti & Cie Banquiers
Karl Stapfer	A Shareholder of Moretti & Cie Banquiers
Wolfgang Graf	A bank inspector

PROLOGUE

Budapest, December 1944

The snow kept falling. Relentlessly.

The woman was in very bad shape. Exhausted from lack of sleep, ravaged by hunger, and weakened by fear, she was barely functional. But she carried on, sustained by willpower alone, dragging her small, emaciated frame around the apartment she and her children shared with three other families.

"Never give up," she whispered as she surveyed the meager rations she kept hidden on the top shelf of her cupboard: some salt, a small bag of beans, another bag of flour, and her treasure and reserve of last resort, two-thirds of a stick of Hungarian dry salami. No sugar, no butter, and no lard. No bread, no milk, and no greens.

She saw she would have to go out to forage for food again before it was too late; otherwise, the children would never make it through the winter. They were already frail. Mike, eight, was seriously underweight for his age, and Andrew, six, had a chronic cough.

And outside, the snow kept falling. Relentlessly.

Her husband was dead, killed in an explosion some weeks earlier as he was crossing the Margit Bridge that had linked Pest with Buda.

It was dangerous to venture into the streets of the Hungarian capital where drunken, marauding Arrow Cross thugs, the Magyar version of Nazi Brown Shirts, roamed in gangs now, looking for Jews to kill. But she had to go out. How else could she hope to keep the children alive?

She could hear the thunder of the Russian siege guns and perceived from their sound that they were still some distance away, though the odd shell was already probing the buildings around her, crashing through nearby walls every now and then.

She had at least another month left to struggle through until spring brought salvation — hopefully. She was determined to keep her promise to her husband: to save the children no matter what and to guide them to a safe haven eventually. To Switzerland.

She looked through the window into the darkness of the late December afternoon and sensed the bitter cold it had brought. Like in Leningrad, the city of her birth. But then it was called St. Petersburg, and her parents had been rich: Father had been one of the Tsar's bankers, and Mother was the daughter of a very, very wealthy lumber merchant. Then came the revolution, and they had all fled — her parents and their parents, her in-laws, and her uncles, aunts, and cousins.

They fled in vain. Ultimately, they had all been caught by the Bolsheviks. Those executed on the spot had been the lucky ones; the ones sent to the Gulag had died slowly from malnutrition, the cold, and disease. Everyone except her. She had been studying in Hungary when the Russian Revolution broke out and had been able to finish her courses at the Jashik Akademia in Budapest. She was talented, and her portraits had found favor with the local *bourgeoisie.*

She was good at painting faces. That's how she had met her famous scientist husband: he had invited her to paint his mother's portrait. They had fallen in love and were married in 1933 — oh so long ago — and had settled in the nation's capital.

Outside the snow kept falling. Relentlessly.

She decided to postpone her foray until the next day.

Mercifully, they still had running water and a source of warmth. A small cast-iron wood stove now disfigured the space that had once been the elegant drawing room of a prominent industrialist's home. It came in handy for cooking and heating the place.

She enjoyed this privilege because her husband had been a Nobel Laureate and the most distinguished inhabitant of the mini-ghetto in which they lived, a *'csillagos ház'*, a building with a large Mogen Dovid, the Star of David, on its main door, signaling that the apartment house was an extension of the city's main ghetto into which the Nazis had jammed dozens upon dozens of families to await deportation "to the East" — a euphemism for death camps.

The home had no electricity and no gas. Only wood that she had managed to scavenge from the ruins of the building adjacent — parquet flooring that was hard to light but, once lit, would smolder and give off heat for a long time.

She could hear the Arrow Cross thugs in the street. They were on a rampage, but did it matter? Even if she did succeed in avoiding them, how would she manage to survive for the next month on her meager hoard of food?

For the moment, her family was safe, protected by the *Schutzpasses* the Swiss Consul had issued when they had moved into the building over which the Swiss flag flew. "Could a flag really protect you?" she wondered.

In the streets the snow kept falling. Relentlessly.

She lit her little kerosene lamp and fetched the flour and the beans and then carefully counted out their daily rations: thirty-six beans, fourteen for each child and eight for her. When the water in the pot on top of the stove came to a boil, she poured the beans into it and, while waiting for the beans to cook, mixed some flour and salt with water. She flattened the mix into little patties and placed them on the hot top for a few moments. Then she cut off four thin slices of salami and placed them on some of the patties.

By the time the patties were ready, her children were sitting next to her, plates in hand. She gave two patties with salami to each child and heaped his respective portion of beans on top.

They ate in silence.

When the meal was over, she turned down the light, and they went to bed still desperately hungry.

Andrew slept in two armchairs pushed together to form a bed — they had used his little bed for firewood. Mike, the eight-year-old, slept with his mother in his parents' bed where there was lots of room now that his father was dead.

And the snow kept falling. Relentlessly.

She fell asleep and dreamt that there were men at her door, trying to smash it down. She awoke with a start and realized that she was not dreaming. The Arrow Cross gangsters had broken in and were already in her room, screaming at them to get dressed and to go down into the street.

The children were whimpering, but they obeyed, as did she.

Downstairs, about a hundred Jews were lined up in a long column. They stood there, bewildered like sheep waiting to be slaughtered, whipped by the freezing winter wind and illuminated by the headlights of the trucks the thugs had brought along.

It was still snowing. Relentlessly.

"Forward march!" someone yelled, and they set out along the Teréz Ring. They passed the Western Railway Station and headed for the Danube, surrounded by Arrow Cross guards and jeering bystanders, some of whom spat in their direction.

She sensed that the end was near and that Fate would soon put "paid" to her aspirations to perpetuate her family's lineage. "At last, we've come to the final act of the horror show," she whispered as she walked on, holding her children tightly by the hand.

When they got to the river, their guards marshaled them into rows of three then tied each row of prisoners together at the wrist with telephone wire. There was a lot of jostling and pushing and shoving, but the boys, disoriented and silent, remained standing on either side of their mother.

The thugs pushed her forward, and she saw that the safety chains connecting the bollards along the Danube's parapet had been removed.

The woman was holding her two boys by the hand when the bullet smashed into her brain. She pitched forward and dragged her terrified children down with her into the freezing, murky river below. Instinctively, they began to tread water hard, fighting to keep themselves and their mother afloat. But they soon tired, mercifully numbed by the icy cold surrounding them.

And the snow, ashamed, stopped falling.

CHAPTER 1

Georgetown, Grand Cayman 2007

Police Commissioner Ian Pocock of the Royal Cayman Islands Police was quite drunk but tried hard to act sober. He had been deep in his usual Sunday night stupor, half comatose, when the call from the Governor had come through, ordering him to meet a trio of bankruptcy liquidators at the office.

Pocock was very put out. "To work...on Sunday night...what damnable cheek — and with bean counters to boot."

Pocock had asked for an hour's reprieve during which he managed to take a cold shower, scald his tongue with coffee far too hot to drink, and put on his uniform. His wife tried to help, but she, too, was under the influence so to speak and kept getting in his way. For which he cursed her soundly.

Thank God for his driver. The man had helped to button his boss's tunic, but that had taken some time. He, too, was drunk.

Everybody drank hard in the Cayman Islands, especially on Sunday night, to escape having to think about what had to be faced on Monday morning: stultifying boredom at the workplace.

✦

The meeting, which took place in the Commissioner's office at Police Headquarters on Elgin Avenue near the building in which the government's administrative offices were housed — the Glass House — was attended by three "bean counters" as Pocock called them. They were polite, alert, earnest, and determined *and* properly attired, wearing suits and ties.

The Financial Secretary was there, too. He was the one who broke the bad news. "The Cayman Islands have experienced unprecedented growth as a tax haven during the last three decades during which we had our share of local financial institutions going under, but none as involved in our economy as the Overseas Bank of Grand Cayman and its subsidiaries. I am very sorry to have to report that the bank's directors have decided to cease operations with immediate effect because the OBGC is no longer able to meet its obligations."

Commissioner Pocock nodded his head sagely and held his tongue. Though still "under the weather," he did discern the import of the news. OBGC had more than a hundred subsidiaries on the island and abroad, including the Cayman Fresh Water Company, the electric utility, the local bus company, two very large construction projects, three substantial restaurants, and the best bar and grill on the island, not to mention acres and acres of choice real estate. Hell, the group employed over 2,000 people, more than 15 percent of the labor force!

The Secretary, who seemed very preoccupied, looked at the policeman. "Do you realize what this means, Commissioner?"

"What do you mean?" Pocock was a firm believer in the doctrine of always answering a tricky question with another question. That way one never got into trouble. He tried to focus but was having a hard time of it.

The oldest of the bean counters, a balding, middle-aged, somewhat overweight man who was sweating profusely, came to his rescue. "My name is Albert Pinsky, Commissioner, and I am the senior insolvency partner in the Toronto Chartered Accountancy firm of Fitzpatrick and Company," he said and pointed to the man sitting next to the Financial Secretary. "You already know Richard

Grant, the partner in charge of our Cayman office. I'll let him explain what the Secretary means."

"The employees of the banking group we're speaking about represent almost 2,000 families and over 10,000 people." Grant was a tall, angular man, wearing enormous spectacles to accommodate the thick lenses he needed to see well. His accent was upper-class British, his education impeccable: Charterhouse and Caius College, Cambridge. "When they find out tomorrow morning that the paychecks they were given on Friday will not be honored, there will be hell to pay. One-third of the island's population will be affected, and most of the people will be very angry. It is my opinion, I'm afraid to say, that some of them will be angry enough to become violent."

Pocock, still at a loss for words, turned to the Secretary for guidance.

"The people will go down to the bank, and by noon there'll be quite a group there." The island's chief financial officer was known for not mincing words. "They'll be looking for someone to blame, and they'll blame the bankruptcy liquidators because they'll be the only ones around."

"How come?" The message was finally getting through to Pocock.

"The managing director of the bank and his family left the island this afternoon," the Secretary said. "Under the circumstances, the mob might attack the liquidators. Therefore, Commissioner, you must provide them with protection."

The policeman shot upright in his chair. It had suddenly struck him that both his wife's and his own savings were with the OBGC because it paid the highest rates of interest locally. And his life's savings were lost — to the men sitting in front of him. Rage made him stutter. "Th...that's absolutely not on," he said decisively, leaned forward aggressively and fell off his chair.

The third, the youngest, bean counter — his name was Jack Brennan — could not help laughing out loud, thereby earning looks of stern disapproval from his colleagues and the Financial Secretary.

CHAPTER 2

Jack Brennan kept tossing and turning in his bed, unable to sleep. The unexpectedly high humidity in his hotel room and the steady but bothersome droning of the air conditioner kept him awake.

Or was sleep eluding him because he was so upset?

The Marriott, located along the famous Seven Mile Beach on Grand Cayman, the largest of the three Cayman Islands situated approximately a thousand miles from the nearest point of the United States, Jack's native land, was definitely not where he wanted to be.

For the hundredth time, Jack asked himself how he could have been so stupid as to allow his uncle to talk him into playing bankruptcy liquidator in the Cayman Islands. Uncle George Rooney, his mother's oldest brother, was Secretary of the U.S. Treasury and Jack's favorite uncle, so when Jack got a call from him two weeks earlier asking for help, Brennan took the next plane from Toronto to Washington. They had lunch in a discreet corner of the Mayflower Hotel's Grill where Uncle George came straight to the point.

"Jack, I didn't want you to come around to my office, and I didn't want you to come out to Chevy Chase for dinner, either. You know why?"

Brennan shook his head and said nothing. He knew his Uncle George. The man hated idle chatter.

"I have a goddamn mole in my office and maybe one in my home, too; that's why."

The younger man gulped. His uncle was not given to swearing.

"I wanted everybody to see me here with you: uncle and nephew having a friendly lunch. Nobody would ever suspect that I'd be telling you state secrets in public, especially not at the Mayflower. Even the walls have ears around here."

Brennan could contain his curiosity no longer. "So why are we really here?"

"What I'm about to tell you is highly confidential." Uncle George looked at his nephew. "Understood?"

"Yes, Uncle."

"I have your word, then, that you'll keep your mouth shut?"

"Yes, sir."

"Here's the pitch, Jack." His uncle lowered his voice. "The Treasury has been trying to penetrate the Chicago Cosa Nostra boys' money laundering and money transferring network for years. We know that the money goes from the states to Grand Cayman and from there to Colombia to pay for the white powder."

The waiter came by to take their order. They both asked for steaks medium rare, mashed potatoes, and green salad.

The waiter continued to hover. "What about something to drink?"

"Double Saint Leger and water," they answered in unison. Scotch drinking ran in the family.

The waiter withdrew.

Uncle George continued. "We also know that there is a lot of black money stashed in the Caymans by the boys as well as by hundreds of ordinary Americans."

"So?"

"I want their names and account numbers, Jack."

"Get your people to go down there, Uncle George, and bribe some of the tellers in the banks. I'm sure there'd be plenty of takers."

Uncle George shook his head. "We tried that a dozen years back and got caught. Since then, the Cayman police keep a very sharp lookout for this kind of thing and, frankly, we've run out of new faces. Besides, the mole keeps tipping them off."

Busy eating, neither man said anything for a while.

When the coffee came, Uncle George broke the silence. "We got a tip from the Bank of Virginia that one of their investments in the Caymans — a fair-sized banking group with strong local involvement — is about to go belly up. Apparently, its directors are looking for a friendly bankruptcy liquidator to help them."

The penny dropped for Brennan. "And you told them to contact my firm's office in Cayman."

Uncle George was very pleased. "You're a bright boy, Jack."

"So?" Brennan knew exactly what was coming but held his fire. He wanted Uncle George to beg a little. He did not expect what happened next.

"I'm not going to beat around the bush, Jack, and I'm not going to beg," his uncle hissed. He was very angry. "We're a family that values public service. Your grandfather was a Medal of Honor winner who served his country in many ways, including a stint in Switzerland as Ambassador during the Second World War, so wipe that knowing smirk off your face and listen up. It's your turn in the barrel, Jack. Your time has come to pay for the privilege of being a member of my family, so I'm not asking — I'm telling you — what you are to do."

"And what would that be, Uncle?" Brennan was quick to adopt a conciliatory tone. He loved his mother's oldest brother and his handsome French wife and had not meant to offend. He was also very proud of the Rooney family's history of public service. Besides, he owed Uncle George big time.

"Your partner in the Cayman office, Grant is his name I think, will be retained by the bank's directors to act as their liquidator, but his staff's not big enough to handle such a large job. He'll ask his Toronto office for reinforcements." Uncle George gave his nephew a hard look. "You are to volunteer to be on the team."

And that had been that.

Uncle George had then outlined what he expected Jack to do. "After you've found your bearings, get chummy with the staff and try to get this Grant fellow to put you in charge of listing the bank's clients and their addresses. This will give you access to information about everybody who ever had money in the bank."

"Got it. What next?"

"Scan the data to identify the really big accounts, say everything with over 50,000 dollars in it, and start looking at what belongs to whom."

Jack more than understood. His uncle had just condemned him to working like a slave for the next six months under considerable pressure far from his familiar hunting grounds, and probably exposed to some physical danger. The prospect of physical danger did not bother him, nor the likelihood of some discomfort. What he did not like was the idea of having to live in an intellectual vacuum while spying on his countrymen on an island with a population numbering less than 30,000 souls.

Jack was a big-city boy, with a highly eclectic circle of friends, a concert-goer, a museum visitor, and a fierce debater on just about everything. To put it mildly, he was pissed. And trapped. There was no way anybody in the family could get George Rooney to change his mind once he had made it up.

The Buffalo Rooneys, of solid Irish stock, were a closely knit family. Their patriarch, "Wild" Bill Rooney, had earned his nickname on the football fields of Ivy League universities. A determined, overwhelming presence, much respected by the opposition, he had gone to war for his country immediately after graduating, and, having distinguished himself by winning the Medal of Honor during World War I, he had gone to work for the State Department.

Shortly before the outbreak of World War II, President Roosevelt had sent Bill Rooney to Bern, Switzerland's capital, as his personal envoy, tasked with evaluating the European situation from an American point of view. An astute observer, the Irishman realized how important advanced information gathering would become for a "modern" nation. After Pearl Harbor, he persuaded Roosevelt to form the OSS, the predecessor of the CIA.

At age fifty-six, Bill Rooney had married a Hungarian woman, twenty-seven years his junior, whom he had met overseas and who had given him three children: George, the eldest, then Patrick and, finally, May, Jack's mother.

George, Bill's son, had also gone overseas, to Vietnam, and brought home a French bride. Patrick, George's younger brother, a Jesuit priest, became Bishop of Buffalo. Their sister, May, married a Canadian, Michael Brennan, from Toronto.

Other than his family, Michael Brennan had two passions – flying and football. He had attended Queen's University in Kingston, Ontario, and had played football there with great enthusiasm and considerable success. He had married May a year after graduating and, very popular, rapidly became a wealthy automobile dealer in Buffalo where he had moved to be near May's family. Passionate about Canadian football, Michael bought a small Cessna and flew up regularly to Montreal, Toronto, Hamilton, and Ottawa – wherever his favorite team, the Toronto Argos, would play.

May and Michael had three children: Mary, the eldest, then Niall, two years her junior and, finally, Jack, who was three years younger than his brother. Jack was born in 1978. A talented, handsome Irish charmer, by the time he left high school, he spoke English, French, and a smattering of Hungarian that he had learned from his grandmother, Ilona, who doted on him.

When Jack was eleven, his father decided to fly up to Toronto to attend the Grey Cup, *the* annual Canadian football epic, and take Niall with him. Jack had wanted desperately to go, too, but his dad said no; he was too young.

"Wait till next year," his father told him. "You'll be old enough by then."

When Jack came home from school on the Monday after the game, he found his mother in her kitchen, weeping uncontrollably. His sister, Mary, five years his senior, was there, too, and in tears, being comforted by Uncle Patrick, the bishop, who, when he saw Jack, took him by the hand and guided him upstairs to his room.

They sat down on Jack's bed and Uncle Patrick put his arms around Jack's shoulders. "Jack," he whispered into the boy's ear, "I'm asking you to be brave and strong because I have very bad news to tell you. Your dad's plane is six hours overdue. We suspect that he lost his way home in the fog. By now, he must have run out of gas, and although we're still looking for him, chances are we will not find him in the dark. You must pray for him, my son."

At first, Jack did not understand. "What about Niall?" he asked. "Is he all right?"

The priest looked at his nephew and his heart broke for him. "I'm afraid your brother is missing, too."

"Oh my God...not Niall...please God, not Niall...not Niall, too...." Jack fell back on his bed. He could no longer hear what his uncle was saying; he was overwhelmed by fear, a fear of being all alone in the world without protection, a fear that was just more than he could bear. Niall, his older brother, his defender and best friend, was either dying or already dead. And his beloved father was probably dead, too.

"There's still hope, my boy..." Jack heard his uncle's voice through the pain of grief, "... you must pray to God for their safety...."

But by the end of the next day, with fog still blanketing Lake Ontario, Jack realized that only a miracle would bring his brother and father back to him.

The search for the small aircraft went on for ten more days with no results, and Michael Brennan and his son Niall were officially declared dead a month later. Because there were no bodies to bury, there was no closure for the family. After the memorial mass, May Brennan and her two remaining children went home and tried to put the shattered pieces of their lives together.

Jack, who had been very close to his father and brother, was devastated. Wracked by guilt about not being on board with them, he seemed inconsolable, tortured by nightmares about Niall's last moments. Had he been conscious and drowned slowly, or had he hit his head and felt nothing? Or had they run out of gas and glided gently to a landing on the lake then waited for hours on board the slowly sinking plane for help that never came, finally succumbing to the cold in the freezing November water?

Jack would wake up screaming in the middle of the night, and the only person who could console him was his sister, Mary, who would take him in her arms and rock him to sleep, crying with him as they mourned their loss together. With no contemporary to turn for help because he was by far the youngest of his generation of Rooneys, Uncle George's children being in their twenties, it took Jack two years to master his grief. By then, he had become an introverted loner who had difficulty making friends at school.

The accident changed Jack in other ways, too. Every traumatic event is followed by a grieving phase then a phase of blind anger that lashes out against everything and everybody. This anger usually subsides after a while, but in Jack's heart, it continued to fester and focused on God, whom he could not forgive for destroying his family. So he gave up on God and refused to accept that there was one. Nor could he, no matter how hard he tried, get over his fear of flying.

On Jack's fifteenth birthday he went to see George Rooney. "What I prize in a person above all," he told his uncle with unusual insight for a teenager, "is courage, physical and intellectual courage. Please, please, help me conquer my fear of flying."

Deeply touched, the older man embraced his nephew wordlessly and held him for a long, long time.

Thereafter, several times each year, uncle and nephew flew up to Canada in a small plane to hunt and fish in the company of Uncle George's trusted companions, one of whom was a behavior therapist, who, knowing the boy's problem, helped him overcome his fear gradually.

During these trips Jack learned how wonderful it was to have a close-knit family and true and trusted friends, how important it was to be loyal to them, and how much one could learn from older people when one listened carefully and with respect.

Jack found that listening, as opposed to just hearing, was an art that yielded incredibly rich rewards. He would always remember the quiet evenings in the fishing cabin on the shores of Lake Sainte Anne, when, after they had cleaned and gutted the fish they had caught and had washed up after they had fried and eaten it, his uncle and his friends would settle down to discuss world affairs, analyze the latest news, and bet on this stock or that. They treated him as an equal, though he was only in his mid-teens, patiently answering his questions and, most importantly, helping him discover at a very early age what really made the world go 'round — who you knew was more important than what you knew.

While fishing and casting, Jack also discovered that he had unusually good eye-hand coordination and that he was exceptionally athletic, talents he used to become an outstanding high-school football player. Unfortunately, he was only five foot ten, so a career in the NFL was out.

To honor his father, Jack enrolled in the international MBA program at Queen's University, a college he had often visited with his father. He had liked the school and the city of Kingston; the town had the feel of a young, rambunctious community, which of course it was and is, because it boasted three first-class institutions of higher learning: Queen's University, the Royal Military College, and the Pen, the Federal penitentiary. It followed that, during the scholastic year, fully a quarter of the town's 100,000-odd population was made up of students and young soldiers from the nearby Canadian Forces Base.

Football helped Jack in many ways. He learned through the school of hard physical knocks that you're nothing unless your mates are willing to back you up and that teamwork is a matter of give and take. He discovered that you're only followed as a leader if you are willing to step up and lead by example and that, to succeed, physical courage must be combined with principled behavior and perseverance in times of adversity.

In his last year at the university, Jack realized that deal making fascinated him. So, after obtaining his MBA, he went to work for a Toronto public accounting firm with international affiliations that had recently started a mergers and acquisitions department. His Irish charm and intelligence, his fame as a footballer, and his easy way with people soon made him a great rainmaker.

New clients flocked to Jack because he had a reputation for being principled, smart and daring. He was just beginning to hit his stride when the call had come from Uncle George, whose request would force him to overhaul his entire value system.

"Let's face it," Jack said to himself on his way back to Toronto, "my uncle is asking me to spy on my fellow citizens, some of whom may have perfectly legitimate reasons for maintaining accounts offshore: couples breaking up...inventors patenting their intellectual property offshore in anticipation of world-wide distribution...people fleeing persecution.... There are dozens of such reasons," he kept on arguing with himself. "I will be running the risk of identifying an innocent guy who will then be investigated for years, which will cause him unnecessary and undeserved grief."

Jack ended up concluding that there was only one way out of his dilemma — he would have to investigate each "suspect" thoroughly before giving his name to his uncle's people. And the more he thought about it now that he was in Cayman, the more convinced he became that he had been right.

"One hell-of-a-lot of extra work," he muttered and finally dozed off.

CHAPTER 3

After a few hours of restless sleep, Jack decided to get some exercise and went for an early walk along the West Bay Road toward George Town, the capital of the islands. He knew from past visits to the West Indies that there is a special smell to dawn in the Caribbean. Just before the sun appears over the horizon, the landward breeze carries with it a whiff of salt and seaweed, a signal for Earth's creatures that a new day is breaking.

At seven, Jack was at the OBGC group's head office on the land side of West Bay Road where he huddled with several of his colleagues, including a nervous Richard Grant and a sweating Albert Pinsky. The older man was calling the shots.

"You look like shit, Jack. What's the matter?"

"Couldn't sleep."

Pinsky was not pleased. "We're short-staffed on this assignment, Jack, so we need every man to pull his weight. You're useless to me tired, so give up your bachelor's habits for the duration and make sure you stop hitting the singles' bars after work."

Stung by the unfair jibe, Jack was about to protest, but just then six local Fitzpatrick employees arrived, and Grant began to hand out assignments.

At ten o'clock, the hour when the bank would usually open, a notice was posted on the front door, informing the general public that the OBGC was closed until further notice. Simultaneously, a police cruiser appeared and positioned itself across the street from the building. Pinsky, who had taken over the office of the bank's president, asked Jack to join him there.

"In about half an hour, the shit will hit the fan, but you and I have an appointment with the lawyers at noon. Be ready."

"But what about —"

"No buts. Talking to the lawyers right off the bat is essential to ensure that we're legally protected on all sides. We'll have to leave Grant and his people to hold the fort here as best they can."

By the time Pinsky and Jack got back to the bank, the situation had turned ugly. There were four police cars on the scene, and the eight officers on site were finding it difficult to control the rowdy crowd of about fifty workers, who were all wearing yellow hard hats with OBGC Construction stencilled on them.

People were shoving and jostling. A brick, thrown by someone in the crowd, came sailing across the street and smashed through a first-floor window. A fifth police cruiser appeared seemingly out of nowhere, and a sergeant got out, bullhorn in hand.

"You are ordered to disperse immediately," he shouted at the crowd. "Those still in the street a minute from now will be arrested and taken into custody."

Reluctantly, most of the workers left, and Pinsky and Jack slid gratefully through the front door.

Just before normal closing time, a bailiff served papers on Pinsky, ordering him and his two co-liquidators to appear in court within twenty-four hours and to show cause why they should not be replaced "by persons more qualified and more familiar with local conditions" than they were.

The hearing took place in the Grand Court before the Honorable Justice Charles Adams. The liquidators' lawyer, James McKenzie, coached by Jack, gave a sterling performance before a crowd of angry creditors. The hearing was unfortunately marred by so many interruptions that the judge finally ordered the courtroom to be cleared of spectators.

This, as it turned out, was a big mistake. By reducing the

transparency of the legal process, the judge unwittingly caused the majority of Caymanians to resent the liquidators for the rest of their time in the islands. In the end, the judge upheld the appointment of Pinsky, Grant, and Jack but changed the bankruptcy from a voluntary to a so-called 'official' liquidation, which meant that Jack and his colleagues, now called Official Liquidators, had a new boss, the grand court judge himself, to whom they were to report on their progress on a weekly basis.

The judge's parting words to the trio had an ominous ring. "Bear in mind that bank secrecy is sacred in the Cayman Islands and that breaching it is a criminal offense punishable by imprisonment, so be forewarned."

This admonishment caused Jack to worry greatly. How was he going to help Uncle George reach his goal of busting the Chicago money-laundering cabal without risking a jail term for his sorry ass and betraying his principles?

CHAPTER 4

Frau Doktor Juris Elize Haemmerle always dreaded the *Pro Nobis* Foundation's annual meetings of its administrators, as the directors of that noble organization called themselves. They were a pack of pompous, self-righteous fat-cat males who held sway over a dominion of companies that billed billions of dollars a year for goods ranging from simple paper boxes to cutting-edge, sophisticated medical equipment and for services as elementary as those offered by modest cleaning establishments and as complex as those supplied by the most advanced civil engineering consultants.

Elize estimated that the Foundation's holdings had a net market value of more than 150 million dollars and that this figure was growing at an annual rate of about 15 percent.

Though its nine administrators, all men and Swiss citizens, had monthly salaries of only a relatively modest 30,000 Swiss francs each, they made millions on the stock options granted them by the companies whose activities they oversaw as directors.

In contrast, Elize had a total compensation package of 300,000 francs a year, from which she was expected to pay for her travelling expenses. These represented about one-third of her emoluments because she was required to act as the Foundation's roving auditor as well as its secretary.

Elize's was a strange life. For three out of four weeks every month, as secretary, she was the prisoner of her office from eight o'clock in the morning until late at night and at the beck and call of the managing administrator. During the last week of each month, Elize, as auditor, would hit the road to check up on the activities of the twenty-odd enterprises in North America and Western Europe in which the Foundation held "significant" interests.

The managing administrator was *Doktor* Helmut Studer, the grandson of the founder of Moretti & Cie Banquiers. The person heading the Foundation was always a Moretti descendant by tradition and preferably a banker, because the Foundation was the bank's biggest client.

Aged thirty-six, Elize was a remarkably handsome woman. Of medium height and beautiful proportions with elegant legs, full breasts, and ample hips, she had full lips in an olive-skinned, oval face surrounded by lustrous black hair, accentuated by pale, strikingly greenish-blue eyes. Her beauty was typically that of an Italo-Swiss woman. She exuded sex appeal.

Elize's dazzling smile conquered the most reluctant executive, and her reserved manner elicited immediate cooperation from those she met because they were all taken by her sincerity. This helped her greatly in gaining people's trust quickly and allowed her to function very efficiently as an auditor. People confided in her, thereby enabling her to identify the occasional bad apple or improper procedure that exists as a matter of course in any organization as extensive and complex as was the Foundation and its affiliated companies.

Elize wore a wedding band on her right hand as was customary for married persons in Europe, but this did not discourage the people, male and female, with whom she came in contact. Many considered propositioning her, and a few actually did. She always let them down gently and politely, never burning her bridges with anyone.

Because of her exceptional intelligence, Elize had been able to finish university at the age of twenty-one and pass her bar exams two years later. For a couple of years, she worked in a well-known patent attorney's office, after which she married her childhood sweetheart.

They were planning to have at least four children. Then, tragedy struck. While she was cooking a festive meal to celebrate their first wedding anniversary, her husband had gone to fetch her parents, her brother, and her in-laws. The station wagon was broadsided by a speeding truck, driven by a drunk who had failed to stop at a red light. Everybody was killed except her brother, Kurt, who was left a paraplegic.

When Kurt was well enough, Elize took him to live with her at her late parents' house — their childhood home — halfway up Zurich's *Sonnenberg,* near the Dolder Hotel. By then, all the insurance money was gone, and she had to find a job well-paying enough to ensure that her brother was looked after properly.

Elize's luck turned. At a seminar, she met Dr. Studer who, impressed by her elegance and sophistication as well as by her professional qualifications and her reputation for discretion, hired her as his personal assistant. That had been eight years earlier, during which Studer kept entrusting her with increasingly greater responsibilities. After five years at the Foundation, he promoted her to secretary and auditor.

Elize's cellphone rang. It was her brother.

"Bist du fertig?"

"Ja, ja, I'm ready. I'll be right down." Understandably insecure since the accident, Kurt would become agitated every time Elize was about to leave him for her monthly inspection trips, so she developed a routine that would lessen his separation anxiety. On the Saturday of her departure, she'd make him brunch, and then she'd go to work for a few hours. The Foundation's chauffeur would drive him to the office in mid-afternoon, and, together, they would head for the airport.

This time, though, she was going away for ten days and not the usual seven because the annual meeting was to take place in New York instead of in Switzerland.

"You've got to listen to this," her brother was saying as the car neared Kloten, Zurich's international airport. Elize could clearly hear the rising anxiety in his voice. "I need to produce the next issue of Western Economic Analysis a week earlier, and I have to have your input as soon as possible."

Now wheelchair-bound, Kurt, an economist, had tried to pull his life together after the accident by getting a job as a lecturer at the university. As time passed, he also began to publish a monthly news-letter in which he'd distill the information his sister would gather from Foundation executives whom she'd meet during her monthly trips. He produced these anonymous four-page musings informally for his friends who would analyze them at the cocktail parties he'd host at his house on the Fridays before Elize's monthly trips.

Elize and Kurt lived a modest and very orderly life, all routines worked out carefully in advance because money was terrifyingly tight. Looking after Kurt cost a great deal of money and took a great deal of time. No concert or dating for her, not even a movie. They'd watch films at home on TV.

Lately, Elize had begun to worry about how long she could keep coping with the stress under which she labored incessantly — at home and at the office — without relief from the struggle for finan-cial survival to the exclusion of almost everything else.

At thirty-six, she was very clear about her mental and physical state of health, keenly aware that her beauty was fading and that however hard she worked at keeping fit, the wrinkles would appear, her proud breasts would start sagging, and her firm buttocks would turn into saddlebags. Mentally, she was still focused, but this, too, would start changing soon; her heightened state of anxiety was beginning to affect her ability to seek escape in deep sleep.

For some time now, Elize had been trying to alleviate the stress by drinking a couple of hefty glasses of red wine with her evening meals, but this didn't help. Instead of relaxing her, the alcohol aroused her sexually and caused her to dream the most incredibly pornographic dreams as she tossed and turned restlessly in her widow's bed. Of course, in her dreams, she was always the main character who would unfailingly awake before reaching sexual satisfaction.

As a result, she'd awake most mornings frustrated and as tense as ever, fervently promising to seek out an acceptable sexual partner as soon as possible with whom she could allow herself to alleviate the ache and longing in her loins without fear of compromising her independence. But where and when and with whom? She never had any time to go looking anywhere, except among the people she'd meet during her auditing trips who were mostly married men always ready for a quick lay with a handsome woman as long as it involved nothing but sex and seldom, if ever, intimacy. And, of course, there was always the danger of STDs, not to mention the possibility of being discovered and exposed by a jealous wife.

Elize was working in a man's world in which the male of the species had all the privileges as long as his "improprieties" were not found out and exposed to public scrutiny in hypocritical, puritanical Swiss society. She sighed and forced herself to face the situation at hand.

"I'll look at your notes during the flight tonight," she promised Kurt who was trying so pathetically to keep her at his side for as long as possible. "I'll email you my comments from Chicago tomorrow."

She kissed his forehead and got out of the car. Leaving him was always heart-rending, even after so many years of monthly goodbyes.

CHAPTER 5

The surface of the rugby pitch west of George Town in Grand Cayman was the hardest that Jack Brennan had ever played on, and he had played on frozen turf in Montreal in the dead of winter. But then, perhaps, it just seemed so damned hard because rugby was played in short pants and short-sleeved shirts without sewn-in padding, or helmet, or other protective gear.

Jack had played Canadian intercollegiate football for four years and had loved the twelve-man setup, the longer field, and the intimate atmosphere of the smaller stadia. He was physically and mentally tough. At five foot ten and weighing only a muscular 170 pounds, he had to be. His teammates and those against whom they played were powerful bruisers, most of them much heavier than he. Jack liked the physical contact of the sport, which was the reason he decided to learn to play rugby in the Caymans. After a long day's boring work in the liquidators' offices, where one stupid, mindless mistake followed the next, he needed a place where he could knock heads together with impunity.

He suspected that most of his teammates and their opponents — mainly lawyers and accountants and bankers — felt the same way. That's why not only the matches themselves but also the piss-ups that followed them were so wild.

The players, composed of English, Irish, Welsh, and Scottish stock and, of course, of superbly athletic Caribbean blacks, had one thing in common: they craved rough, physical contact.

Jack's mentor was an Irishman by the name of Rhyall Gallagher. Six foot three and weighing 230 pounds, he was very fast for his size, but Jack was faster. On the other hand, Gallagher could drink more than Jack, and when he drank, he became indiscreet. For this, Jack became eternally grateful, because Gallagher's indiscretion ultimately helped him get out from under the pressure his uncle George was exerting on him.

Months had gone by since the start of the liquidation, and Jack's abode was no longer the Marriott. He had rented a furnished condo in the Villas of the Galleon where he lived the typical life of an ex-pat bachelor, buying groceries only in amounts necessary for minimal culinary activities. There was no need for more. Most weekday nights he worked late, so he restricted himself to one main meal a day, lunch, which he ate in the company of his like-minded colleagues at one or the other of the island's English-style pubs.

The exception was rugby night when, after the game, the team would go for a monumental piss-up at the Cayman Arms, where they'd consume large quantities of beer accompanied by various dishes of very unhealthy fast food the likes of hamburgers, steak, and kidney pie.

Jack spent his weekends on the beach, resting, reading, and chatting up girls, some of whom he had no difficulty bedding. As for cultural activities, there were few, mainly the occasional visit to the Harquail Theatre to see productions of musicals, drama, and concerts featuring principally local amateur talent. Cultural contact with the outside world was mainly through satellite TV and visits of short duration to Miami.

On the whole, Jack's was a boring, routine existence, exacerbated by a feeling of isolation. He sensed that his friends and contacts in Toronto — the "community" that he had created for himself there — were slowly slipping away from him as his life as a transient, a nomad, dragged on.

He also realized that he was beginning to run out of excuses with which to keep Uncle George off his back. Finally 'fessing up during a visit to Washington, Jack told the Secretary that helping the U.S. Treasury would mean breaching the Cayman Islands' Bank Secrecy Act, a criminal offense for which they would send him to prison.

"If they caught you."

"True, but I simply can't risk it, Uncle. Once charged with a criminal offense in the Caymans, I would never be able to get a job anywhere in the British Commonwealth's financial community, and my ability to travel would be severely limited."

"How come?"

"I couldn't go to any country that had an extradition agreement with the Caymans."

"Big deal."

"Just think Canada and the U.K. on one end of the scale and Monaco on the other."

"Monaco?" Uncle George was laughing. "You must be joking."

"No. I looked it up. Besides, breaking the law is not right."

George Rooney was undeterred. "Jack, there's law, and there's morality. At times, they're in conflict. Every decent man has to come to grips with this dilemma sooner or later." The uncle looked at his nephew with a speculative eye. "As I said when we first talked about your assignment, Jack, you're a smart boy. I'm sure you'll find a solution to your problem *soon*."

CHAPTER 6

The liquidation dragged on till Christmas when Pinsky called a halt to proceedings and sent everyone home for two weeks' vacation. Jack spent ten days in Buffalo visiting family, especially his grandmother, Ilona. The crusty old woman, in her nineties, was still very much alert, and Jack enjoyed listening to her talking about the post-Second World War life that she had lived both in Europe and in the United States.

On his way back to Cayman, Jack met Gallagher for a booze-up in Miami before returning to the salt mines.

"I'm set for months to come," the Irishman bragged.

"What's that mean?" Jack couldn't follow.

It was eleven o'clock on a Sunday morning, and they were drinking tequila shooters with beer chasers at the liquidation's apartment in the Sheraton Towers on Brickell Boulevard.

"I've lined up enough pussy to provide for steady variety until Easter."

"What's your plan?"

Gallagher grinned. "You know how crazy I get when I can't get off that damned rock at least once every six weeks?"

Jack nodded. All the bachelors condemned to work in Grand Cayman felt the same way.

"I usually leave on Friday after work, spend Saturday and Sunday in the bars and restaurants of Coconut Grove, and then I hightail it out to Chicago on the last flight, visit my clients there, and give them copies of their accounts. Late Tuesday, I fly back to Cayman."

"Not really a restful regime." Preoccupied with his painful meeting with Uncle George the day after Christmas, Jack wasn't really paying much attention.

"To think I used to waste a whole day and sometimes more, trying to line up poon-tang in Miami," Gallagher was saying. "Well, that's over with."

"How come?" Jack was just being polite. His mind was on how to meet Uncle George's ultimatum. The Rooney family's patriarch had been firm. "I need results from you by Easter, Jack. Otherwise, I'll have to look elsewhere," he had said. This meant that Uncle George's disposition toward Jack would change drastically and that someone else would begin to enjoy his benevolent support. Not a career-enhancing situation when your uncle is the U.S. Secretary of the Treasury.

Gallagher droned on, oblivious to his friend's discomfiture. Apparently, he had met a very foxy lady in the Coconut Grove Hotel's lobby and hit it off with her right from the start. They spent a long weekend screwing each-other's brains out. Then she told him that she ran a very discreet call-girl ring.

"So?"

"We struck a deal," said Gallagher proudly. "In return for a 250-dollar monthly retainer, she'd let me date as many of her employees as I want."

"Per month? Where's the profit for her in that?"

"Jack, don't be obtuse. I have time to overnight in Miami only about six times a year."

"Well, then, where's the bargain for you?"

The Irishman had it all figured out. What he'd save on not having to wine and dine the women he had to chat up before getting one to go to bed with him would make up for more than the retainer.

"There are three advantages: I'm guaranteed to get laid, I'm guaranteed variety, and I save a ton of time."

"When does this thing go into effect?"

"February 1."

"And when do you go to Chicago next?"

"In March, a week before Easter."

The word "Easter" did it for Jack. He now knew exactly how to obtain the information Uncle George was after — and without breaking the Cayman Bank Secrecy Laws to boot.

He called the Secretary at his home in Chevy Chase that evening and spent half an hour on the phone with him.

CHAPTER 7

Elize Haemmerle's North American trip was rapidly degenerating into a nightmare. In Chicago, she discovered that the airline had lost her luggage. Because she had to visit three cities in five days, her clothes didn't catch up with her until the following Saturday when she checked into the Regency on New York's Fifth Avenue, less than an hour before she was to attend the administrators' annual dinner.

Her escort for the evening was to be her male assistant who had flown in from Zurich to organize the event at which twenty-one chief executive officers, their chief financial officers, and their wives were to dine, dance and mingle with the seven administrators and *their* spouses. Exactly one hundred people at ten tables of ten, bursting with false *bonhomie* in a desperate effort to create Swiss-style *gemütlichkeit*. Crushingly phony and boring, but attendance was *de rigeur!*

Elize made do somehow because she was a practiced war horse. She did her best to charm her table companions, two of whom, a man and a woman, openly signaled that they were more than fleetingly interested in her physical attributes.

The event's highlight was a send-off for the oldest of the seven administrators. The eighty-four-year-old Dr. Petitmaitre, who had served the Foundation for fifty years, took leave of his many friends and resigned as administrator with immediate effect in a moving farewell ceremony that left not a single eye dry.

Pleading near exhaustion immediately after the speeches, Elize fled the ballroom and retired to her bed to crash. On Sunday, finally her elegant and radiant self again after eight hours' sleep, she attended the brunch for CEOs that the Foundation arranged annually at which each guest was allowed five minutes to speak about his previous year's achievements.

At three o'clock in the afternoon, she got ready for what she hoped would be the last official engagement of her North American tour: the administrators' annual meeting.

Dr. Studer opened proceedings by announcing that yet another administrator, the Foundation's scientific advisor, Dr. Frederik Faerber, who taught physics at the university, also wished to retire.

"I'm very sorry," the good doctor told his assembled colleagues, "but the state of my health requires me to lighten my load. I resign with regret because I enjoy serving the Foundation, which I have done for the last seven years."

The scientist's resignation was duly accepted, and Elize was instructed to pay Faerber the customary retirement fee for administrators who had served for more than five years: half a million Swiss francs.

"We now have two vacancies to fill," Dr. Studer went on, "but presently have no suitable candidates to fill them."

Enrico Moretti, Dr. Studer's cousin and, like Studer, also a grandson of the bank's founder, raised his hand. "Would I be out of order if I suggested that we consider reducing the number of liquidators from seven to five?" Moretti, the managing director of the Moretti Bank, was a soft-spoken man.

How convenient, Elize thought. Moretti was an administrator of the Foundation and the boss of the bank, and Studer was a director of the bank and the boss of the Foundation. And they were family. Another administrator, the youngest of the lot, Hans-Ruedi Schmidt, was the bank's senior vice president. Therefore, if the number of administrators were to be reduced to five, the bank would have a stranglehold on the Foundation's operations — three administrators out of five.

Schmidt cleared his throat. At forty-five, he was a mere child compared to the others, most of whom were in their late sixties. "I find that to be a very good idea," he said enthusiastically. He was an outsider and would always remain one, however much he would try to brown-nose his way in.

"It would simplify administration considerably," he added and looked at Elize with open malevolence. Ever since she had rebuffed his sexual advances a couple of years earlier, he had had it in for her. God, she hated that man.

"Would you then care to make a motion to that effect?" Studer asked.

Schmidt's reply was prompt. "I so move." He had been a professional accountant and systems and methods expert whom the bank had sought out some years earlier to overhaul its chaotic and antiquated accounting system and who was nothing more nor less than Moretti's puppet.

Studer nodded to Elize who made a note.

The remaining two administrators looked shocked. They had accepted serving the Foundation with the understanding that four out of the seven administrators would be independents, that is to say persons not affiliated with Moretti & Cie Banquiers. But they said nothing because neither had been with the Foundation long enough to qualify for the five-year retirement bonus. Studer had them where he wanted them — at his mercy.

Elize shuddered. She had just witnessed the transformation of a semi-public, independent, and civic-minded Foundation into a virtual subsidiary of a predatory bank. It was only a matter of time before the remaining independent administrators, and she as well, would be asked to resign. And Schmidt would take over her job.

The motion to reduce the administrators' number was passed, and after spending another hour on housekeeping matters, Studer formally ended the meeting. On his way out, he signaled for Elize to follow him. She did so with her heart in her throat.

"Of course, you'll have dinner with Heddi and me as usual," he said, giving her a friendly smile, then added, "I'm sorry I did not tell you in advance what Enrico and I had decided to do this afternoon, but I just couldn't find you anywhere."

To a degree that was true. She had, indeed, been busy from the moment that she had arrived for Saturday night's dinner.

"Please do come, and let's make it an informal affair. My wife is so looking forward to our annual gossip *cum post mortem* meal." He sounded genuinely friendly and concerned, so she accepted, as she did every year.

When she got back to her room that night after a delightful dinner at Le Papillon, she found a note from him, accompanied by an immense box of chocolates and a Neiman Marcus gift certificate for 500 dollars.

"I need a special favor," Studer had written. "Would it be possible for you to type up the minutes of our meeting early tomorrow morning so that I can get them signed by everybody before they leave for home at noon?"

She complied with his wish, even though it meant forgoing the secret day trip to Bermuda she had planned so carefully for Monday.

Twice a year, when in New York on Foundation business, she would take a day off "for shopping." In fact, she would use the time to visit her attorneys' office in Hamilton, Bermuda, to check up on her bank account — her ticket to financial independence.

Her offshore activity had come about quite by accident. She was waiting for the VP of Finance in the staff cafeteria of a German company she was inspecting. Since he had told her that he'd be late, she had brought along a copy of her brother's mimeographed newsletter and became totally engrossed in it.

"Reading a love letter?"

Startled, she looked up. It was the VP.

"Actually, it's sort of a newsletter." She was blushing. The man had caught her off guard. He laughed and sat down beside her.

"A likely story."

She handed him the paper. "Here. See for yourself."

After glancing at the newsletter, he stuck it in his pocket absent-mindedly, his attention already focused on how to solve the problems they were going to talk about during lunch.

A couple of weeks later, he called her.

"That was a damned fine piece of work."

"What was?" She didn't follow.

"That newsletter you gave me. I showed it around a bit, and my colleagues found it interesting, too. They'd like to read the next issue. How often is it published and where?"

One thing led to another until the newsletter became a regular monthly publication in English and German. The VP talked it up with his counterparts in the Foundation's other affiliates, and most of them decided to subscribe. This created a dilemma for Elize. She feared that the administrators would not approve of her being involved in a commercial enterprise that dealt with "the Foundation Family."

She solved her problem by setting up a numbered company in Bermuda through a lawyer friend in Vaduz, the capital of the Principality of Liechtenstein, less than an hour's drive from Zurich. Bermacor was to be a publishing company that she would own through bearer shares, which meant that once she took possession of them, only she would know who their owner was.

Bermacor was to be run by the company management services arm of a large international public accounting firm called Nexior from its Hamilton, Bermuda, offices.

Elize would give the Lichtenstein lawyer the newsletter's text on the last Friday of every month, and the lawyer would email it to Nexior. Nexior would then print up the required number of copies, which it would mail to the subscribers. Nexior would also look after billing the subscribers and keeping the subscription list up-to-date.

All bills were to be sent out on Bermacor letterhead and the money that came in deposited to Bermacor's bank account in Bermuda. The process appeared complicated, but it was not. There were only a couple of dozen subscribers, all Foundation-related companies that paid their 500-dollar monthly subscription fees with clockwork regularity.

Being a conservative and cautious Swiss woman working in an

overwhelmingly male-dominated environment in which every man she met seemed intent on only one thing, bedding her, Elize had developed a paranoia that was much aggravated by her having to look after an invalid brother. Forever afraid that Fate would double-cross her again, she had Bermacor open a second bank account, this time in Grand Cayman, to which Nexior was to transfer monthly all funds remaining in the Bermuda bank account after the payment of expenses. Her instructions were crystal clear. The Cayman account was to operate on a "one-way only" basis — that is to say "money in but never out." *Under no circumstances were Nexior and Bermacor to send correspondence or documentation having to do with the Cayman account to Switzerland.*

As a result, Elize's only way of keeping track of how her money was growing offshore was through her twice-yearly visits to Bermuda during which she'd pretend to be there on Foundation business as auditor.

CHAPTER 8

Jack was watching the sunset through the windows of Pinsky's sixth-floor office, always an impressive sight, especially when there was nothing obstructing the line where the sky met the sea. He hoped to catch a glimpse of the green flash produced by the sun on a cloudless day at the precise moment its crown sank below the horizon.

The liquidators labored in a surreal world. They worked in a multi-storey, modern, hermetically sealed and air conditioned building in which the inside temperature was a pleasant twenty-two degrees Centigrade during the day — shirt-sleeve weather. But after sundown, as the outside temperature cooled and the air conditioning kept working full blast, the offices became frigid to the point where dew began to form on the windows and the people inside had to don sweaters to stop their teeth from chattering.

Meanwhile, on the beach, the tourists were running around in bathing suits.

"Where are you at?" Pinsky wanted to know.

"We're six months into this thing. Albert and I've sold most of the major real estate, except for the land in Mexico."

"You have an offer on it, though, don't you?"

"I do, but knowing the Mexicans, it will take at least three more months to close the deal. Remember, vacation time is fast approaching."

"What else?"

Jack looked at his notes and, in a few brief sentences, summarized what remained on his plate.

Pinsky was pleased. "We seem to be getting ahead of the curve, so we may as well start looking at items with lower priority."

"Meaning?"

The older man grabbed a file off the top of the pile on his desk. "Here's a bothersome one. I call it *post partum* pain." He was chuckling.

"What on earth do you mean?"

"Lighten up; it's just one of my bad jokes." Pinsky was fully aware of what his colleagues thought of his efforts at levity. "Look at the stuff in the file and apply your devious mind to the problem of returning the money involved to its rightful owners."

He got up and headed for the door. "Come, I'll take you to dinner at the Wharf. Seems like a good night for dining on the terrace. There's almost no wind."

✚

Ten days later, Jack was back in Pinsky's office with a mug of coffee and the file in his hand. His boss noted with pleasure that the folder had grown thicker by a factor of three. Jack was shaking his head in disbelief as he sat down. "It's hard to make sense of what's in here," he said and took a sheet of paper from the file. "I don't know where to begin."

Sensing that he was in for a long session, Pinsky leaned back in his chair and put his feet on his desk.

"When the bank closed, it had over 15,000 clients. They were from all over the world, and their accounts were denominated in American dollars, Canadian dollars, Australian dollars, rubles, and euros."

"And Japanese yen."

Jack nodded and took a sip of his coffee. "Some of the clients had more than one account, so we had to examine about 22,000 ledger cards. Roughly half were deposit accounts — say, about 10,000

— and I concentrated on these. I found that just under 10 percent of their owners could not be contacted during the first few weeks of the liquidation. Then we began to advertise world-wide and that whittled the number down to less than a third."

"You mean to less than 3 percent of 10,000."

"You've got it right — to 289 to be more specific."

Pinsky was pleased. "So, out of 10,000 depositors, we were able to contact everybody except these last few. I'd say that that's quite an achievement, wouldn't you? Nobody can accuse us of not doing our job."

"Absolutely. Legally, we're in the clear."

"What's so unbelievable then?"

"Most of these last few, as you call them, had only small amounts on deposit — a couple of thousand dollars or less in most cases. I guess they couldn't be bothered with contacting us. It was just not worth their while. "

"You mean because they felt they had lost most of their money anyway with no hope of getting more than about one-tenth of it back max?"

Jack nodded again and began to fiddle with a paper clip he had picked up off his boss's desk. "That's the dividend you said you were projecting, Albert."

"So it's your opinion, then, that we needn't bother with the *post partum* file any longer?" Pinsky knew the answer to his question but wanted to see whether Brennan had done his homework.

"Not quite. There are seven accounts on which further work should be done. Their owners keep sending us money for deposit because they don't seem to know that OBGC has gone belly up. Whether we like it or not, in the long run, we'll have to refund all the moneys received after the date of the bankruptcy."

"Are we talking about big money?"

Jack began to laugh. He knew exactly what Pinsky was trying to do.

"No, Albert. As you well know, the sums are small, except in one case where we're looking at over 100,000 dollars." He got up and threw the paper clip at the head liquidator who ducked.

"What do you propose we do?" Pinsky was grinning broadly.

"Okay, okay, Albert, I'll do you a favor. On my way to Europe on my vacation, I'll look in on my rugby-playing friends in Hamilton and find out whatever I can about what we all call the 'mysterious Bermuda account.'"

CHAPTER 9

Senior U.S. Treasury Agent Dennis Benson was in a quandary. In his opinion, the simple task his superior, the Acting Assistant Deputy Undersecretary, Harry Cohen, had thrust on him the previous Friday — five minutes before he was to leave on two weeks' vacation — had seemed unworthy of his seniority.

The forty-four-year-old Benson was in charge of the Treasury Department's Miami regional office, and the last time he had taken part in a "wet" operation had been ten years earlier. He had tried to explain this to Cohen, hoping the man would cut him some slack, but to no avail. He was ordered to reschedule his leave and supervise the action personally. Period.

Because the tip-off had come from "way up high," Benson decided to play it safe. He summoned two of his trusted Cuban-American operatives, Rivero and Canisares, and his best technical man, Ed Lewkowski, to a Saturday morning meeting at the office. Then, satisfied that he had spread as much of the misery that had befallen him among as many of his people as possible, he went home where he got the height of hell from his wife who had been looking forward to a couple of weeks' stay with her family in California.

This had not done much to improve Benson's disposition when he met his men on Saturday morning.

"Here's what we're up against," he started off, bleary-eyed from drinking heavily and fighting sporadically with his better half through the night. "Some British prick who runs a small bank in the Caymans has hooked up with a call-girl madam here in Miami. He pays her a monthly retainer so that he can get his pipe cleaned here without fuss or bother or the need to go hunting for pussy when he's short of time."

The older of the two Cubans, Canisares, yawned. "So what else is new?" What his boss had just told him was SOP — standard operating procedure — among the thousands of businesspeople who visited Florida on a regular, repetitive, basis.

"This limey is special," Benson continued, sounding irritated. "His bank is supposedly doing extensive business in Chicago with the boys we've been trying to nail."

"In connection with money laundering and drug dealing in the area?" This from Canisares.

Benson nodded. "Yep."

The silence that followed was enough to hear a pin drop. Suddenly, everybody was all ears.

"Problem is we can't just grab this guy as he comes through here and force him to tell us what he knows by making him sweat, because the political consequences would be diplomatic disaster."

"How come?" Canisares wasn't buying.

"We can't show probable cause. The guy is as clean as a whistle. I checked. He travels on a British passport with valid multiple entry visas, he does not accept employment in the US, has not created a public disturbance, and has never stayed longer in this country than twenty days."

"Can't we get the Cayman police to lean on him?" Canisares kept insisting. "Isn't there some sort of an agreement about money laundering and drug dealing that covers this?"

"That's just it; there is. But we have to show probable cause in the Cayman courts before asking for help from the police there."

Lewkowski nodded. "And we have no proof, right?"

"Right."

"And when is this paragon of virtue scheduled to pass through here again?" The technician fancied himself a bit of a wordsmith because he was working on completing his first novel.

"Our tipster says next Thursday, so we have very little time to set things up."

The lights went on in the younger Cuban's brain. "Got it. You want me to set a honey trap for this limey so that while he's getting laid Ed here can photograph everything in his briefcase."

"That's exactly what I've got in mind, Rivero. The madam's name is Diana Breton. Here's her business telephone number, registered to a D. Breton in South Kendall. " Benson handed the Cuban a slip of paper. "Get your ass out there and have a talk with her. See if you can get her to cooperate."

"Today?"

Benson shook his head. "Better tomorrow. First, because by tonight I will know what the FBI has on her if anything; second, because tomorrow is Sunday and people scare easier on Sundays; and third, because by tomorrow morning I will have her income tax file from the IRS. I'll email you the info by noon."

Benson looked at Canisares. "You had better go with Rivero. Keep him company in the intimidation department and stop him from saying too much to the lady."

Rivero looked hurt. "Have I ever fucked up a honey trap?"

"No, but there's always a first time. I've got a funny feeling about this operation. It looks too easy." Benson rose to signal that the meeting was over.

Lewkowski piped up. "What about me, Boss? What do you want me to do?"

"Polish up your micro and macro photo skills and then go home to your wife and make nice to her." Benson gave his three cohorts a pensive once-over. "We'll meet here at eight sharp Monday morning and decide who is to fly to George Town, Grand Cayman, to eyeball the target."

✢

After much reflection, Benson finally decided to send Lewkowski to Cayman because the photographer looked the least cop-like of his troops. The man duly reported back that the target, named Gallagher, was a tall, burly, hard-drinking Irishman, popular with his clients as well as with his employers. He was, indeed, planning a four-day trip to the U.S. and was quite open about it. He expected to spend a couple of days in Miami then visit Chicago.

Gallagher had a wide-open type of personality and Lewkowski, playing the timid stranger (his favorite disguise, principally because he *was* basically shy), had no difficulty getting into a conversation with him at his regular booze-up place, the Cayman Arms, to which Gallagher repaired daily for a stiff vodka and tonic after work.

"He's totally unaware of being of interest to us," the technician reported via telephone. "The man chatters like a magpie and is very indiscreet. Even so, I didn't dare ask him what flight he was taking to Miami on Thursday."

"Never mind about that," Benson sounded decisive. "I'll find out from the airlines. There aren't that many flights from Cayman on Thursday afternoon."

"Anything else you want to know?"

"Yeah. Where's he planning to stay in Miami?"

"At the Mayfair Inn and Spa. He always stays there. His secretary told me he gets a special rate."

"Shame on you."

Lewkowski was confused. "Why? What have I done?"

Benson chuckled. "And you, a happily married man."

"That I am boss, so what's the beef?"

"Tell me, Ed, did you just get friendly with her, or did you get laid?"

"You're being unfair, Boss."

Benson was very happy. Lewkowski's information confirmed what Rivero had learned from his talk with Diana Breton, the madam, on Sunday afternoon.

The Mayfair Inn was one of the more fashionable watering holes in Coconut Grove, an oasis of lush palm trees and rhododendron bushes around a gorgeous swimming pool in a well-sheltered garden adjacent to the elegant bar. The hotel sat opposite the popular Shops in the Grove — and Benson hated everything about it.

As far as his needs and wants were concerned, the place was too close to a shopping mall, it had too many exits, the rooms had electronic locks with identity readers, and the corridors were too long, with no place to hide if things went wrong.

On Thursday morning, Lewkowski returned to Miami, picked up his gear at the office, and met Benson and his gang shortly after lunch in the Mayfair Inn's presidential suite.

This time, there were seven of them, including the lookout (Miriam, a woman agent dressed like a chamber maid), the driver and his sidekick, and a very fit rookie with special training, who would act as muscle if need be. His name was Harry Dunn.

Benson kept the briefing short.

"Canisares will meet the target's flight and trail him to his hotel just in case the info we have from the madam is inaccurate."

"Is she trustworthy?" As soon as Lewkowski, the constant worrier, uttered the words, he realized how stupid his question was.

"Of course not," Rivero remarked. "But we've got her plenty scared. She said she'll do the trick herself to make sure things work out as planned."

Benson continued. "She'll let him lay her as soon as they get into his room. Then she'll suggest that they have dinner at the Versailles on *Calle Ocho*. I suppose they'll shower and then get underway around eight thirty for dinner, which she'll drag out for a couple of hours. This will give Ed plenty of time to take pictures of everything Gallagher has in his briefcase."

"Piece of cake." Lewkowski was happy.

"We'll have Miriam stand guard in the corridor while Ed's in the room, just in case. Harry will be with him."

"Is that wise?"

"It's safer," Canisares said. He was the most experienced of the lot, with decades of service.

Things began to go wrong almost from the start.

Gallagher's flight was ninety minutes late. He didn't arrive at the hotel until eight, two hours behind schedule, after having spent the time drinking while waiting for take-off. As a result, he was slightly drunk and churlish.

He categorically refused to go as far as *Calle Ocho* for dinner and initially wanted room service to send up a meal and champagne to his suite on the fourth floor. Diana finally managed to get him to leave the inn around ten. He made her drive him to a bar-grill called the Foxhole a few blocks away where he began to drink again, and quite heavily. He became argumentative and, after a very quick and unsatisfactory steak sandwich, demanded to be driven back to his hotel.

Fearing a scene, she complied.

At the hotel, he made her park in the underground garage and insisted that she come up to the room. By then, he was becoming dangerously physical so she had no choice but to do as she was told.

Rivero and Canisares who had been following the pair, duly reported their every move to Benson who was in the presidential suite with Miriam. He sent her down to the fourth floor and then called Ed and Harry.

The two were still at work in the suite because they had found nothing of interest in the Irishman's briefcase and had to spend time searching for a likely place where the banker could have hidden the information they were after. Lewkowski had finally stumbled onto the cleverly hidden secret compartment in the banker's roll-on, but opening it without leaving a trace had used up another fifteen minutes. The photographing operation wasn't quite finished when Benson called.

The two Cubans following Gallagher and his date did not see them take the express elevator from the garage directly to the fourth floor because they had not dared to follow the madam's car into the underground parking area. Benson, who had gone down to the lobby to watch for them, realized this only when Miriam called to advise that their target was almost at the door of his suite.

By then it was too late to call Ed and Harry again.

On the fourth floor, Miriam did her best to hold up Gallagher's progress. First, she called out to him in Spanish, and then she wheeled her maid's cart around to block his path but to no avail. Gallagher pushed her aside roughly just as Ed and Harry emerged from the suite.

As soon as Gallagher saw Lewkowski and his large camera case, he instinctively understood everything and, with a roar, took off after the photographer who sprinted away down the corridor, running for his life. Gallagher tripped the photographer from behind with a flying tackle and tore the case from his shoulder. By then, Harry Dunn had caught up and tried to kick Gallagher in the head. The Irishman rolled away, grabbed Dunn's leg and twisted. Dunn fell on top of Gallagher and got his arm around the larger man's head. Gallagher struggled, and Dunn gave the head a jerk.

Gallagher went limp. Dunn had broken his neck.

By the time Benson reached the scene, Gallagher was dead.

That's when Diana Breton lost it. She was going to scream, but Benson saw the scream coming and slapped her face to shut her up.

"Get out of here, NOW!" he commanded. "Remember only what happened up to the time you drove your date into the garage *and said good night to him there!*"

She looked at him blankly. "But, but..."

"No buts. I have two witnesses who saw him leave you in the car. You drove home and read about the accident in the Monday morning papers."

"What accident?"

Benson gave her a withering look. She got his drift and left without a word.

The Treasury agents swung into damage-control mode. Miriam helped the five men carry Gallagher's limp body to his suite. They were going through its half-open door when an elderly couple emerged from the elevator.

Miriam waved to the man as she was closing the door, and the man winked at her, reassured by her maid's uniform.

Benson called for a clean-up team. Its members arrived at midnight and smuggled Gallagher's body out through the garage at three o'clock in the morning. Everybody else left then except for Dunn, who stayed behind to impersonate Gallagher for the next couple of days. He stayed at the suite until Sunday morning when he called reception to say he was going to "check out a little late...around two."

After walking through the streets of the Shops in the Grove, Dunn turned right and headed toward the corner of Matilda and Grand where he was conveniently "hit by a taxi," courtesy of Benson and his team, as he was crossing the intersection.

An "ambulance" took him to the Orthopedic Institute of South Florida, a medical facility on Campo Sano Avenue in Coral Gables that specializes in complex compound fractures. From there, he called the hotel and told the manager on duty about what had happened.

"My bags are all packed, so have the bellboy take them downstairs and put them in storage. Please pay my bill and check me out of the hotel by using the imprint you already have of my credit card." It was easy to make himself sound slightly Irish. He remembered the accent from his grandfather.

The manager was very solicitous. "I'll look after everything, Mr. Gallagher, don't worry. Just make sure you get yourself fixed up all right. If there's anything else I can do for you, just holler."

"I will. In the meantime, hang on to my luggage. I'll send someone to pick it up in a day or two if I can't come myself."

On Sunday night, using Gallagher's computer, Dunn sent messages from his "bedside" to his clients in Chicago, explaining his situation and asking them to postpone their meetings for a few days until after the doctors had "set his leg," an "operation" scheduled for Tuesday afternoon. He also wrote his assistant, Rex Rankin, in Grand Cayman, asking that Rankin call him on Monday so they could talk about what Rankin had to do in his absence.

Of course, when Rankin called, he was told that "Mr. Gallagher was having some tests done and X-rays taken" and that he was unavailable but would call back. Gallagher never did. Tuesday evening, it was reported that he died on the operating table of a "massive stroke caused by a blot clot, probably caused by the accident."

Rankin only found out about what had happened on Wednesday and got around to notifying the Chicago clients on Thursday morning. After contacting his late boss's next of kin in the U.K., he made copies of the Chicago accounts and rushed to deliver them in person to the clients the following Monday.

Thus, Benson and his crew had a full ten days before having to worry about being discovered. In fact, the sting became public knowledge only about a year later when the Chicago "boys" were arrested, prosecuted, and found guilty of drug trafficking and money laundering based on the evidence submitted by operatives of the Treasury Department.

CHAPTER 10

Gallagher's death upset Jack profoundly, principally because it had come about so unexpectedly. Although the two had not been bosom buddies, they had been close, and Jack missed the gregarious Irishman, especially on the rugby field. The thought of foul play never crossed Jack's mind. He presumed that any intervention on the part of Uncle George's people would have had to have been over long before Gallagher died on Tuesday.

A week after Gallagher's death, Jack took a ten-day leave of absence to visit his family in Buffalo. He wanted to attend the annual Rooney family Easter dinner organized traditionally by his beloved grandmother, Ilona Pásztor, who had turned ninety-four in February.

When Bill Rooney met Ilona, she was working as a secretary in an export-import firm in Bern where her language skills were much valued. In addition to speaking French, English, German, and her native Hungarian, she was also fluent in Spanish and Italian, having spent years in Barcelona where her parents had sent her to study when she was twenty.

Ilona was an orphan. Having somehow made her way into Switzerland illegally, she was on the verge of being deported when Rooney, who had fallen madly in love with this fiery Hungarian beauty of elegance and intellect, pulled some strings and obtained an extension so she could stay.

He promptly hired her and then married her within a year, even though she was less than half his age.

"An old fool's folly," his friends told him, but he and Ilona persisted. She bore him two sons and a daughter, and their marriage lasted till death parted them when William Rooney died after twenty years of wedded bliss.

Ilona resided in a large mansion in the Orchard Park area not far from the Our Lady of Victory Basilica where her son, Patrick, the Roman Catholic Bishop of Buffalo, held court and where she would attend mass more or less regularly on Sundays.

For the last fifteen years, she had two live-in caregivers, Lani, a Fillippina and Zsóka, originally from Hungary. Their efforts were supplemented by Vali who cooked on weekdays for Ilona Hungarian-style, and Zoltán, the handyman-chauffeur.

Ilona had built up her retinue with care; she was in the process of returning to her roots. Though somewhat fragile, she was still very active, playing a mean hand of bridge with her friends on Tuesdays and Thursdays and inviting members of her family for Sunday afternoon tea on a regular basis. Sharp as a tack, she kept track of all their many activities. In other words, she was still very much the family matriarch.

The dinner turned out to be, as always, a boisterous and highly successful event. As she surveyed the twenty faces around her table (including seven great-grandchildren), Ilona noted that all seemed to be smiling, and for this she was very grateful to God.

Of course, she talked to Him every day anyway because she could not thank him often enough for having given her a full and healthy life, and a great family, and for having spared her the hardships of World Wall II.

"What are you thinking about, Grandma?" It was Jack, her favorite grandson, who asked the question. He was sitting immediately to her right, his reserved place every year. She smiled and put her hand on his arm. "I was thinking about how lucky we all are to be here together in peace and prosperity." Then she looked at him, her eyes searching. "What's bothering you, my grandson?"

"Why do you think anything's bothering me?"

"I can see it in your face. Is everything all right?"

He grinned and put his hand over hers. "Absolutely. It's just my job. Grand Cayman is not a place one wants to stay in too long."

She nodded knowingly. "In other words, no girls or perhaps not the right kind."

He burst out laughing. "You might just have hit the nail on the head."

"Perhaps it's time to settle down, no? How old are you now anyway?"

"I'll be thirty in July."

"It's definitely time you started to think about settling down." She sighed. "Time goes by so fast. To me it seems that only yesterday you were running around in short pants." She held out her plate to him. "Now be a good boy, mister hotshot football player, and get me some more ham and mashed potatoes."

He kissed her on the forehead and, always the obedient grandson, went to the sideboard to fetch her some food.

Later, as the party was breaking up, Uncle George collared him. "Come upstairs for a moment with me, Jack."

Jack was surprised. "What's up, Uncle?"

The older man started up the stairs without a word. His nephew followed.

"I was hoping to have a quiet word with you tomorrow morning. Just the two of us. But something's come up, and I have to leave for Washington early."

They were in Grandma Ilona's upstairs sitting room. Uncle George closed the door, sat down in his mother's favorite armchair, and motioned for Jack to sit opposite him on the little sofa. "My boy, I wanted to thank you personally for what you've done for us at the Treasury."

Jack felt ill at ease. "Did you get the material you were after?"

His uncle nodded. "And some." Then he lifted his two hands toward his shoulders in a gesture of resignation only to drop them on his knees. "I'm sorry about your friend," he said softly. "We didn't intend for him to die. It was an accident. He returned to his room sooner than expected."

Jack felt as if a horse had kicked him in the gut. He wanted to throw up. Ever since Gallagher's untimely passing he couldn't help feeling that *he* was somehow responsible for the man's death. He could not explain how a healthy, extremely fit young man in his late twenties could suddenly die of an embolism on the operating table.

And now, his uncle had just confirmed what he had suspected all along.

"You mean —"

Uncle George cut him off. "These things happen, my boy. Don't sweat it. You've done your duty, that's all. Nobody can blame you for anything."

Except I myself, Jack thought. *I'm doing this job because my family expects me to "take my turn in the barrel," as Uncle George had put it so inelegantly not so long ago. Am I also expected to sacrifice my principles for the family's record of public service?*

He got up because he knew he had to leave the room before he lost his temper and struck his uncle.

Just then, he hated everything that had to do with his family and the way all ties and obligations were so complexly intertwined as to make a murderer out of one of their own. Or so it seemed to Jack who felt he would never be able to forgive himself for not only having betrayed a friend but also having caused his untimely death. Although not actively practicing, Jack was a Catholic; he couldn't help but be one. Born into the religion of his ancestors, he had been inculcated with the Roman dogma since early childhood. At the time of his brother's and father's tragic deaths, he had made a conscious choice to deny the existence of an Almighty, but he could not rid himself of the Catholic's sense of guilt that was now exacerbated by what his uncle had let slip.

CHAPTER 11

When Elize returned from New York, she found her desk piled high with files *Herr* Schmidt had placed there. The note accompanying them instructed her to "correct the contents to reflect the new situation."

The files, she saw after flipping through them, all related to the activities of the two ex-administrators, Petitmaitre and Faerber, who would now have to vacate their directorships in the companies in which the Foundation had interests.

A simple matter but with far-reaching consequences for Elize because the Foundation was proposing that *Herr* Schmidt be appointed in their stead. Seeking confirmation, she sought out her boss. Studer, polite and aloof as always, was quick to apologize. "I'm so sorry," he said. "It completely slipped my mind in New York to tell you about Schmidt. You see, its time the Foundation started to project a new image, an image of youth and vigor. Schmidt fits the bill admirably. He is relatively young but mature and certainly vigorous."

"Does this mean that I have to clear my auditor's reports with him before submitting them to you?"

"Regarding the companies in which he will now become director, yes."

Although she had tried to hide her feelings behind a poker face, Studer knew her too well not to sense her disappointment. "*Frau*

Doktor Haemmerle, please do not worry. You know that you have my complete trust and that these reviews are only a formality."

Like a good soldier, she nodded. "Very well, *Herr Doktor,* I shall act accordingly." She made for the door, but he stopped her.

"Please sit down for a moment and allow me to ask you a question." He pointed to one of the chairs in front of his huge, beautifully polished and hand-rubbed desk. "Why do you dislike *Herr* Schmidt so much?"

Elize was surprised. During the eight years that she had worked for Studer, he had always been unfailingly polite, respectful and caring, especially at the beginning of their association when her grief over the loss of her family was still fresh. Studer and she were, of course, still not on first-name terms after all these years and would never be. Swiss banking tradition would not allow it. Nor would it allow personal feelings to influence office behavior.

She couldn't help but blush. The question was so personal and so uncharacteristic of him that, at first, she couldn't think of a diplomatic way to answer because she could not bring herself to tell him the truth.

"It is not that I dislike him. I am just not comfortable working with him."

He shook his head. "That is a pity *Doktor* Haemmerle because *Herr* Schmidt is our rising star. It would help your career with the Foundation if you made an ally of him. I am certain he would be delighted to work closely with you." There was a slight emphasis on the word "closely."

Elize understood at once. *She* was no longer the rising star — she had been supplanted by Schmidt. Unless she welcomed his advances, she would soon find herself being gently nudged out of her job, never mind her eight years of loyal service, the long extra hours, and the stress of having to criss-cross half the world to make sure the Foundation did not get cheated.

Thank God she had her little nest egg offshore. If she could hang in for another year or two, she'd have enough, with the Cayman money and the pre-arranged separation settlement the Foundation would have to pay her, to survive for the time she'd need to find another well-paying job. And her brother wouldn't have to go without, especially if the subscriptions to the newsletter continued. Which they would, unless, of course, Schmidt found out about them and did something to have them canceled, just so he could show her who is the boss.

Or was she worrying for nothing, just being her neurotic, frightened, insecure self? Why was she incapable of heeding her late mother's advice: "Don't start worrying in advance about bad things that have yet to happen, and, above all, don't paint the devil on the wall if you don't want him to appear"? Why was she so hesitant behind her mask of unflappable levelheadedness and self-assuredness? How come she could not dominate her demons?

She knew the answer to this question, a question she had asked herself a thousand times, whenever she choked up with fear: she had no financial reserves to speak of. She desperately needed the money she was earning to be able to look after her invalid brother. And to earn that money, she needed two things: a well-paying job, such as the one she now had, and good health to be able to continue doing her work.

God knew what would happen to Kurt if she fell ill. Her health insurance plan certainly did not cover all her needs under such a contingency.

She stood up and squared her shoulders.

"Thank you, Dr. Studer, for your kind comments. As you know, I value your counsel highly, and I will certainly follow it."

There, you pompous, ungrateful bastard, she thought. *I vocalized what you wanted to hear, but you can bet your last Swiss franc that I will use every second of my time to find ways of undermining Schmidt's authority. Don't you worry,* she went on to herself, *I'll have him eating out of my hand in no time. Then I'll let him have it right between the eyes.*

CHAPTER 12

Karl Stapfer and his wife, Clara, ten years his junior, lived in an old farmhouse built in the Swiss tradition into the side of a mountain: the master bedroom, the living room, the kitchen and the bathroom were on the ground floor, the rest of the house — the two guest bedrooms — upstairs, with access to a magnificent terrace. This terrace could also be accessed from the garden. The steps were a bit of a challenge, but Stapfer did not mind. At age ninety-five, he considered climbing the twenty-one stairs that led to the terrace four times a day to be a wonderfully worthwhile exercise. It kept him mobile and rewarded him every time with a breathtaking view of the lake that lay below his home.

And the view was never the same. It changed with the time of the day, with the time of the year, and, of course, with the weather.

The couple's routine seldom varied. Whenever weather permitted, they took their meals on the terrace to maximize the time they could spend enjoying nature's beauty around them. The Stapfers had inherited the house from Clara's grandfather who used to grow grapes and make wine before land in the Italian part of Switzerland became too expensive for viniculture. It was situated above the *Via Sotto Chiesa* in Carona, a small town about six kilometers south of Lugano.

Clara's father had subdivided the vineyard and had made a fortune selling lots to foreign investors who wanted to live in the temperate climate around the *Lago di Lugano,* near to their tax-sheltered money in the fiscal enclave called *Campo d'Italia.*

Karl was originally from Zurich. After finishing *Kantonalschule,* or high school, he wangled a job as a clerk at Moretti & Cie Banquiers through family connections, no mean feat at the height of the Great Depression. The year 1936 was not a year when twenty-three-year-old young men without a university education could find jobs easily. But Karl was intelligent, personable, and diligent. He was also willing to work for a pittance, which endeared him to Aldo Moretti very much. He hired Karl as his personal go-for and was pleased to find that the young man spoke English fluently, having picked up the language working at various local hotels.

Karl made it his business to learn everything he could about private banking and, more specifically, about the internal work-ings of the Moretti bank. During the two years immediately before World War II, he also attended night courses during which he was introduced to the mysteries of creative accounting and the rudi-ments of economics.

In 1946, Moretti finally made Karl a junior partner and gave him a small share in his bank, about 15 percent, as compensation for his hard work and loyalty during ten years of devoted service at starvation wages. Karl promptly married Clara, but their union produced no children.

Moretti could afford to be generous. The private banking busi-ness in Switzerland was booming, fuelled by the huge amounts of capital these institutions had accumulated from the war's victims who had entrusted their money to the Swiss for management.

Another ten years went by during which the banks continued shamelessly to enrich themselves further by refusing to return the funds belonging to the relatives of Holocaust victims and its survivors.

In the late seventies, Aldo Moretti died, and his heirs decided to liquefy — that is to say, convert into cash — their inheritance by taking the bank public through listing its shares on the Zurich Stock Exchange.

They went about it in a clever way. They valued the bank at 100 million Swiss francs of which only one-half was represented by tangible assets. The other half was so-called goodwill, meaning the bank's name, its reputation, its clients, and its management's know-how and track record. The much-touted main feature of the know-how and track record was the presence on the board of directors of Karl Stapfer, an old-time Swiss banker who could boast of forty years' experience as one of the bank's senior executives.

Moretti's heirs received 40,000 Series "A" common shares worth 1,000 francs each and 45 million francs in cash. The cash came from the sale of 45,000 Series "B" common shares to those people who were lucky enough to be able to buy shares at the 1,000-franc issue price. They were lucky because the demand for shares was so great that the price reached 1,180 francs per share the day after they were issued.

Karl Stapfer received 15,000 "A" common shares, which meant that, on paper, he was worth over 16 million Swiss francs, about 12 million U.S. dollars. He was rich, and so was his wife who had inherited her share of her father's considerable estate.

Very few people who bought them realized that the "A" common shares issued to the heirs of Aldo Moretti and to Stapfer had ten votes each at shareholders' meetings, while the "B" common shares that the public bought (the public shares) had only one vote per share as long as the bank kept paying the yearly 4 percent dividend that the Zurich Stock Exchange had ordered the bank to pay to compensate "B" shareholders for their disadvantage vote-wise. This meant that out of a total of 595,000 votes, the Moretti heirs had 400,000, and that, although they only owned 40 percent of the bank, they had more than two-thirds of the votes. In other words, *as long as the annual dividend was paid,* they would still have absolute control over operations and could make the bank do whatever they wanted it to do, though they no longer had a single penny invested in the business.

Of course, in any year that the dividend would *not* be paid, the public shares would automatically acquire the same rights as the heirs' shares had, namely ten votes per share. Under such circumstances the heirs would have 400,000 votes, the public would have 450,000 votes, and Stapfer — with his 150,000 votes — would be the key man, the person whose votes would decide the outcome of any issue on which the shareholders were asked to vote.

This did not concern the heirs overly for two reasons. First, the bank's financial position was rock-solid and a payment of a 4 percent dividend on 45 million francs — a paltry 1,800,000 francs — would never be a problem. Second, good old, faithful, grateful, and predictable Stapfer would always vote with the Moretti heirs, wouldn't he?

At one point, one of the heirs, waxing eloquent, had asked with considerable pathos: had Stapfer not demonstrated over the years time and again that not blood but loyalty flowed in his veins?

Famous last words.

CHAPTER 13

The alarm bells began to ring in Elize's head during the mid-May meeting of the Foundation's administrators the moment Hans-Ruedi Schmidt put his hand up when it came time to discuss "other business," the last item on the agenda. He wanted to make a motion.

This caught Elize by surprise. Usually, she would be advised of all matters ahead of time, including 'other business', that were to be discussed at monthly meetings. This enabled her to prepare relevant information in advance — standard operating procedure for large organizations. It made it easier for everybody to talk intelligently about the subject being discussed.

"I see from the monthly financials," Schmidt began, "that for the sixth month running, the Foundation shows cash on hand at the end of each of these months in excess of 10 million francs. I also note that, on deposit with the bank, these funds bear annual interest at only 2 percent." He looked at Elize with open hostility. "I am surprised that our internal auditor has not drawn management's attention to this lamentable situation."

Elize blushed with rage but kept her cool. The question was obviously prompted by malevolence and intended to provoke. "What situation, *Herr* Schmidt?"

"These funds should have been invested in short-term commercial paper of some kind that would yield a higher rate." He sounded very smug, very sure of himself.

Elize gave as good as she got. "Two points, if I may, *Herr* Schmidt. First, the cash position is reviewed by me weekly with Dr. Studer. It is up to him to decide where and how the Foundation's funds should be invested and not up to me. Second, you may have forgotten that six months ago, the board had instructed management to keep at least 6 million francs — 4.5 million dollars — instantly available in case the Foundation decided to intervene in the Sterling Drug proxy fight."

Schmidt was furious. He hated being put down, especially by a woman. He began shuffling through his papers, looking for a way to justify his position. "That's just the point," he finally said. "The Sterling situation is going nowhere. You should know that. You had just visited them."

She looked at Studer, but he refused to come to her aid, even though they had discussed cash investment alternatives as recently as the previous Friday when he had specifically told her to leave things as they were.

Emboldened, Schmidt continued. "I hereby move that, to correct the situation that has arisen as a result of this oversight, 6 million francs be placed on deposit with our bankers for a term of 180 days at a correspondingly higher yield than is now being achieved."

"Anybody wants to second the motion?" Studer promptly asked.

His attitude upset Elize very much. Her boss should have supported her by at least insisting on a less ambiguous wording that would clarify that no blame attached to her. Instead, the man seemed to be encouraging Schmidt.

To her utter amazement, Moretti put up his hand. "I second the motion."

Why on earth would a banker second a motion that would force him to pay a higher interest rate on money that was already deposited in his bank? she asked herself, shaking her head in wonderment.

"Those in favor?" Her boss put the question quickly, thereby cutting off any opportunity for her to voice her opinion.

Studer's, Moretti's, and Schmidt's hands shot into the air. The remaining two administrators did not vote.

"Carried." Studer announced firmly then turned to Elize. "Is there any other business to be transacted?" he inquired.

Numbly, she shook her head. It was the first time since her appointment as auditor and secretary that her opinion on a matter involving finances had not been solicited. Something was very wrong, but what?

Back in the safety of her office some time later, Elize tried to analyze the situation. She knew that Studer was a very political and wily animal who would not go on record with anything that was against the Foundation's interests. He was also manipulative and a director of Moretti & Cie Banquiers. A position of clear conflict of interest.

From the Foundation's point of view, the action taken was obviously advantageous. It would *receive* more interest on its money. On the other hand, as far as the bank was concerned, it now had to *pay* higher interest on money that was already on deposit with it. Elize marveled at the way in which her boss had managed to maneuver Schmidt into doing his own and Moretti's dirty work.

He should never have voted on the motion, nor should have Studer or Moretti, the lawyer side of her brain was telling her. *The three of them should have abstained. They were all in a position of conflict of interest.*

So why the whole exercise? They knew the law as well as anyone. She could only come up with one answer: The Moretti Bank must be short of cash and is trying to defend against a run on it. The bank's latest quarterly statement lay on her desk. Dated March 31, it had just been placed there. She flipped through it and saw that although all the required ratios seemed to be within reasonable limits, there was quite a chunk of the bank's cash invested in what it called ABCP — Asset Based Commercial Paper. She did not find this particularly worrisome because she noted with relief that most of it was due to be redeemed within five months.

So that's it, she mused. *They wanted to use the proceeds of the redemption to pay the Foundation back its money in case the Foundation needed to have it back. But with the latest arrangement in place, the money could not be reclaimed by the Foundation before six months went by.*

Mentally, Elize congratulated both Studer and Moretti. *Very neat.* They certainly knew their business. She filed the statements in their appropriate place and then wrote herself a reminder memo. It said, "Discuss ABCPs and bank ratios with K. during next visit," and marked it for follow-up in June.

"K." of course, was Karl Stapfer, her dear old friend and a director of Moretti & Cie, whom she had met the day after she had started work at the Foundation and who instantly volunteered to become her mentor in banking matters. Stapfer was then eighty-seven and would remain a director of the bank for another three years.

The relationship between the young lawyer and the wise old banker remained close, even after Stapfer left the bank. His home near Lugano became a haven for Elize and her brother where they could relax and forget about the pressures of life in Zurich. After a while, it became a tradition for Elize and Kurt to spend their summer holidays with the Stapfers in Lugano, and the old couple began to think of Elize and Kurt as their children.

CHAPTER 14

Jack Brennan was utterly disgusted with himself. He had lost respect for his Uncle George, his career was on hold, and he had nobody in whom to confide his shame: he had betrayed a friend and had become an unwitting accessory to murder.

Unwitting? Not really. Deep down in his tortured, guilt-ridden, Catholic soul, he knew for certain that sooner or later he would be called to task and forced to atone for his act of betrayal.

"I should never have told Uncle George about that woman," he muttered as he got ready to go golfing with his Bermudian rugby buddy, Henry Keiser, the Nexior Partner in Bermuda in charge of the famous accounting firm's Company Services Division.

Although on vacation, Jack found it hard to relax. The liquidation had exhausted his patience. It had taken him ages to close the Toluca land sale in Mexico, which had meant that he had had to delay his vacation by two weeks. Bad enough, but now, after Pinsky had finally consented to his taking off, he had to detour to Bermuda to keep his promise to try to find out who owned the mysterious Bermuda account into which money kept flowing on a regular monthly basis.

✚

It was a beautiful Saturday morning in June, and the pristine fairways of the Princess Hotel still glistened in the early sun from a light morning shower. Keiser was waiting at the putting green, keen to get going. Bachelors both, he and Jack, like all natural athletes, were imbued with the competitive spirit, and they tried constantly to best each other in just about everything: on the rugby pitch for tries, on the golf course for strokes, and in the pubs for girls.

In their encounters, it was usually Jack who came out the winner but not this particular time. He lost by four strokes.

"You played like shit this morning" Keiser gloated. "What's the matter? Too many girls or too much booze?" They were having a late breakfast on the terrace.

"I wish. I guess not enough of either."

"Oh? You don't sound like the Jack Brennan I know. What's up?"

"It's that damned liquidation. And then, of course, there is Gallagher's death."

Keiser was quick to agree. "A nasty business. Rumor has it that his bank is having a hard time finding someone to replace Rhyall."

Jack's mood turned somber. "I guess that's true, in more ways than one."

"Come on, Jack, cheer up. Tell me why you find it so frustrating to work for the liquidation."

That was the opening Jack had been waiting for.

He told Keiser about the crazy construction workers who wanted to do him harm, about the tough guys with the broken noses from Marseille who wanted their money back and the hell with the law, about freezing his butt off in air-conditioned offices on a hot and humid tropical island, about the corrupt Mexican judges who held up the sale of OBGC's most valuable asset to force the liquidators to pay them a huge bribe, and about the Thai general laundering illicit commissions on the arms purchases by his country. Finally, he got around to mentioning the mysterious Bermuda account.

"Perhaps I feel most frustrated when I stumble onto a situation in which I could actually do some real good only to find that I'm stopped from doing anything by stupid arrangements put in place to protect confidentiality and that achieve exactly the opposite of what they were originally put in place for."

Keiser didn't follow. "That was one hell-of-a sentence, Brennan. What exactly do you mean by it?"

"Let me give you an example. There is an account on OBGC's books that shows a credit balance in the high five figures. Of course, most of this money is lost. The owner will likely not recover more than a maximum of 10 percent of it."

"That little?"

"I'm afraid so. Pinsky is projecting a dividend of from 8 to 10 percent."

"Go on."

"However hard we try, we cannot get in touch with the owner of the account because he or she or it has not gotten in touch with us."

"How come?"

"Probably because the owner does not know that the bank has gone belly up."

"What makes you think that?"

"He keeps sending us more money every month, which we will have to return to him in the end, but God knows how. The only contact we have keeps stonewalling us, citing bank secrecy laws and confidentiality instructions it says it cannot, or is not willing, to break."

"And who is this asshole, this contact?"

Jack had been dreaming about this moment for a long time, so he took his sweet time to answer. He emptied his cup, leaned across the table, looked his friend squarely in the eyes, and then let Keiser have it.

"You are."

CHAPTER 15

During his stint as a liquidator, Jack had accumulated thousands upon thousands of air miles all of which he intended to "spend" during his vacation. He flew from Bermuda to New York, spent a long weekend going to the opera and taking in a couple of plays, and then, still on Pinsky's tab, he bought a business-class return ticket to Zurich. The plan was to spend a couple of days in Switzerland to identify the owner of the mysterious Bermuda account and then to keep on going on his free air miles to Budapest and points beyond.

Budapest was a must. He had been planning to find out firsthand for quite some time about the place where his grandmother was born, but somehow he had never gotten around to visiting Hungary. Little did he know that this project would turn out to be no less daunting than the Bermuda account gig.

Admittedly, business class air travel was a luxury, and Pinsky had been reluctant to authorize it until Jack had pointed out that the expense could be legitimately charged to the Bermuda account. So Jack chose to fly Swiss at a discounted rate, not a winning decision. The company's in-flight entertainment equipment was on the fritz, but Jack didn't mind. He had enough to think about to keep him busy.

After Keiser realized that it was he who had been keeping information from the Cayman liquidators, thereby creating hardship for whoever was at the other end, he couldn't do enough to make things right. They went to his office straight from the golf course, and he retrieved the file so that they could look at it together.

It contained precious little of use to Jack.

"This is a very simple operation," Keiser was saying as he leafed through the binder. "We get a monthly text from a lawyer in Vaduz, Lichtenstein, print it up, mail it to the subscribers, collect the subscription fees, pay the printers and ourselves, and then send whatever money is left in the account to Cayman."

"All the money?"

Keiser glanced at the papers in his hand. "No. We have built up a 2,000-U.S.-dollar cushion over the past eighteen months just so we're not out-of-pocket if we have to wind up the operation."

Jack nodded in agreement. "That's wise and understandable."

His host kept flipping through the file then suddenly stopped. "Here's an item that may help you." He handed a business card to Jack. "How I could have completely forgotten about her I do not know."

Jack looked at the card. It said: E. Haemmerle, Auditor, The *Pro Nobis* Foundation. "I don't understand. What do you mean by 'her'?"

"Her." Keiser pointed at the paper in Jack's hand. "The auditor."

"You mean E. Haemmerle is a woman?"

Keiser began to laugh. "She sure is, my friend, she sure is." He shook his head. "What a looker!"

"And the *Pro Nobis* Foundation? Who are they?"

"Some obscure Swiss charity that has a diversified North American investment portfolio."

"How do you know this? There's no address on the card."

"Ms. Haemmerle told me when we first met. Apparently, she is the internal auditor of the Foundation, and she travels around the world checking on the activities of the companies in which the Foundation has money invested."

Keiser took the card out of his guest's hand and looked at it again. "Typical European style business card." He nodded knowingly. "Simple but arrogant."

"What do you mean?"

"It gives you the least amount of information possible, thereby sending you a clear message."

"Which is?"

Keiser chuckled. "Believe it or not, the message is 'If you don't know who I am and where to find me, I don't want to hear from you.'"

Jack was amazed. Where he came from, people gave their business cards to other people so that they could find them, not to play hide and seek. "Tell me more."

"Nothing much else to tell. The subscribers to the newsletter, which, by the way, is very well written and shows a deep understanding of how economic cycles work, are all senior executives of leading public corporations."

"What else?"

"I suspect they all have one shareholder in common, and that is the Foundation."

"Does the newsletter indicate who writes it?"

Keiser picked up the file and put it away. "Jack, I've helped you as much as I can. I have no contact name or phone number or address for the Caymanian account's owner, nor any other useful information to give you."

"You have the auditor's name."

"Yes, but I doubt she is the owner."

"Who else can it be then? Certainly not an important and well-known person because the amount involved, though steadily growing, is relatively small."

Keiser looked at his watch and stood up. "I really have to go, so let me tell you briefly what I think, and you'll just have to take it from there yourself."

"Shoot."

"I think the whole setup is owned by the Foundation itself. The newsletter is a neat way of circulating the combined wisdom of all these companies' executives without appearing to be giving away insider information."

"And the auditor?"

"She's just that, the Foundation's internal auditor."

"So where do I go from here?"

"I suggest you go to Switzerland and find out whatever you can about the Foundation and then call the auditor and make an appointment to see her."

"What about going to see the lawyer in Lichtenstein instead?"

Keiser shook his head emphatically. "I'd rather you didn't do that because it would get me and my firm into trouble. He'd immediately guess who gave you his name. Besides, I'm sure that the lawyer does not know about the Cayman account."

"Why?"

"Because it was set up by us here and not by him. Come to think of it, she was the one who instructed us to open it."

"So she must know all about it."

"Exactly. She examines the statements every time she passes through here."

"How often is that?"

"About every six months or so. In fact, she's overdue. We haven't seen her since last July."

CHAPTER 16

Elize was having a hard time coping with the pressure that Schmidt was exerting on her.

His method was simple. He made it a point to load her down with work every Wednesday and Friday evening just as she was getting ready to go home. This forced her to stay late and to work during weekends. What she found the most infuriating was his insistence that she personally do the work he was dumping on her immediately, even though it was of a trivial nature and certainly not urgent or confidential.

After a month of such harassment, she went to see her boss.

"I followed your advice, *Herr Doktor,* and made a real effort to satisfy *Herr* Schmidt's special requirements, but he doesn't seem to appreciate what I'm doing for him. He just keeps piling more work on my desk as if there were no tomorrow."

"Are you telling me that you cannot keep up?" Studer sounded unsympathetic.

"I am keeping up, *Herr Doktor,* but only just, and because I am working overtime almost every night and on weekends, too. I've never been as busy as this in the past. And it's trivial work that someone less senior, such as *Herr* Schmidt's secretary, could easily handle."

Studer leaned back in his chair and considered the problem. Then he scribbled a note on his pad and looked at Elize. He seemed curiously preoccupied.

"Let me see what I can do," he finally told her. "Leave this with me."

✚

When Elize walked into the monthly administrators' meeting ten days later, during which the workflow from Schmidt had seemed to increase rather than diminish, she had the strangest feeling. There seemed to be a sort of tension in the room, a tension created by her or because of her. And Schmidt was looking too smug, too cocky.

Don't be silly, she chided herself. *Put it out of your mind. You're being paranoid. Stop feeling so insecure.*

But the feeling of insecurity returned with a vengeance when Studer, having disposed of routine matters, asked if there were any other business to be discussed, and Schmidt again raised his hand unexpectedly.

None of the administrators had given advance notice of wanting to include additional items on the agenda.

"It occurs to me," he started off pompously, "that we are complicating the administration of the Foundation's affairs unnecessarily by registering the ownership of our investments as being 'The *Pro Nobis* Foundation In Trust.'"

"I don't quite understand what you mean," one of the independent administrators said, looking puzzled.

"Let me explain." Schmidt was bubbling with enthusiasm. "We buy shares in let's say, Microsoft. We write 'The *Pro Nobis* Foundation In Trust' in the space reserved for the shareholder's name."

The administrator nodded his understanding. "And the Foundation holds the shares in trust for the owner of the money with which the shares were bought."

"That is correct."

"And who is that?" the administrator wanted to know.

Schmidt looked to Studer for the answer. He obliged. "The money and, thus, the Foundation, belong to a client of the bank who owns it through a numbered account. His identity is confidential and is known only to senior banking officials. It is also registered with the Swiss Bankers Association."

The administrator turned to Schmidt. "What are you proposing?"

"That we incorporate a company, which we will call SIL Limited. We will then transfer all of the Foundation's investments to it and sign a contract between the Foundation and SIL, whereby the Foundation will manage SIL's affairs and investments for a fee. All future investments will be made in the name of SIL."

"Who will own SIL?" Elize held her breath. This was the crux of the matter!

"SIL's entire capital will consist of 1,000 ordinary shares represented by *one* share certificate. This share certificate should be issued in the name of the beneficial owner of the account, but, in the present case, we will use the account number itself."

Elize let out an audible sigh of relief. The arrangement made sense, was entirely lawful, and continued to respect the rights of the account's owner. Unfortunately, her relief was short-lived. The next item on the agenda that Schmidt dragged up was a direct attack on her.

"I'm told," he said while looking straight at her, "that *Frau Doktor* Haemmerle feels she is being overworked. I entirely sympathize with her and feel partly responsible. I must admit to having been guilty of giving her extra work, and for this I apologize."

He looked at Studer who nodded as if to say that he accepted the apology.

Schmidt continued. "I have thought about the problem and I have come up with what I think is a workable solution. I propose that *Doktor* Haemmerle's duties as the Foundation's secretary be taken over by the Moretti Bank's in-house counsel, *Doktor Juris* Von Tobel. As for the work I have been giving her, I'll switch it to my secretary."

"Very cooperative of you," Studer said and thanked him. The other administrators said nothing.

Studer finally looked at Elize. "How long will it take you to familiarize Dr. Von Tobel with your work?"

She was at a loss for words. Her boss had just betrayed her. He had sold her out to Schmidt. "About a month or so, Dr. Studer," she finally managed to stammer.

"Well then," he said, studiously ignoring her discomfort. "Let us aim for July 1 as the date for the official handover. That way we won't interfere with your vacation plans." He turned to Schmidt. "Do you think Von Tobel could live with such a timetable?"

Schmidt nodded, and Studer got up. "Well then, lady and gentlemen, our business is done. Allow me to suggest that we schedule our next meeting for the first week in July."

"I so move," said Moretti. Schmidt seconded the motion, and they passed it unanimously.

Schmidt was very pleased. With Haemmerle out of the way, he could start implementing his secret agenda.

CHAPTER 17

Elize Haemmerle had felt as if a truck had run over her. She just couldn't function. Near tears when she had gotten home after the meeting, she kept berating herself all the way up the *Sonnenberg* for not having foreseen how Dr. Studer would react to her complaint about too much work. Heaven knows, she had felt justified. During her eight years with the Foundation, she had never complained before or refused to put in extra time. She would not have minded now, either, but the type of work she was being pressured into doing was ridiculously trivial.

The board meeting on Thursday had been bad enough, but what was to happen on Friday morning would devastate her.

Funny, she thought as she headed toward her boss's office that day. *I was sure he would understand. But he seems preoccupied of late — not his courteous, considerate self. I wonder what's bothering him.* She shrugged and entered.

"Please sit down, Dr. Haemmerle, and take coffee with me." He poured a cup from the thermos he kept on his desk, and she relaxed. It was obvious he was trying to make amends.

She couldn't have been further off the mark.

"I wish to tell you that I intend to supervise the transition personally so that it goes as smoothly as possible."

Taken aback, she could hardly speak. "What transition, *Herr Doktor?*"

He looked away. "The change in your role at the Foundation, of course."

"What *exactly* do you mean, *Doktor?*" She gave as much emphasis to the word "exactly" as she could.

Studer took a deep breath. "Once your resignation as secretary becomes effective, some of your other duties will also have to be modified. Of course, your role as internal auditor will not be affected," he added quickly, "but the work you are doing for me personally will."

"Meaning?"

"I will engage a personal assistant to do most of the work you are doing for me now. This will leave you free to devote your entire attention to auditing. Of course, you may be required to spend somewhat more time on the road, but the Foundation will compensate by giving you a special traveling allowance. Needless to say, your present compensation package will continue for the time being."

The lawyer in her kicked in. "You are then talking about a new employment contract, are you, Dr. Studer?" She was furious.

He didn't like her question. "Not really, just a small adjustment." He sounded put out.

She couldn't have cared less. Her back was up. She felt betrayed and abused, but she knew she had to keep her cool. It was always easier to defeat the enemy from within than from the outside. "Let me give it some thought over the weekend, *Herr Doktor.* I'm sure we'll be able to work something out."

She got up and left.

Her entire Saturday was spent fuming about the ungratefulness of people, the spinelessness and disloyalty of employers, and the duplicity of men like Schmidt. She was, however, a hard-nosed realist who understood where the real power lay, so very early on Sunday morning, she went to her office and copied all the documentation that she thought might be relevant to any legal action she might want to take against the Foundation.

Her brother sensed that something was wrong, though she had not shared her bad news with him. He tried to cheer her up and, at one point, remarked out of the blue, "Hang in there, my sister. Vacation time is less than a month away. You'll feel better when we're in Lugano and you see the Stapfers again."

She bent down and gave him a tight hug. "Thank God for you, Kurt," she whispered in his ear. "You always know what to say to cheer me up."

On Monday morning, Elize's chauffeur failed to materialize at eight. When he still hadn't shown by twenty past, she called him. He was surprised. "But *Frau* Haemmerle, Dr. Studer called last night to say you won't be needing my services for the time being. I thought you knew."

After mumbling some sort of an explanation, she hung up and took a cab to the office.

Her Monday morning was spent with emergencies that took longer than expected, and she had to skip lunch. In the afternoon, she composed a letter to Studer in which she confirmed her understanding that her duties had been redefined but that all other terms of her employment contract, which was due to expire on June 30 of the following year, remained valid except that she no longer had to pay for her traveling expenses from her present remuneration package.

To clarify the matter, she added a clause whereby the Foundation agreed that she was entitled to traveling in business class wherever she went and that she was allowed to charge all traveling expenses to a credit card for which the Foundation would pick up the tab monthly. As a final act of defiance, she requested confirmation that she had the right to use the Foundation's limousine and the services of its chauffeur.

She stuck her signed letter in an envelope, sealed it and, after addressing it to Studer by hand, slid it under the locked door of the head administrator's office.

She took a taxi home.

CHAPTER 18

Zurich is a city that takes itself too seriously. Jack realized this as soon as he got off the plane at Kloten at the crack of dawn on Wednesday morning, after a seven-hour flight from New York.

Everything was overengineered: the luggage carts at the airport with their extra brakes; the plethora of traffic lights at intersections for cars, trams, and cyclist; the complicated white markings on the asphalt directing traffic hither and yon; and the multitude of directional indicators that required a university degree to figure out.

He took a cab to the Hotel Baur au Lac where, his grandmother had told him, she and his grandfather had taken tea in the afternoons and had danced to the music of Charlie Kunz, the talented Swiss Jazz pianist. His room was not ready, so he walked down to the Bürkli *Platz* and watched the boats on the Zürich *See* for a while.

At eight, he had a light breakfast in the hotel's garden solarium: orange juice, *brötli* (delicious freshly-baked rolls) with lots of butter and jam, and strong coffee.

Half an hour later the *lohndiener* (bellboy) came by to say that his room was ready. After a leisurely bath and shave, he put on lightweight gray slacks, Bally loafers with socks to match his pants, a light-blue shirt from Turnbull and Asser of Jermyn Street, and a sporty dark-blue blazer he had picked up at Gieves and Hawkes on Saville Row when he had visited London the last time. He did not bother with a tie. He was on vacation.

Slowly, he made his way along the *Bahnhof Strasse,* perhaps the world's most expensive street for shopping and ended up at the *Hauptbahnhof* shortly before noon. He took the midday express to Bern and, after a fifty-seven minute train ride, was at the U.S. Embassy on *Sulgeneck Strasse* at a quarter past one.

He was starving — jet lag.

The Chargée d'Affaires couldn't do enough for him. She took him to lunch, listened to his story, and, while they were eating, called one of her people with instructions to find whatever information the embassy had on the *Pro Nobis* Foundation. Having an uncle who is the U.S. Secretary of the Treasury was obviously a great asset.

After a splendid lunch, Jack took the train back to Zurich, and when he opened his computer at the Baur au Lac that evening, he had all the material he needed. The embassy had provided him not only with the Foundation's address on Tal *Strasse* but also with background information on its administrators and its investments.

There was also a brief mention of *Frau Doktor Juris* Elize Haemmerle, the organization's secretary and internal auditor. Apparently, she attended embassy functions sporadically and visited the U.S. regularly, presumably to check up on the Foundation's investments. She was a widow and lived with her invalid brother, a professor of economics.

In addition to her direct line at the office, a home address and a private telephone number were also provided. Jack was in a quandary. It was too late to call the office, but he could call her at home and make an appointment for the next day.

He decided to wait. Calling her at home would alarm her. She'd start wondering about how he got her private number. Besides, he was too tired. He had slept only for four hours on the plane.

CHAPTER 19

The meeting, called for Thursday late afternoon in the oak-paneled study of Enrico Moretti's palatial residence took place in the utmost secrecy — only Moretti, Studer, and Schmidt were present.

The maid was off, but, as instructed, she had left a plate of roast beef sandwiches, mineral water, and coffee for the participants. There was also beer but no hard liquor.

"I've asked you to attend this meeting because I need your help." As always, Moretti spoke softly, and his guests had to strain to make sure they heard every word clearly. They knew very well that their economic survival depended on it. "I want your word that you will not share with anyone what we discuss in this room tonight."

He looked at Studer. "Do I have your word, cousin?"

"You do." Studer looked worried.

"And yours, *Herr* Schmidt?"

"You have my word." Schmidt could barely conceal his excitement. He had finally arrived: he was one of the big boys now!

"When our bank went public twenty-eight years ago," Moretti began, "the twenty-odd heirs of Aldo Moretti converted 45 percent of their total holdings in the bank to cash by selling 45,000 shares to the public. We still kept control of the bank by granting our 'A' shares ten votes per share and the public 'B' shares only one vote per share. A further backup for keeping control was the 15,000 'A' shares held by Stapfer, who it was assumed would always vote with the family."

Ignoring an irrelevant comment by Studer, Moretti continued. "Unfortunately, to make the original public issue more attractive, a needless gesture as it turned out, and at the insistence of the Zurich Stock Exchange, the family agreed to include in the offer a guarantee that, in the event that the bank failed to pay a 4 percent dividend in any year, the voting rights of the 'B' shares would automattically be increased to ten votes per share"

"I don't see the problem," piped up Schmidt, "it seems clear to me that we are covered both ways." Moretti gave him a frosty smile. "*Herr* Schmidt, please do not interrupt me again with your thoughtless comments."

Studer was beginning to perspire seriously. He sensed from the sharp tone of his admonition that Moretti was leading up to discussing a serious problem, "We have been paying these dividends religiously, have we not?"

"Yes, we have, cousin, but, as you know, we have also been paying dividends on the other shares. This means that during the last twenty-eight years, we added only about 2 to 2.5 million francs to our bank's value each year."

"How much did we pay out in dividends on average per annum?"

Moretti had all the answers at his fingertips because he had known what kind of questions his colleagues were likely to ask. "One point eight million to the public each year and 2.5 million to the heirs and Stapfer."

"That makes it about 4.3 million in dividends and leaves about 2.5 million that the bank must have added to its worth each year."

Moretti gave Schmidt a withering look. At that moment, he hated his obsequious, ingratiating deputy with all his heart. He took a deep breath to control his anger but could not refrain from adding: "I believe that is what I have just said *Herr* Schmidt. I would appreciate your not interrupting me constantly by repeatedly stating the obvious."

Studer, always the diplomat, attempted to diffuse the tension. "Let's not squabble. What you're telling us, Enrico, is that the bank, which had a worth of 100 million Swiss francs twenty-eight years ago is now worth…" he looked at his calculations on the note pad in front of him, "… is now worth about 170 million." He was tremendously relieved. "Considering that the heirs lived pretty handsomely off the business during all these years and that they still own 40 percent of a bank that is worth close to 200 million, I'd say that we haven't done badly at all."

Moretti bit his lip. "That's just the problem. Everybody expects us to keep on doing well, but profit margins are being squeezed, and I had to find ways to generate new types of revenues to be able to compete with the large international banks."

"And you did — brilliantly, if I might add." A firm statement from Schmidt uttered in abject ignorance of the true situation. Moretti abruptly left the room, afraid that he would lose control and physically assault the smarmy bastard.

When he returned a minute later, he had the bank's latest quarterly financial statements in his hand.

"On March 31, our investment portfolio, excluding the Foundation's assets, which are segregated, was over 1 billion Swiss francs. Of this, about a quarter billion is invested in Asset Based Commercial Paper, which we bought from our major U.S. correspondent banks because these securities offered a high yield and were guaranteed by these banks." He looked at Schmidt with loathing. "Although you encouraged me in this, I must assume full responsibility for making the investment."

"And I still stand by my judgment," Schmidt said haughtily. He was miffed.

"That's because you don't have the connections with old money that I have, and you never will." Moretti could no longer hold back. "Old money always knows in advance what is about to happen and only whispers it aloud very softly if at all and exclusively to members of the elite club that makes up old money."

"And what is old money whispering?" Studer asked.

"That at least half of the ABCP securities in circulation are rubbish, cousin."

"Rubbish?" Schmidt could not believe his ears.

"Yes, *Herr* Schmidt, rubbish — in a word: worthless."

"Which means..." Schmidt turned pale when he realized the enormity and far reaching consequences of the problem.

Moretti continued relentlessly "...that the bank will have to report a loss of at least 60 million francs in the third quarter of this year..."

"...which will wipe out most of our retained earnings that total only 70 million francs as we speak..."

"...and almost certainly another loss of 70 million francs in the last quarter of the year when knowledge about the ABCP problem becomes widely known..."

"...thereby reducing the worth of Moretti & Cie from a value of 170 million francs to a value of 40 million...." Schmidt completed the narrative for Moretti in a whisper.

Studer felt like retching. "*Je l'ai échappé belle,* as the saying goes in French," he said to himself. He had escaped disaster by the skin of his teeth and thanked the gods that he had had the foresight and strength of character to resist Schmidt's insistence that the Foundation invest money in ABCPs. His relief was short-lived because with relief came the realization that his share in the bank had become worth a quarter of what it had been. But all was not lost, his mind kept insisting. The Foundation was sound, and the bank was still worth money.

Then Schmidt delivered the *coup de grace.*

"According to corporate law, a public limited liability company may not declare and pay a dividend if the dividend would encroach on its capital."

"Which means?" Studer felt like retching again.

"Don't be dense, Helmut," Moretti snapped at his cousin irritably. "With our retained earnings gone and our capital diminished to 40 million Swiss francs, we cannot pay the dividend on the shares held by the public."

"And the shares would get the right to ten votes each instead of one," Studer whispered to himself. Then it hit him. "Oh my God! We would lose control of the bank."

"Not if we could make sure that Stapfer voted with the heirs," Schmidt volunteered. "Or if we could find some way of inflating the bank's capital to 172 million."

"Impossible. We could never generate those kinds of profits in six months."

"Maybe not, but there are other ways," Schmidt continued. "I have an idea, but I'd like to think about it some more before putting it forward for consideration."

"Why? There isn't a moment to lose." Studer was near panic.

"I need to look into the legality of my scheme, *Herr Doktor,* because it is very complicated and borderline."

Moretti and Studer kept pressing him, but Schmidt would give no further details other than saying that his plan involved the Foundation.

CHAPTER 20

By Friday morning, Elize was a nervous wreck. On Tuesday, she had gone about her business as if nothing had changed but took great pains to copy all relevant confidential documents that crossed her desk that day. This included the minutes of the last administrators' meeting, duly signed.

Although she had heard nothing from Studer, she was not particularly concerned because she had known that he had outside appointments all day. On Wednesday morning, he had advised her in a brief and rather cold email that he would not be in the office before Friday. This had surprised and worried her. Studer was a consistent man, a creature of habit, not one to change plans abruptly and without explanation.

She had become somewhat more concerned during the day when Schmidt's secretary had appeared in her office with yet another pile of files for her review.

"*Herr* Schmidt will be absent for the week but would like the work completed by next Monday," she had announced primly and had left without another word.

Were Schmidt and Studer away together? Elize had slept badly that night, tossing and turning and worrying about what would happen to her and her brother if she lost her job. Repeatedly recalculating the amount of money she would dispose over should she find herself in the street didn't help her sleep, either. They had about

20,000 francs in their joint bank account and maybe another thirty invested in *Kantonalische Schuldverschreibungen* — nice, secure bonds, issued by Switzerland's provinces called Kantons. "Their interest rates are nothing to write home about," she had mused while awake between nightmares, "but they are safe and not likely to lose their value."

Then there was the house. Mortgage free. She could sell it for a million francs, 600,000 euros, if push came to shove. Her termination pay would amount to 200,000 francs after five years' service, as per contract. The amount was set to increase to 300,000 after ten years' service, but she only had eight.

There would be no income. Except perhaps the money from the newsletter, which amounted to about 6,000 dollars a month, if Schmidt didn't stumble on it and stop the flow of money. But she needed more than that because caring for Kurt was very costly. He needed help in the morning to bathe and dress and someone to help him go to bed at night. And she needed a housekeeper.

She would take the money from the house, add to it the termination pay and what they had in the bank, and invest it all into a life annuity for Kurt. What kind of an annuity would he receive on 1.25 million francs invested? Perhaps 10,000 a month. Not enough.

She'd need to find a well-paying new job — and fast. How long could she live on her secret money in Cayman? *By now there must be at least 150,000 dollars in the account. Twenty-five times 6,000.* Enough for a job search lasting eight months. And she wouldn't have to sell the house or anything.

She had finally fallen asleep at three o'clock in the morning and had awoken at six thirty.

Deeply engrossed in her work on Thursday afternoon, exhausted and feeling very insecure, Elize did not hear her assistant's knock on her door, so he came in.

"Excuse me, *Doktor* Haemmerle, but the American gentleman is here."

"What American gentleman?"

"The one I told you about this morning. You agreed to see him at four o'clock."

"Oh my God," she exclaimed. "I completely forgot about him."

Her assistant seemed to hesitate. "Shall I tell him to come back tomorrow?"

"No, no, we can't do that. Did you not say he was from the embassy?"

"No, *Frau Doktor.* I said that he said that he got your number from the embassy." *What's the matter with the boss, anyway?* he asked himself. *She's been acting very strange of late. Can't remember a thing from one minute to the next.* Then he shrugged. *Must be on the rag,* he added and immediately regretted the thought. *God knows, the poor woman has enough on her plate. Office gossip has her on her way out — and she with that invalid brother to look after.* He liked his boss and he was ashamed of having been uncharacteristically unkind to her even if only in his thoughts.

He tried to make amends because he didn't relate to guilt. "Why don't you powder your nose a bit while I chat with him?"

"Do I look that awful?"

He gave her his best smile to make up for his bitchiness. "It does look a little bit too shiny."

"What does?"

"Your nose."

She took out her compact and returned his smile. "Thank you. Give me five minutes."

She found the man who entered her office a few minutes later incredibly attractive.

He was wearing a beautifully tailored, obviously bespoke, light-gray suit that offset his deeply tanned, handsome face admirably. His pink shirt and exquisitely matching tie looked very expensive and would have looked effeminate had it not been for the man's jet black hair and his piercing gray-green eyes that sparkled with intelligence.

He crossed the room with athletic grace and extended his hand. "How do you do, Dr. Haemmerle? I'm Jack Brennan." He took her hand and bent over it to brush it with his lips without really touching it.

No simple American, he, she said to herself and inhaled sharply. The man exuded sex appeal. "I am Elize Haemmerle," she replied in English, "and I am sorry to have kept you waiting. May I offer you a coffee? We make a very fine espresso here."

"Yes, please. I'm afraid I'm still a bit jetlagged." He had just a hint of the Irish in his way of speaking.

They chatted politely while her assistant busied himself with the fine silver and porcelain service he trotted out to impress those important visitors whom he liked. Dr. Studer had drilled into everybody that to be important you had to look important. To be taken seriously, you had to act seriously. Elize's office, as all the offices of the Foundation's executives, was spacious and tastefully furnished and decorated without being ostentatious.

Satisfied that the coffee was ready to be served, her assistant left the room.

Elize was watching Jack's strong hands as he manipulated the sugar pincers with ease and blushed when she realized that she was wondering how his long, slender, suntanned fingers would feel on her breasts.

Don't go there, she commanded. *This man is dangerous for you.* Aloud she asked: "When did you come over?"

"I left New York Tuesday night."

"How come you are so suntanned?"

He looked up at her, and she felt his gorgeous eyes boring into her soul. "I live in the Cayman Islands."

Shaken, she looked away. "And what is it that you do there?"

"I am a liquidator, Dr. Haemmerle, a bankruptcy liquidator, who liquidates banks. And I have a colleague in Bermuda whom I believe you know."

Elize felt dizzy. She was afraid of what this man would say next, but she had to ask.

"What is his name?"

"Keiser, Henry Keiser."

"But he is not with a bank."

"No, Dr. Haemmerle, he is not. He works for a management

company that services clients with businesses offshore. I believe that you are the auditor of one of his clients. Am I correct?"

She nodded, dumbfounded and totally lost. What did this beautiful man want from her? Why was he here? Whom was he working for?

Numbly, she whispered. "You are correct." She mustered all her strength. "Now please tell me what you want from me."

"I need to speak with the client about his bank account in the Cayman Islands. Could you help me get in touch with him?"

She was finished, betrayed.

She stood up and faced him. "I am the owner of the publishing company that owns the Cayman account."

Something clicked in Jack's brain. "And your brother is the author of that excellent monthly newsletter."

"That is so." Her lips were quivering. This man knew everything. "Now tell me. Why are you here?"

So he told her about the OBGC bankruptcy and when he got to the part where he had to admit that most of her money was lost, the beautiful, haughty, elegant but insecure and stressed-out *Frau Doktor Juris* Elize Haemmerle burst into tears and began to sob uncontrollably.

The sight of the weeping woman jolted Jack back into the past by twenty years. In his mind's eye, he saw his mother again in their kitchen, sobbing her heart out at the loss of a beloved husband and a precious son. He also saw Mary, his sister, in his own bed, hugging and kissing him to comfort the tortured, guilt-ridden lost soul that he was then — a frightened little boy without a friend in the world.

What he did next was pure instinct. He enfolded her in his embrace and held her tight until the sobs subsided. Then he held her away from his face, looked her in the eyes and gently kissed her on the lips. He intended the kiss to be a brotherly one, but she held his head to her until they were both out of breath.

When they finally separated, he took out his handkerchief and began to wipe her tears away.

"I am so ashamed, Mr. Brennan." She dared not look at him. "I should never have lost control."

He gave her a big smile that seemed to light up the entire room. "Don't be silly. It happens in the best of families. Just remember, what goes around comes around."

"I don't understand."

Taking her gently by the hand, he guided her to the sofa and made her sit next to him. Then, still holding her hand, he told her about his father and his brother, Niall, and about his sister, Mary, and the way Mary had helped him retain his sanity.

When he had finished, he got up and took his leave. "Go home now and get some rest. I'm busy during the day, but I'll call you at home tomorrow night. We'll get together on Saturday to work out how we can salvage at least part of the situation."

He was gone before she could give him her home phone number.

And she was not in the book.

On Friday, Dr. Studer, looking haggard and worried, asked her to have lunch with him at Lindt *und* Sprüngli, just around the corner from the office. The restaurant was upstairs. Its windows overlooked the busy *Paradeplatz,* or "Parade Square," where an endless stream of gleaming tramways seemed to go around in incessant circles, their metal wheels grinding harshly against the rails sunk into the roadbed. They could hear their screeching through the large dining room's windows, even though these were triple-glazed.

Studer ordered soup and *Bouchée á la Reine* for both and insisted that they have a glass of white wine with their meal. When their drinks arrived, he raised his glass to hers and said, "Contrary to what you may think, I am not your enemy. We have worked together for eight years, and I have never had reason to complain about your work or your loyal devotion to duty."

She said nothing.

When their main course arrived, he raised his glass again. "I have reviewed your letter and agree with its contents, except for one thing."

"And what is that?"

"I cannot make the limousine and the chauffeur available

for you."

She was surprised. It was such a small thing — picayune. After all, he had just agreed to a 10 percent salary raise *and* a reduced work load.

"Why not?"

His answer surprised her. "I'd rather not go into it. Besides, in due course, you'll work it out for yourself." He reached into his inside pocket and extracted two copies of her letter. "I have not bothered to have your letter retyped. I just struck out the last paragraph. After you've initialed the change, I'll sign the letter in the space you provided."

He held out his pen. After she initialed the change he signed the letter with a flourish and handed her a copy with a sad smile. Then he raised his glass for a third time.

"Friends again?"

Baffled, she nodded. "Friends again."

She thought she understood why he was sad. He must have suddenly realized that their relationship would never be the same again. For her part, she sensed that he was concerned about something that he could no longer bring himself to share with her, which meant that her contract would not be renewed next July because he no longer trusted her.

At least, she reflected on her way home in a taxi, the week had not been a total disaster. She got a substantial raise, her responsibilities were reduced, she had gained a full year in which to recover at least a part of the money she had lost, and she had met a man who seemed to be sensitive enough to merit her companionship. He said he would call her at home, so she'd leave it to him to prove that he was a man of his word, resourceful enough to find her private telephone number in time to make the call as promised. She decided there and then that she would make no effort to try to track him down.

Then she laughed out so loud that the startled driver could not stop himself from looking back at her. "You're being silly" she muttered. "If he doesn't call, you had damn better be sure to go after him because men like him are rare to find. And look how happy you are just thinking about him."

Her mood turned somber after she had paid off the cab. *Maybe he is married or has a girlfriend? No, he mentioned his mother and his sister, and he was not wearing a wedding ring. Or was he?* She couldn't be sure.

Sighing, she entered her house and went to greet her brother. At least she could count on him.

CHAPTER 21

Jack could not stop himself from reviewing the widow Haemmerle's circumstances over and over again. She was alone in the world, *that* he knew, except for her invalid brother whom she had been looking after for years. And that was expensive.

It had never occurred to him that the Bermuda account's auditor would turn out to be its beneficial owner, nor had he expected this beautiful woman to break down before his eyes. And beautiful she was, breathtakingly so.

Her lips had been velvet against his when they had kissed, and he had felt her passion for him rise while he was holding her. What a classy woman!

There was something, though, that he couldn't understand. The money she had lost in the bankruptcy had not amounted to much, relatively speaking, only about 100,000 dollars. She still had 55,000 dollars left in a good account, and money kept flowing into it at the monthly rate of about 6,000 bucks, money that she was not using and seemed not to need.

"She must have a reasonably high salary," he mused. "Just look at the stylish office she works in." So why the tears? What was the real reason for her being so upset?' He felt sorry to have been the one who had to break the bad news to her but very glad to have been there to console her. And he could hardly wait to see her again.

After sending out his suit to be dry-cleaned in hopes that the thorough Swiss would be able to remove the mascara and lipstick stains from the garment, Jack ate a light dinner, went for a walk, and then was off to bed. He fell asleep, thinking about Elize and his grandma Ilona. "Time to settle down, Jack!"

Friday was a red-letter day for Jack. He had an appointment with a friend of his grandmother's, the legendary "Doctors" (a European aberration when one had not one but two doctorates) Hans Arbenz, Nobel Laureate and Professor Emeritus of Chemistry at several universities. Yes, *Doctors* in the plural. Arbenz had at least two PhDs.

Grandma Ilona and her husband, Bill, had met him in Bern during the Second World War. They became lifelong friends, and Ilona still corresponded with Arbenz, though the scientist was 102 years old. Jack had never met a man as old as that and did not know what to expect.

Arbenz knocked his socks off. Absolutely.

He lived in an apartment occupying the top two floors of a building along the *Stadthaus Quai,* part of the embankment of the Limat River. The care-giving arrangements in place to keep him going resembled those surrounding Grandma Ilona except that Arbenz's servants were all male.

Jack had been told that the best time to see the old man would be at eleven o'clock, just after he had finished breakfast. He would be rested and sharp and ready for a chat until lunchtime. If the conversation was to his liking, he'd invite his visitor to a light lunch around one thirty. Then it was off to bed at three for a long siesta. At six, he'd watch the BBC news and, after a snack, do battle on the chessboard with selected co-practitioners of the game three times a week. His wife was long dead, but he had lots of family — more than a dozen great-grandchildren.

When he got to Arbenz's place, Jack was shown to the roof garden. He found the old man looking toward the river through binoculars.

"Come over here," he commanded, "and have a look at the view." Jack took the glasses and began to scan the buildings on the other side of the Limat.

"Don't be dense, man," his host said with a chuckle. "Look at what's *on* the river, not across it."

Jack did as he was told and let out a great guffaw. The 102-year-old Nobel Laureate and professor emeritus was ogling the women taking the sun in the ladies' *Badeanstallt* (bathing pavilion) anchored in the middle of the river. Most of them were stark naked.

"When I bought this place about seventy years ago, there was no roof garden. Then I built one and my late wife, God rest her soul, almost killed me. She called me a dirty old man. I wonder what she'd be calling me today if she saw me trying to corrupt a young innocent."

He winked at Jack. "But, frankly, you don't look too innocent to me."

Arbenz took the armchair elevator down to the top floor, and Jack joined him there. He was amazed how spritely the old man was.

"Tell me about Ilona."

Jack obliged while the valet served them lemonade. It was a sunny, warm June day. The windows in the spacious study were wide open, and the sunshine streaming through them bathed the room in a brilliant light. Floor-to-ceiling shelves burgeoning with books, monographs, and manuscripts of all shapes and sizes lined the walls. Jack couldn't find a spot where one could have inserted yet another volume.

"Amazing these Hungarian women, you know." The professor became serious. "You should have seen how beautiful Ilona was when she was young. And Bill, your grandfather, was absolutely crazy about her."

"I understand that there was a lot of opposition to their marrying."

Arbenz chuckled. "That there was, but Bill would have none of it. Just swept it aside. And so did she."

The old man kept on sipping his lemonade in silence for a while then lifted his head. "Tell me, what brings you to Zurich?"

"To meet you, Professor."

"Very flattering, I'm sure. But be serious now. Tell me the real reason."

Jack told him about his job and quickly summarized the

mysterious Bermuda account problem. He was surprised to find that his host's familiarity with offshore tax havens was right up there with the accounting professionals.

"You know, we Swiss thought up this whole concept during the *Hitlerei*."

"What is *Hitlerei?*"

"The time during which Hitler persecuted the Jews, the Bolsheviks, the gays, the mentally ill and the gypsies — all the non-Aryans, whatever that means."

Jack's host looked at his watch. "If you are free, have lunch with me, and I'll tell you how this tax haven business started."

The meal — soup, smoked salmon, and a little potato salad, and, for dessert, a vanilla sherbet — was good, but the conversation was much better, bordering on the outstanding. Arbenz spoke knowledgably about a number of topics and had the knack of making his listener live the story he was telling. Jack was mesmerized.

When the professor heard that his guest was going on to visit Hungary, his mood turned somber.

"I had a Hungarian colleague once." He was whispering. It was evident that he was getting tired. "Perished during the war. A great pity. A brilliant man, he never got the chance to develop his potential fully." Arbenz rang a little silver bell, and the valet appeared at his side immediately. "I have to rest for a while, but come back around six, and we'll watch the BBC news together. Remind me to tell you about my Hungarian colleague."

At six, Arbenz was fresh as a daisy again. After the newscast, he told Jack about his Jewish Hungarian Nobel Laureate friend and how the man got himself blown up by accident.

"What about his wife and kids?"

"They got killed, too. The Hungarian Nazis shot them and threw their bodies into the Danube. She was a wonderfully talented painter and a sweet woman, I was told. Also Jewish, of course. Her father had been the Tsar's banker. Shvedov was his name."

"And your friend? What was his name?"

"Gombos, Dr. Peter Gombos. Nobel Laureate in Physics. Got his prize the same year as me, 1936."

In the lobby, as Jack was bidding his host farewell, Arbenz held out his arms to him. "Come here boy, and let me give you a hug. Carry it to your grandmother for me, and tell her she has every right to be proud of you."

CHAPTER 22

Elize was in the kitchen, sipping a glass of red wine, her third, and warming the meatloaf and the vegetables her housekeeper had prepared for dinner. Usually, she tried to limit herself to only one glass, but it was Friday and she needed a buzz; her week had been stressful, to say the least.

She was also discouraged. Jack Brennan had not called, and she wasn't sure what to do about him. Her heart and body ached for him, but her mind kept insisting that he was just another good-looking man, easy-going and unreliable, who, once he bedded her, would fade away like the others.

Kurt was yelling something from his office, so she went into the hall to hear him better.

"What is it?"

"When's supper, Sis? I'm starving."

"Give me ten minutes."

Quite disconsolate, she returned to the kitchen and took a major slug from the wine in her glass.

The phone rang, and she ran to pick it up.

"Hello, auditor lady. I hope I'm not interrupting your dinner."

The feeling of immense relief that swept over her made it hard to speak. "No, Jack, we haven't started yet," she finally managed. Then she caught herself. "May I call you, Jack?"

"Don't be silly; of course you can. I'm phoning to invite you for lunch tomorrow at the Hotel Eden au Lac's restaurant. I've reserved a table on the terrace so we can eat and watch the sailboats at the same time."

She was bowled over. "How did you manage that? The terrace is always fully booked for lunch on Saturdays. You must reserve a month ahead in June. They have a waiting list."

"Ah, but I have connections." She could hear him laugh. "I guess this means you accept, so I'll pick you up around noon, and we'll have a drink first. My reservations are for twelve forty-five *pünktlich*."

Her heart was singing. He even knew the right word in German for "punctually." *Yes, we Swiss are very* pünktlich, *to a fault. And boringly so,* she said to herself.

Then she became suspicious. "Are you staying at the Hotel Eden?" What would be easier than getting her tipsy and then taking her upstairs? And she wasn't sure she could resist him.

"No, I'm at the Baur au Lac. My grandmother told me that in her days they had *Thés Dansants* in the garden pavilion at four o'clock in the afternoon on weekends. We could have a sail after lunch and then check it out."

"Sounds as if you plan to spend the whole afternoon with me."

"And the evening. We have much to discuss." He laughed again, a happy, full-throated laugh. "I'll pick you up at noon, *pünktlich*." Then he hung up.

And how are you going to do that? she asked herself. *You don't know where I live.* Very few people did. Then her insecurities kicked in again. *This man seems to have extraordinary connections in Zurich. I wonder how come? May be he isn't really who he says he is.* Jack Brennan was dangerous.

She took their dinner into the dining room and called Kurt to come and eat.

The next day, Jack picked her up in a limo at twelve noon sharp. He was wearing an ultra-light, navy blue cashmere blazer, a sparklingly white silk shirt open at the neck, beautifully fitting grey slacks with razor-sharp creases, and Gucci loafers without socks.

To Elize, he looked like a fashion model from the social pages of

Paris Match. The overall impression he created was that of understated elegance and sophistication. To avoid his meeting Kurt, she cut him off at the door and did not ask him to come in. This seemed to take him aback.

"I didn't want you to meet my brother yet," she explained in the car. "He doesn't know about the Cayman account. Frankly, I'm afraid to tell him about it."

"But you must."

She kissed him lightly on the cheek. "I promise I will. Just give me time," she whispered in his ear.

Once or twice in a lifetime, if one is lucky, the heavenly powers provide one with an extraordinary set of circumstances in which everything seems to work perfectly. If one is super lucky the circumstances prevail for a whole day. For Jack Brennan, the first day he spent with Elize Haemmerle was such a day, a day he would never forget.

There wasn't a cloud in the proverbial blue sky when they took their seats on the Eden's terrace and ordered mojitos. The weather was quite warm, but there was a light breeze and the large awning kept the sun away from their faces. They decided to eat outside and watch the sailboats on the lake.

Well sated after a splendid meal during which they somehow managed to talk just enough business for him to know what she wanted him to do with the money in her "good" account, they walked down to the steamboat wharf and took a short cruise on the lake. They were back at the Baur au Lac by half past four where the band in the garden was about to start playing. After ordering tea for two, Jack asked Elize to dance.

And from that moment on, they both knew that it was all over, that to resist was no longer possible. As soon as he took her in his arms, Elize melted. Her desire for him became so strong that she lost control over her trembling legs and had to sit down.

To her amazement, he understood perfectly. He poured her some tea then took both of her hands in his. "I want you to know how I feel about you." His whisper had an urgent intensity. "The chemistry between us is so strong that it's choking me. I suspect the same is happening with you."

She nodded wordlessly.

"If I asked you to come to bed with me right now, you would say yes, wouldn't you?"

She nodded again, not daring to say anything.

"I know you're under a lot of stress, and I don't want this thing between the two of us to be just a casual fling. If you can bear to wait for a few days until you're sure you want to get involved with me, come to Budapest with me for four days next weekend."

"Thank you," she said softly but firmly. She knew exactly what she wanted and what she needed. "I don't want to wait. Bed me now, Jack, *and* take me to Budapest next weekend."

CHAPTER 23

Budapest used to be the Austro-Hungarian Monarchy's second-most important city, but whereas Vienna was pompous and full of self-importance because it was the seat of government and the hub of the empire, Budapest refused to take itself seriously. Its architecture resembled that of Paris and not that of the Austrian capital, and its inhabitants loved wine, women, and song more than holding their noses to the grindstone to make money.

Jack, who had taken the last flight to Budapest from Zurich on Sunday night, was met at Ferihegy airport by his friend Ákos who drove him to his hotel, the Four Seasons, overlooking Roosevelt Square.

Prior to becoming a hotel, the building was called the Gresham Palace, a fine example of Art Nouveau Architecture, and *the* address for the local gentry and for resident British aristocrats Pestside before World War II.

Ákos, a banker whom Jack had met in London on liquidation business, was Jack's only contact in Hungary. Grandma Ilona had been of no help. Always evasive when it came to talking about her background, she said that she had no living friends or relatives in the region. After all, she had left the country as a young woman, barely twenty — and that had been three-quarters of a century earlier. At Jack's insistence, she had finally volunteered that she was born in Budapest, that her father's name was Béla Pásztor, and that her mother's name was Irma Szabó.

When Jack got to his room and the bellboy opened the curtains to show him the view, he gasped. The fully illuminated Chain Bridge stretched across the Danube like a string of glowing pearls and connected with the tunnel on the other side of the river that burrowed into the mountain below the castle, its entrance also brightly lit. Above, the ancient seat of Corwin kings brooded in somber majesty, and to its right, the Fishermen's Bastion glittered brilliantly, its reflection sparkling in the river's waters.

The sight was heartbreakingly beautiful, and this made him think of Elize. Their lovemaking on Saturday afternoon had been spectacular. He had felt her hunger and had striven hard to satisfy it. She responded with incredible tenderness and a torrent of tears. When it was over, they clung to each other for a long time without speaking. Finally, she broke the silence and told him about her brother, her job, the intolerable chauvinism of the male world in which she was forced to live, the disloyalty of her long-time boss, Dr. Studer, and the threat Schmidt represented.

"Then you came along with your bad news, and all the lights went out. I broke down." She had snuggled closer to him. "But I'm glad you've finally arrived."

"Meaning?"

"I've been waiting for a man like you ever since my husband died."

"But you hardly know me."

She had looked at him mischievously."That's where you're wrong. I saw enough to know that I know."

That had made both of them laugh, and the mood was broken.

She had then taken him home to meet her brother. Kurt and Jack hit it off right from the start, and that had been good, too.

Jack closed the curtains and went in search of a snack. He didn't know how he'd manage without her during the next three days.

He spent Monday sightseeing and then let Ákos and his wife, a freelance fashion photographer, take him to dinner. The next day at the Embassy on Vörösmarty *Tér,* the Chargé d'Affaires, Geoffrey Moffat, received him as if he were the President himself. Uncle

George's magic worked even in Hungary.

"To get a handle on your grandmother's background, you'll need to visit the Ministry of the Interior. That's where they keep the records of births, deaths, marriages, and so forth."

"Do you know anyone there?"

Moffat was quick to oblige. "There's a woman at the ministry who acts as liaison between us and them." He handed Jack a card. "Here's her name and number. Call her, and tell her I sent you."

Jack secured an appointment and went to see her at the Interior Ministry on Andrassy Street the next morning. Mrs. Pázmány spoke perfect English. After hearing Jack out, she made a couple of quick phone calls then gave Brennan the bad news.

"We're in the process of transferring our database to computers, and it's taking more time than we expected. Logically, we started with the most recent data first and are working our way back into history." She looked at her visitor and gave him an encouraging smile before telling him that no data was available on computer that related to events before World War II — that is to say before 1939.

"But my grandmother was born in 1914. What can be done?"

The woman was sympathetic. "We'll have to undertake a manual search, which takes time and costs money."

"How long and how much?"

She laughed. "You Americans are always very quick to cut to the chase, but before answering your question, let me explain. The year 1914 was when the First World War broke out. By the way, on what day was your grandmother born?"

"March 30."

"That makes it easier." Mrs. Pázmány said. "The monarchy's records were well kept. We will probably have no difficulty finding the register in which the birth was recorded, provided it was not being stored in an area damaged during World War II."

"And if it did?"

"We'd try to obtain the data from a secondary source."

"Such as?"

"The Passport Office, for example."

Jack nodded. "That makes sense. Grandma must have obtained a passport some time during the early 1930s. She traveled to Spain around that time."

The woman made a note. "That's useful information. I presume she must have traveled under her maiden name."

Jack nodded. He liked his hostess. There was something very no-nonsense about her. "Where did you learn your excellent English?"

"I worked at the UN in New York for five years."

No wonder she was so American in her ways.

"So what's the bottom line?"

"For a pre–World War II 'normal' search, nine months and 20,000 forints."

Jack bit his lip. "That's a hundred bucks and time enough to have a baby."

"If you want results more quickly, you must pay more."

"How much more?"

"The best we could do is three to four months for 200 dollars."

And that's where they left the matter.

Jack filled out the required questionnaire and gave Mrs. Pázmány 200 dollars in cash for which he received an official-looking receipt.

"We'll send the results of the search to your friend, Mr. Moffat, at the embassy."

"Why?"

"If it looks like the request had come from the embassy itself, it might speed matters up a bit."

"Good idea," said Jack. He wanted the information as soon as possible but, in any event, before Grandma's ninety-fifth birthday. The Rooneys were always bragging about how they could trace their ancestry as far back as the Revolutionary War with the British. On such occasions, his grandmother would sit in pained silence and say nothing.

He intended to surprise her by tracing the family tree of the Pásztors.

CHAPTER 24

Jack found the next three days heavy going. He did the obligatory sights of Hungary's capital city and even ventured into the famous Rudas thermal and medicinal baths that still retain a strong Turkish atmosphere, (they were built by the Ottomans in 1566), but his heart was not into sightseeing. His body and soul were pining for Elize.

She arrived on Thursday night, and by the time the taxi got them to the Four Seasons, they were half-crazed with desire for each other. They went straight to bed and, totally out of control, tore at each other with savage want over and over again.

Their need was not only physical. During long post-coital conversations, they admitted, first timidly then openly and tearfully, that neither had ever recovered from the deeply traumatic events that had taken place in their lives.

After the death of his father and his brother, Jack had spent his teen years fighting loneliness and guilt, overcompensating for his deep insecurity by constantly seeking to please everyone and to over-achieve. Elize confessed to having hardened her heart in self-defense to the point where she trusted no one and was incapable of responding to love offered — until now. She saw in Jack the suffering she herself had endured, while he, in turn, recognized that by making her able to love again, he would somehow heal his own hurt. And this meant that he would have to share her life.

Was he ready to do so? He wasn't sure. Would she want him to do so? It was too early to ask. Impasse. He resolved to wait and see and to be kind, loving, decent, and considerate.

They spent their time together in Hungary alternating between lovemaking and limited touring, and all of a sudden it was Sunday, their last full day in Budapest and time for lunch with Ákos and Judit Almási. They decided to eat on the terrace of the Robinson Restaurant, which is located alongside the artificial lake in the *Városliget,* the city's largest park.

While on their second post-lunch espresso, Judy suggested that they visit an interesting art exhibition at the BAV's main showroom.

"They're auctioning off antique jewelry, and I'd like to take some pictures," she announced.

"What's a BAV?" Elize asked.

"BAV stands for *Bizományi Áruház Vállalat* and is a two-and-a-half centuries' old business started by the Empress Maria Theresia who, in an effort to limit usury, created a gigantic imperial pawn-shop enterprise. BAV is the successor business that holds regular exhibitions — auctions really — where you can find, buy and sell all sorts of stuff, including antiquities and paintings. People bring their items to BAV on consignment, and BAV tries to sell them."

"They charge a commission, I suppose."

"Yes. And if they haven't sold an item after a year, you have to pick it up; otherwise, they charge you for storage."

Elize was fascinated by the idea. "Is it run by the state?"

"Sort of."

She looked at Jack. "Would you like to go?"

"Sure. Why not?"

A fateful decision, although taken in a most offhand manner. It would dominate the rest of their lives.

They got to BAV's Váci street showroom about a half-hour before the auction was to begin. Elize and Judit headed straight for the display tables, leaving Ákos and Jack to wander around the huge premises crammed with carpets, paintings, furniture, lamps, knick-knacks, and all other kinds of *objets d'art.*

On their way back to rejoin the women, a picture on the wall caught Jack's eye. It was a portrait depicting two very smartly dressed little boys in front of a blackboard on which their teacher seemed to be writing something. The card at the left of the picture read: portrait of Nobel Laureate Dr. Peter Gombos and his family, painted by his wife Svetlana Shvedova. 1943.

He called for Ákos to have a look. "Have you ever heard of this guy before?"

"Can't say that I have."

"Where could we find out how much they want for the picture?"

"Come with me." Ákos took him to the back office where a harassed clerk looked the price up on her computer. "One hundred and fifty thousand forints," she said in English

"How much is that in U.S. money?"

"About 750 dollars."

Jack made up his mind in a flash. "I want to buy this painting for a friend, but I have to call him first. How much money do I have to give you to hold it for me for a week?"

"Ten percent."

Jack gave the clerk seventy-five dollars and asked Ákos to fetch Judit. "I need her to take a really professional photo of this picture. You know — high resolution, faithful color reproduction, large, hard copy...."

When Judit arrived, he told her about Arbenz and the man in the painting. "So you see," he finished up, "I don't want to give the old man the picture unless he really wants it, but to want it, he has to see it. How big a print could you make without losing resolution?"

"Fifteen by eighteen centimeters. Would that do?"

"Perfect."

Later that evening, Jack and Elize agreed that he'd return to Zurich with her on Monday so he could show Judit's photo of the Gombos family to Arbenz. He felt strongly about wanting to demonstrate how much he appreciated the old man's hospitality by bringing him a memento from his past.

"And after?" Jack could hear the anxiety in her voice.

"You're going on vacation with your brother in July, aren't you?"

"What do you have in mind?"

"Maybe you, Kurt, and I could spend some time together to see how we get along."

She stepped toward him and buried her face in the crook of his neck. "Thank you," she whispered. "I'll speak with Kurt."

CHAPTER 25

Nobel Laureate Arbenz was delighted with Jack's second visit, thrilled to hear that he'd located a likeness of his old friend Gombos, and tickled pink when he laid eyes on Dr. Elize Haemmerle. He loved the company of beautiful women.

"So the picture is up for auction. How much do they want for it?"

"Professor Arbenz, never mind that. Tell me if you like it, and I will have it shipped to you from Budapest. I've already put down a deposit on it."

Arbenz picked up a strong magnifying glass and extracted the photograph from its frame. "Yes, it definitely is Gombos," he said after examining the picture carefully. "I never met his wife or the children." He continued to scan the photo. "What a bizarre distortion!" he suddenly exclaimed.

"What is?"

"Look at the first formula, Jack."

"I'm afraid you lost me, Professor."

"There are four equations on the blackboard in this picture. The last three seem to be calendar dates, but the first one is a misrepresentation of Einstein's famous theory of relativity. Einstein stipulated that $E = mc^2$, which is to say that energy equals mass multiplied by the speed of light squared. How could a renowned and brilliant physicist and mathematician get such a well-known formula wrong?"

Elize chimed in. "Perhaps he did it on purpose."

Arbenz looked at Elize with new interest. "Very intuitive." He handed her the picture. "What else do you see?"

"As you know, Professor, I work for a Foundation that is connected with a well-known private bank, so I think about 'private banking' every time I see a reference to banking."

It was Arbenz's turn to be mystified. "Where is the reference to banking?"

"In the window, *Herr Doktor*. If you look carefully, you can see the picture of a building through the window with Bank written over its entrance."

Arbenz became very excited. He snatched the picture from Elize's outstretched hand. "By Jove, you're right." He took a deep breath and turned to Jack. "Come to think of it, when Gombos and I got back to Zurich from Sweden, I insisted that he put some money away in a safe place, just in case he got into trouble. I even introduced him to Otto Graf, the managing director of Banque Julius Odier. I seem to remember that we all had dinner together."

Elize sucked in her breath. "*Die goldene Bank*," she whispered.

"What does that mean?" Jack was completely lost.

"Darling, the bank we are talking about has been in business for almost 300 years. It is considered to be so solid that its nickname in financial circles is 'the Golden Bank.'"

Elize looked at the picture again. "The first formula says AU = c^2m. AU is the universally recognized symbol for gold. To me, this means that, if I'm right, Professor Gombos's account number at Banque Odier is either c^2m, or that c^2m is a code for the account number."

For some reason, he couldn't explain why, the hackles began to rise on the back of Jack's neck. "And what do you think the second equation represents?"

"Probably the password."

"What an intriguing idea." Professor Arbenz closed his eyes for a few moments and then looked at Jack and added, "Certainly worth following up."

CHAPTER 26

No sooner had Elize returned from her long weekend than Schmidt began to badger her again. He wanted everything done before she left on vacation — the handover of her work to her successor *and* the reregistration of all the Foundation's securities in the name of SIL Limited. Jack watched her struggle with her heavy workload for a few days and then visited Kurt and had a word with him.

"Your sister is killing herself with work and worry," he told her brother, "and we are partially to blame for the situation."

Kurt was taken aback. He was not accustomed to such a direct frontal approach, especially not from a relative stranger. Typically Swiss, he hardly ever expressed his true feelings and expected others to act in the same way. And he was convinced that everybody had a hidden agenda — always. So why should this perpetually smiling Irishman be different from everybody else? What did he really want? Was it not enough for him to have succeeded in worming his way into his sister's heart so that he could crawl into bed with her?

He felt mildly insulted. "Frankly, Jack, I don't really think that this is either your business or mine. Elize knows what she's doing, and I think we should just leave the matter at that."

Jack surprised him. He drew up a chair and faced him squarely.

"Look, Kurt, I don't want any misunderstandings between us. I think I know how you feel and relate to your concerns because I have an older sister just like you do. Believe me, she, too, had her share of sorrows, like Elize and you and me." He leaned forward. "You feel that you must protect her at all cost and that it is your duty to be wary of me. I'd feel the same way if I were in your place."

"What do you want then?"

"I met your sister two weeks ago, and we fell in lust."

"Lust? What is that?"

"Our hormones made us hunger for each other so much that we were driven to become lovers. We are still in that stage of our relationship, but, at least as far as I'm concerned, our feelings have begun to evolve into more than just being bedmates."

"You are in love? After two weeks?" *This man is telling me lies,* the economist said to himself. *He thinks we have money because Elize is a senior executive and we live in an expensive house. So he's after our money. After he finds out that we haven't any, he'll drop Elize like all the others and go back to America. And Elize will be heartbroken — again.*

"I did not say that." Jack was getting upset but tried not to show it. "We may well be on the way to falling in love, but neither of us is sure about it. We need more time together."

Kurt was embarrassed. He did not know how to cope with the other man's way of baring his feelings so openly. "What do you propose?"

"Elize wants to satisfy her boss and you and me, all at the same time. She's rushing to finish her job so that we can go away on vacation soon. In the process, she's exhausting herself needlessly." Jack came to the point. "I propose that we postpone our vacation for two weeks. I'll report back to my superior in Cayman and bring him up-to-date, then I'll swing by Buffalo for a week to see my family, and then I'll come back here and drive the two of you down to Lugano, as promised."

"Elize will never agree to this."

"I count on you to persuade her."

✦

The second secret meeting to address the problem of the eventual shortage in Moretti & Cie's capital account took place in mid-July.

"The theoretical solution to the situation is simple." Schmidt reported. "The bank has to buy something and pay for it with its shares."

"Such as?"

"The shares of SIL held by the Foundation."

The answer did not surprise either Studer or Moretti. They were expecting it.

"How do you see that happening?"

"When the bank went public, it obtained the right to issue an unlimited number of 'B' common shares..."

"...of which we sold 45,000 to the public..." Studer cut in, and Schmidt nodded agreement.

"I propose that we issue some more of these shares to buy SIL from its owner."

"And how would that work?"

"Thanks to Dr. Haemmerle's dedicated work during the last month, SIL Limited now owns everything that the Foundation used to own, and the person who used to own the Foundation now owns all the shares of SIL Limited. We will buy these shares from him by giving him 'B' shares of Moretti & Cie."

Although Schmidt had tried to make the deal sound simple, Enrico Moretti knew better. He asked two crucial questions. "How many shares would we have to give him? In other words, how would we establish relative value?"

Schmidt bit his lip. "That's the problem. To make the sale legally binding and irreversible, we must obtain an independent valuation of the bank as well as of SIL Limited." He raised his hands in a gesture of frustration and made a face. "We must have these two valuations completed within three weeks."

"Why such a rush?"

"We must seal the whole deal before the end of the third quarter — before news gets out about the problems with our ABCP investments. Otherwise, the experts will value the bank at such a low figure that we'll have to issue too many shares, and we'll lose control over the bank and the Foundation with it."

Moretti was doubtful. "I can't see how we can get everything done in time."

Schmidt decided to step up to the plate to show that he could be counted on. He squared his shoulders. "Leave the matter with me. It will cost a lot of money, but I'll get everything done in time. I have already spoken with a couple of reputable business valuators whose certification will be acceptable to the Zurich Stock Exchange."

Schmidt had his own reasons for making sure the transaction he proposed would take place as soon as possible. Soon after he had been promoted to take over the directorships held by the two administrators who had recently retired, he had decided to steal part or all of SIL. It was an ambitious undertaking fraught with obstacles that could result in jail time for him, but what the devil — wasn't a fortune of almost 200 million dollars worth taking a risk?

Of course, he realized that he had to be patient, perhaps as long as a couple of years. His rather complicated plan involved a number of steps that he knew he would have to complete in their proper sequence for his undertaking to succeed. But, then, was the light not worth the candle?

The first step had been to eliminate, or at least severely limit, Elize Haemmerle's influence over Helmut Studer. This, he felt, he had achieved when Studer stopped using her as his personal assistant. The second had been to simplify the structure through which the Foundation held its investments. This, too, he had managed to accomplish through creating SIL Limited, the holding company to which the Moretti Bank had ordered the numbered account owning the Foundation to transfer all its holdings. As for the third step — well, he had just managed to complete it by having Moretti put him in charge of engineering the acquisition transaction. Step four would be a real challenge, finding a "beard," a *Strohman,* through whom to scare Enrico Moretti into doing his bidding without the banker finding out who was behind the scheme. After that, step five, the elimination of all traces leading back to him, would be a cakewalk.

CHAPTER 27

The Stapfers fell in love with Jack as soon as they saw how caringly he helped Kurt. This came naturally to Jack, He was used to having to help physically incapacitated men from time to time — his teammates. And it wasn't a problem for him to help Kurt in and out of his wheelchair or bed whenever required. Jack was strong.

Initially, Kurt felt awkward about being around the American in pajamas, but he overcame his shyness when Jack started telling locker-room stories and recounted some of his experiences in the showers during his ten-year stint as a football player.

The first two weeks of the Lugano vacation at the Stapfers' place went by in a flash. Then Elize began to worry about what mischief Schmidt was up to and decided to pay a surprise visit to the office. She left for Zurich by train at the crack of dawn on a Friday and was back in Lugano by eight o'clock at night, exhausted, annoyed and very perturbed.

"When I got to the office, I found three men working in my room," she told her friends over a late dinner in the Stapfers' dining room. "I told them who I was and asked them to leave. They became very apologetic and explained that their firm had been retained to prepare a rush valuation of SIL Limited, a company for which the Foundation was acting as financial advisor. They said they needed to have at least ten people working on the file to finish the job on time. Workspace was at a premium so Dr. Studer had given them permission to use my office."

Jack was very surprised. "How come your assistant didn't tell you about all this?"

"That's just it. He was scheduled to take this week off as part of his summer vacation. I called him on his cell, and he said he was never told about the valuation."

"So it was a surprise to everyone?"

"Not really. I nosed around a bit and found out that Schmidt's staff had known that it was going to happen. What's the strangest about all this is that a woman I know who works for Moretti & Cie told me in the elevator that the bank is also undergoing a valuation."

"By the same valuation firm?"

"No, another one but just as well known."

"Did you see Studer?"

"He was very busy with the valuators, but he broke away for a few moments to speak with me. He asked why I had not let him know that I was coming back to work for a day." Eliza paused. "Come to think of it, he was very ill at ease."

"Was Schmidt around?"

"I didn't see him."

"Did you pick up any scuttlebutt?"

"What's that?"

"Gossip."

"I did, and that's what frightens me. I ran into one of the independent administrators at the *Hauptbahnhof* who kind of likes me. He told me in confidence that he thinks SIL and maybe also the Moretti bank are being put up for sale. That's why they are doing a valuation of both."

Jack pursed his lips. "That makes sense only if the bank intends to buy SIL. I wonder," he continued, "if that is what Studer has in mind, or if he and Moretti intend to solicit bids."

Stapfer, who had kept his counsel up to that point, spoke up. "Elize tells me that SIL is a private company so the rules for going to market with it are pretty informal. Studer could get away with selling it as long as he could prove to the owner that the price he got for it was at fair market value."

"And a price established by a reputable valuation company would go a long way toward doing just that." Jack glanced at Elize. "By the way, who *does* own SIL?" She looked to Stapfer for help who then explained what the obligations of a custodian bank were under Swiss law.

"SIL is owned by a bank account, which in turn is owned by someone whose true identity is known only to a very limited number of the custodian bank's senior executives as well as the Swiss Bankers Association. For obvious reasons, in most cases, the names and addresses that were given to the Swiss banks during the period between 1934 and 1945 were false."

"So the banks react positively only to those customers who show up knowing their account numbers and passwords." Kurt thought he understood.

"Almost correct. In exceptional cases, where people know the true name of the original account holder and the claimant is his documented heir, the banks acknowledge ownership and release the money.

"Such was the case with some Holocaust victims," Kurt commented.

"Again you are right." Stapfer continued. "But if nobody shows up, to use your expression, then, after twenty years, *alles ist forüber,* everything is finished. The account is closed and the money and whatever else belongs to the account is transferred to the Swiss National Bank."

"No exceptions?" This from Jack.

"No exceptions, but, of course, we are talking about totally inactive accounts."

"What do you mean by that?"

"No activity whatsoever in the account for twenty years."

Elize intervened. "But this is not so in the case of the account in question. Am I not right, *Herr* Stapfer?"

"I'm not supposed to discuss banking secrets with people who are not officers of the bank, but, of course, you as the

Foundation's auditor know everything about the account except the owner's identity."

Jack was intrigued. "Might I ask what makes the account that owns SIL so special?"

Stapfer hesitated then plunged, "The account is not inactive because the original owner was a very intelligent person. The way he set things up the account will remain active forever."

"How?"

"Every year, there is one deposit made *into* it from a certain bank and then a payment is made *from* it to yet another bank."

"So two different banks are involved in addition to Moretti's bank." Kurt was no less fascinated than Jack. "Who knows the identity of these two banks?"

Elize had the answer, "I do and so do Dr. Studer for one, and, of course, Enrico Moretti. The bank's chief accountant and its senior vice president, Hans-Ruedi Schmidt, are also in the know."

Jack gave her a meaningful look. "Your nemesis."

They went outside and sat on the terrace to watch the lights shimmering on the Lake of Lugano in the distance. It was a balmy mid-summer's night, and the ambiance became very relaxed after everyone had a sip or two from a bottle of Pflümli, a plum *Eau de Vie,* that Stapfer passed around.

All was peace and quiet, an ideal moment for quiet talk and reminiscing.

Jack spoke about his family and his grandparents' remarkable marriage, about the death of his brother and father, and, finally, about his plans to trace his grandmother's lineage in Hungary. Then Elize told the Stapfers about her meeting with Nobel Laureate Arbenz, an old friend of Grandma Ilona. In the middle of her narrative, she suddenly remembered the Gombos picture. "What did you do about the painting you were going to give Dr. Arbenz?" she asked.

Jack was noncommittal. "Nothing. He didn't want it. Said he had enough clutter around him and that as a memento, the photo was enough."

Stapfer wanted to know more about the picture, so Elize told him the whole story, including the bit about the golden bank and the four strange formulas.

The next morning, as Jack and Elize were breakfasting on the terrace, Stapfer came out and joined them. He looked haggard and seemed agitated.

Elize became concerned. "What's the matter, Uncle Karl? Did you not sleep well?"

"I did not. That strange story about the picture kept me awake for most of the night."

"How so?"

"Aldo Moretti hired me in 1936 when I was twenty-three years old. His bank was not as large as it is now and certainly not mechanized. Everything was recorded by hand so we clerks knew just about everything that was going on, but we kept our mouths shut for two reasons: we didn't want to get fired, and we didn't want to go to jail."

"Jail?"

"Yes, jail. In Switzerland in those days, it was a criminal offense to divulge bank secrets. Anyway," Stapfer continued, "six years after I started working for the bank, I was promoted to senior ledger keeper with the responsibility of doing the bookkeeping for all the bank's so-called numbered accounts."

"How many of them were there?"

"About 200 when World War II ended, and the flow of this kind of business diminished to a trickle."

"What happened next?"

"I continued to keep the books for another five years during which Aldo Moretti made some great investment decisions that yielded a lot of money for his clients, especially for one particular account that grew like a mushroom in the dark and ultimately became the Foundation."

Stapfer helped himself to some orange juice. He drank deeply then continued. "I remember the account well because it had a couple of particularities. Nobody came forward to claim ownership of it after the war, but it could never be closed because of what I told you yesterday."

"So what kept you awake half the night?"

"What you said about *die goldene Bank*. Every spring, since its creation, the account that owns SIL receives 500 dollars from the Golden Bank even today, when there are millions in the account."

"So you think the owner of SIL has a bank account at Banque Odier from which he transfers money to Moretti & Cie to keep his account at Moretti's bank open?"

"No. I think the owner has died long ago and that his heirs — if he had heirs and if the heirs have survived the war — don't know that they own a fortune worth over 150 million dollars."

"Who then makes the annual transfer to the Moretti account?"

"I think it's being generated automatically by what we call a 'standing order.'"

"And where does Banque Odier get the 500 dollars?"

Stapfer laughed. "Why ask a question, Jack, when you know the answer to it?"

Jack was taken aback. "I do?" he was stymied for a moment. Then he, too, burst out laughing. "Of course! Every year, the Moretti account sends money to an account at a certain bank, which then sends some or all of it on to Banque Odier, which then sends 500 dollars to the account in the Moretti bank."

Stapfer nodded. "That's one possibility. But you should also consider the possibility that more than three banks are involved."

Elize ran into the house to fetch pencil and paper. She was incredibly excited. "Let's see. We know that Odier is sending money to Moretti, and I can get the account number at Odier by looking at the account at Moretti & Cie. Let's call the Moretti account the 'major' account."

"But we don't know what name was used to open the account at Odier, and we don't know the password to it, either." Jack was, to say the least, skeptical, underwhelmed.

"True." She bit her lip then brightened. "I can also get the third bank's name and the account number in that bank by looking at the 'major' account."

"Where we again don't know what name was used to open the

account or what the relevant password is."

Stapfer was shaking his head. "Now you know why I couldn't sleep last night. I kept thinking about all these things and got very upset, so please summarize the situation for me because I'm afraid I'm lost."

Jack held up his hand. "Wait," he said. "I'll get the second copy of the photo Judy Almási took of the picture. It's been in my briefcase ever since my visit to Dr. Arbenz."

CHAPTER 28

Jack was back within minutes. "We may be in the process of making a huge mistake here," he said. "We're assuming that the owner of the SIL bank account was this Hungarian scientist, but we have no proof to that effect."

Elize was insistent. "There are just too many coincidences for it not to be true."

"Such as?"

"His wife paints a painting in which there is reference to the Golden Bank —"

Jack was quick to interrupt. "That's not so. I grant you that there is a reference to gold in her painting, but concluding that this is a reference to the Golden Bank is a rather ambitious leap of faith."

Elize would not be deterred. "Dr. Arbenz said that he had introduced Gombos to Odier's managing director, and now we find that Odier makes regular — and ridiculously small, I might add — transfers to the Moretti account —"

Stapfer cut in. "Let's not argue. Dr. Gombos either was or was not SIL's original owner. If he was not, we're wasting our time with the picture and its equations. But let's assume he was."

Excited, he got up and began to pace up and down just like Jack's accountancy professor at Queen's University used to do when getting ready to address his large class. The old banker abruptly stopped and faced his audience. "Don't you think we should start by trying to find out how Gombos died and what happened to his family? Bear in mind that even if we do solve the equations and identify him as the original owner, the money would go to the man's legal heirs and nobody else."

This sounded eminently logical to Jack. "You're right, Uncle Karl." He looked around him. "We must form two teams; one to try to decode the equations and the other to check on Dr. Gombos's background. And whatever these two teams do," he added, "they must do it quickly because time is of the essence."

Elize was puzzled. "Why?"

Jack put his arm around her."Because, my darling, your friend Dr. Studer, is in the process of trying to find a way in which to sell SIL to Moretti & Cie at a bargain basement price and probably in exchange for paper and not money."

"Why on earth would he want to do that?"

Jack shrugged. "Just a hunch, based on what you told us yesterday about the bank and SIL undergoing valuation audits at the same time."

Stapfer turned pale. "You mean..."

"Yes Uncle Karl, I do. I suspect that the bank is in some kind of financial squeeze and needs to make a spectacular deal to recoup."

The silence that followed could have been cut with a knife.

CHAPTER 29

Hans-Ruedi Schmidt was having a hard time getting the purchase of SIL by Moretti & Cie done in time to save control of the bank slipping through the fingers of the Moretti family. This he could not allow to happen, not if he wanted to succeed in stealing the assets of SIL! Unfortunately for him, the two valuation audits were not going the way he wanted them to go. First, progress was too slow. At the rate the valuators were advancing in their work, their report would never be ready before October. Second, the values being projected did not fit well with what Schmidt had in mind.

"We may be in trouble," he reported to Moretti. "As we now stand, the valuators are saying that, on the one hand, the bank is worth about 100 million Swiss francs, more or less the same as it was worth when it went public about thirty years ago. That means that each bank share is worth a thousand francs."

"But that's shocking! What has happened to the profits that we made during all those years?" Moretti was close to gagging; he was so upset.

"Some were paid out in dividends; the rest was lost when the valuators wrote off part of our investment portfolio's bad portion." Schmidt was quick to set the record straight. "We're lucky that the valuators picked up only about half of what is worthless."

The implication was clear: Enrico Moretti's management of the bank's affairs during the past few years had been totally inept, maybe even criminally negligent. The shareholders would be sure to demand his head on a platter at the annual meeting, which was scheduled for December — if the bank survived that long.

Schmidt continued. "On the other hand, the value of SIL Limited, calculated on the same basis — that is to say, taking SIL's goodwill into consideration — will probably come in at about 230 million Swiss francs, or about 190 million dollars."

"Which means?"

"That to buy SIL, Moretti & Cie will have to pay 230,000 shares of Moretti 'B' shares to SIL's present owner, which, as you know, is the numbered account for which the *Pro Nobis* Foundation acts as administrator."

"These are the same type of shares that we sold to the public thirty years ago, right?"

"Yes. They have one vote each as long as the annual dividend due on them is paid. And we have the right to issue an unlimited number of them, so we don't have to waste time trying to get permission to increase our capital structure."

Moretti made a quick mental calculation then wiped his forehead with an immaculately white handkerchief. "Then we're safe," he announced with a sigh of relief. "As long as Stapfer votes with us, we retain control no matter how anyone else votes."

Schmidt was not that confident."You are right, as long as Stapfer votes with us. The heirs have 400,000 votes, Stapfer has 150,000 and the rest would have 275,000."

"How do you get to that figure?" Moretti interrupted.

"Add the 45,000 shares issued to the general public when the bank went public to the 230,000 shares we would have to issue to buy SIL, and you get 275,000."

Moretti nodded. "I see."

Schmidt continued. "But if Stapfer votes against us, it is mathematically possible that we could lose control if all the others join Stapfer in voting against us."

Moretti looked at his senior vice president with pity in his eyes. "*Herr* Schmidt, you still do not grasp fully the situation, do you?

Who do you think will vote the bank's shares held by the owner of SIL?"

"The owner, of course."

"And who is the owner?"

"The numbered account for which the *Pro Nobis* Foundation acts as administrator."

"And who owns the numbered account?"

"We don't know."

"Have we heard from him recently?"

"Not to my knowledge."

"Precisely. So who will have the right to vote those shares?"

"Either the custodian of the account — which is our bank — or, if this right is disputed, no one!"

Schmidt could not stop himself from chortling when he realized the meaning of what he had just said. "Not only is this a win-win situation for us, but it is also a tremendous bargain." he said to his boss. "We are really buying SIL for a price that is automatically discounted by two-thirds."

"What do you mean?"

"Taking into consideration that the bank's investment portfolio's value is still overstated by about 60 million francs, each share of the bank is only worth 400 francs and not 1,000."

"You are quite right, Schmidt." Moretti was very pleased. "Win-win it is, thanks to you. So stop worrying. Just get the paperwork done in time."

Schmidt was beside himself with joy. For the first time since he had started working for Moretti & Cie Banquiers, the head of the bank had actually paid him a compliment.

CHAPTER 30

Everyone agreed that Jack would take charge of researching Dr. Gombos's background and that the rest would attempt to decode the equations they presumed represented the passwords of the three accounts.

"We have a starting point," he told them," because, thanks to Elize's work, we know the solution to the first equation, AU = c^2m."

Stapfer was surprised. "How come?"

"Elize looked it up in her files. The account number in Banque Odier is 35220. That's from where the annual payment comes into the account that owns SIL; it shows clearly on the account card. Therefore, c^2m is equal to 35220, which means that c is 35 and m is 20. She also looked up the names of the banks involved in the annual triangulation — you know, the sending of money around in a circle."

"Which are they?" Kurt asked.

"Odier, Moretti & Cie, and Bank Lamarche, Lambert." Jack continued. "After this, things get quite complicated. Although we can apply the knowledge we have developed so far to the remaining three formulas and assume that they represent the passwords to the accounts in the three banks involved, we cannot know for certain in what order they are reflected in the painting."

"Explain." Kurt had difficulty following.

"The second formula in the painting is P + S = OCT 14 1934. Is this the code for the password to the account in the Odier bank, or is it the password for the account in the Moretti or the Lamarche, Lambert bank?"

"Does the order matter?" This from Stapfer

"Yes, it does, because the money moves from Odier to Moretti in the spring and from Moretti to Lamarche, Lambert in the autumn."

"And when do you think the money moves from Lamarche to Odier?"

"Sometime between the autumn and the spring, but it doesn't matter when exactly. The order is 'Odier-to-Moretti-to-Lamarche-to-Odier,' or, if you prefer, from A to B to C to A, but we must somehow establish which bank is the A bank."

"How on earth are we going to do that?"

"We must decode the three equations, and Elize must then ask one of her lawyer colleagues to write to the Odier bank and ask."

They all stared at Jack as if he had two heads. "Just like that?"

He had smiled at them. "Well, not quite. I'll let you know what to say in the letter when I finish researching Gombos's background." He turned to Kurt. "I figure that the code is a simple one that can be broken without much of a hassle, but we can't be sure." He handed the economist a piece of paper. "Try this for starters. As you can see, I wrote out the alphabet and numbered the letters from 1 to 26. Then I reversed the order and made A number 26 and Z number 1. See if, by applying this grid to the formulae and also by using the values we already have for S and M, you can come up with something that makes sense."

"What will you be doing in the meantime?"

"Googling Dr. Gombos in earnest to see what I can find out about him."

Before going upstairs to attack his computer, Jack put in a call to Moffat at the U.S. Embassy in Budapest.

"I'm glad you called," he told Jack. "I was wondering about how you made out with your search of your grandmother's ancestry?"

Jack summarized his problems relating to that matter then told Moffat that he was working on yet another research project, one that involved the Hungarian Nobel Laureate, Dr. Peter Gombos.

"That shouldn't be too difficult," the diplomat said and powered up his computer. Within minutes, Jack was reading an email summarizing the life and death of the man. Unfortunately, there was little information in the document about his wife, his children, or his parents.

"This is a damned good start, and I thank you for it," Jack said," but I need more in-depth stuff."

"Such as?"

"Where did he go to school? Where was his family from? Did they all die? What about his wife's family? Where did *they* come from? That's the kind of background info that I'm after."

Moffat sighed. "You're not easy, are you?" He thought for a moment then brightened. "Here's an idea. Go to the university archives and dig around a bit. Maybe you'll find some answers to your questions there."

"But my Hungarian is poor, and I cannot read the language. Can you find me a qualified guide who could help me in my research? Someone who is fluent in Hungarian and who also speaks English and perhaps one or two other languages."

"Meaning?"

"German and French would be nice."

"Better throw in Slovak or some other Slavic language. In Gombos's days Greater Hungary had all kinds of Slavic-speaking inhabitants." Moffat made a note on his pad. "Give me a couple of days, and let me see what I can come up with."

Just before dinner, while researching, Jack found an obscure article in the *Scientific American* written five years earlier by a student of Dr. Gombos. The substance of the paper was far beyond Jack's ken as far as the science went, but the biographical note at the end of the article made him very happy. It read in part, "Dr. Gombos was born in 1900 in Stomfa (then part of the Austro Hungarian Monarchy). He attended Pázmány Péter University in Budapest then studied at the ETH in Zurich where he obtained his doctorate. He worked for a number of years with Niels Bohr, the Danish scientist (Nobel Laureate in Physics in 1922). At age thirty, Dr. Gombos was made

Professor Emeritus at his alma mater in Budapest, where he continued his work on particle physics. For this, he was awarded the Nobel
Prize in Physics in 1936. He was accidentally killed in 1944."

None of this information was new to Jack. He had seen it all in
the report on Gombos that Moffat had given him earlier. But he
argued that if the author was able to write about Gombos's work
exhaustively and append a biographical note, he must have either
known Gombos or researched his life in depth.

The article was signed by a Dr. Andrew Szilard, Professor
Emeritus of Mathematical Physics at Cornell University in Ithaca,
in the State of New York, a town less than 200 kilometers from
where the Brennan family lived in Buffalo. Jack Googled "Szilard"
and managed to find his email address. He fired off an explanatory
letter to the eighty-nine-year-old man then crossed his fingers and
hoped that Szilard was not only alive but also still *compos mentis*.

CHAPTER 31

"We tried to do what you suggested yesterday." Kurt reported to the group the next day at lunch, again on the terrace and again under a beautifully clear, cloudless summer sky, "but the system doesn't work. It's not consistent."

"How so?" Jack wasn't surprised. It would have been too easy had it been otherwise.

"If you look at the grid you gave us yesterday, c is either 3 or 24 and m is either 13 or 14. What's more, the difference between 3 and 13 is 10 and 24 and 14 is also 10, so we have a consistent shift one way or the other of 10. But according to Elize's work, c is 35 and m is 20. The difference between these two values is 15."

"So what's your conclusion?"

Kurt laughed, "We're working with the wrong grid."

Stapfer was concerned. "Do you have any further suggestions, or have you run out of ideas?"

"Don't worry, Uncle Karl, I have lots more." Kurt tried to sound confident, though he was far from being so.

Elize turned to Jack. "What about you? How's your work coming along?"

"I'm afraid I have to leave here for a few days to follow up a lead I've developed."

Elize made a face. "How long will you be away?"

"I should be done in about ten days, sweetheart. But I'm not going alone. I want you to come with me."

"Where would we be going?" Taken aback by his answer, she barely managed the question.

Jack looked at her lovingly. "I think it's time for you to meet my family. We're first going to Buffalo then on to Ithaca where I have a meeting scheduled with a Professor Szilard who has just emailed me that he'd be very pleased to receive us."

She rewarded him with a grateful smile and mouthed "I love you" at him when she was sure nobody else could see it. Then she blushed.

His heart skipped a beat. She had never said that to him before.

CHAPTER 32

Elize was overwhelmed. The entire Rooney family was at Uncle George's immense summer home on the shores of Lake Erie near Lakeview to welcome her and Jack. He had not told her that the day of their arrival would coincide with the family's annual get-together weekend.

The lot on which the house stood had a lakefront footage of over a thousand feet. This allowed for marvelous nautical activity for the dozen or so children present to splash about, row around in Uncle George's rubber dinghy and dive off the dock that stretched into the water for about ten paces.

In the swirl of people that included cousins and their families, Elize had little opportunity to get to know any of them well, except Jack's mother, May, and grandma, Ilona, who had driven out to Lakeview for lunch. The old lady bonded with the Swiss woman instinctively and immediately.

At the end of the day, just before leaving, Ilona asked her grandson for a word in her car, the only place of tranquility in a sea of shouting, squealing great-grandchildren.

"This one is a keeper," she told Jack. "Don't mess it up."

Jack was happy. "When can I come to see you, Grandma?"

"How long are you staying?"

"A week, but we have to go to Ithaca tomorrow."

"Come by Wednesday afternoon. We'll have tea. And be sure to bring Elize."

✚

Dr. Szilard lived near the Cornell campus. The eighty-nine-year-old scientist was cared for by his wife, Catherine, twenty years his junior, and their spinster daughter, Vilma. Their home, an immaculately kept cottage on Roberts Drive, comfortable and full of light, overlooked Fall Creek Gorge. When he discovered that Jack had recently visited Arbenz, Szilard became very excited.

"I knew that Dr. Gombos had known Dr. Arbenz." He spoke nearly perfect English but with an atrocious Hungarian accent. "But, of course, our relationship was not that close. Dr. Gombos was a highly respected, world-famous professor, and I an impoverished student on a scholarship."

Mrs. Szilard, who was serving coffee and cakes, cut in. "Andrew, enough already with the false modesty. Tell the man the whole truth."

Szilard took a bite out of his wife's excellent coffeecake and addressed his visitors. "Nobody has ever accused a Hungarian of being modest, so, please indulge me." He turned to Jack. "I was a bit of a mathematical genius, and my work was brought to Dr. Gombos's attention by my high-school professor. Dr. Gombos then immediately arranged for me to become one of his advanced students."

"Before you finished high school?"

"Actually, no. I graduated, but when I was in my second year at the university, I was so advanced in mathematics that he took me on as a special case."

"Then what happened?"

"I worked with him during 1943 and early 1944, but then the Germans came, and the university authorities withdrew his teaching privileges because, as you know, he was a Jew."

Jack nodded. He had learned about Gombos's conversion from Judaism to Catholicism while researching the man's life on the Internet. "When the Nazis started to round up the Jews in earnest,"

Szilard continued, "Dr. Arbenz arranged for Dr. Gombos and his family to move into what was known as a Swiss protected house."

"How do you know this?"

"Dr. Gombos told me. He and I continued our work at his home during the summer of 1944. His quarters were cramped, but we managed. That's when I met his wife and children."

"Tell me about them."

"His wife was originally from Moscow and was visiting Hungary when the Bolshevik Revolution broke out in 1917. Her parents were killed — I think he was some sort of a banker and originally very rich, but then he lost everything — so she stayed on in Hungary and became a well-known painter."

"Did you ever see any of her work?"

"Of course I did. Her pictures were hanging on the walls of the place where we worked."

"What became of her?"

"I don't dare to tell you. The last time I saw her and her two little boys was when I had to tell her that her husband's body was washed ashore and found by the police in Csepel, a southern suburb of Budapest. He had been in the wrong place at the wrong time and got blown up by accident." Dr. Szilard was visibly upset. He shook his head. "Those were terrible times, terrible times."

Jack's mind was spinning. Trying to cope with his emotions, he had taken Elize's hand while Szilard was speaking and was squeezing it so hard that she winced.

Szilard continued as, in a voice barely above a whisper, he described the circumstances of his professor's death. Then he stopped talking for a while.

"After the siege of Budapest I went back to the house to see what happened to her and the children. The building's janitor told me that all the tenants had been killed, shot to death on the banks of the Danube. I asked him how he knew that and he said he saw it happen." Tears were running down Szilard's cheeks, and Elize was crying, too.

"When I asked him why he and the other onlookers hadn't tried to stop the carnage, he said, and I quote him verbatim because I'll never forget his words: 'Are you crazy? Have you ever been near a lynch mob? If we would have lifted a finger in the Jews' defense, they would have killed us, too.'"

"So the janitor saw Mrs. Gombos and the children die." Jack could barely speak. He was deeply moved. 'How could civilized people behave like this?' he kept asking himself over and over again. Was all virtue lost? Was compassion dead? And where was God, if there is one, when all this was going on?

For a while, no one said anything. Then Mrs. Szilard reappeared with a pitcher of cold water and some glasses.

"Drink some water. It will calm you," she said to Elize who was sobbing openly.

Old man Szilard dried his eyes. "I have told this story many times, Mr. Brennan, and I cry every time I tell it." He sighed. "But it is my duty to tell it every time someone asks me to tell it."

"Why?"

"To bear witness. To make sure these things don't happen again."

"But they do, don't they, Dr. Szilard? Look at Vietnam, look at Cambodia, look at the Taliban who are killing women for wanting to go to school, look at ISIS, cutting innocent peoples' heads off."

The professor looked at Jack speculatively for a while without saying a word. "But you and your friend haven't traveled this far just to hear this sad story. What is it that you are after?" he finally asked.

Jack told him about the Foundation and the painting and his far-fetched theory that the two were connected.

Szilard's reaction was immediate. "I remember the painting. It was painted by his wife on the occasion of their older son's first communion.The last time I saw the picture it was still hanging on the wall of the apartment where the Gombos family lived.."

"When was that?

"In March 1945."

CHAPTER 33

Stockholm, December 1936

As he sat waiting for his Swiss friend in one of the first-class carriages of the Stockholm–Berlin Express, Dr. Peter Gombos never suspected that his Nobel Prize of 159,850 Swedish krona would, one day, be worth a fortune in excess of 150 million dollars.

The train was just about to depart, and this disappointed Gombos. It seemed he would have to make the voyage by himself, though he was still hoping that his colleague, Dr. Hans Arbenz, who, like Gombos, was passing through Berlin on his way home to Zurich, would turn up at the last minute to accompany him.

The two men greatly enjoyed spending time together and had much in common. Both were newly minted Nobel Laureates — Gombos in Physics, Arbenz in Chemistry. They were young (the Swiss only thirty, and Gombos thirty-six) and absolutely brilliant. Having cooperated on a number of scientific projects during the last five years, they had enormous respect for each other. But they also had fundamental differences, principally about the intentions of *Herr* Adolf Hitler, the new German *Reichkanzler*.

No wonder.

Arbenz, a bachelor, was a robust, rotund Protestant Swiss German, returning to his native land, while Gombos, a thin, ascetic-looking secular Hungarian Jew, was on his way back to Budapest via

Zurich where he was to deliver a lecture on particle physics at the *Eidgenössische Technische Hochschule,* the prestigious ETH, Europe's finest Science and Technology University.

Ironically, Arbenz was far more concerned about Hitler than was Gombos.

A week earlier, they had attended the Nobel Awards Dinner in the Golden Hall, or Gyllene Salen, of Stockholm's City Hall. The venue, illuminated by twenty-four crystal chandeliers, the lights of which were intensified by over 18 million gold mosaic tiles on the walls, could accommodate 700 people for dinner. After a sumptuous meal under the glittering lights, the elegant guests had broken into small groups to mix and mingle.

Gombos had been mildly surprised when the Swiss had suggested they meet at an informal luncheon he was organizing at his hotel the next day,

"Including you, there would be four of us," he had explained. "Russell the British literary Laureate, and also *ein Amerikaner,* Bill Rooney." They were conversing in German, a language Gombos spoke like a native.

"The Englishman, I know who he is, but not the American."

"He works unofficially for the U.S. State Department and has an office in Bern. He wants to meet you, Peter. Just for a friendly chat," Arbenz had added hastily when he saw his friend demur.

The lunch turned out to be a thinly veiled recruiting effort aimed at getting Gombos to emigrate from Hungary to the United States,

"War with Germany is inevitable," Rooney told his listeners. "It's only a matter of time." He then addressed Gombos directly. "Hitler intends to eliminate all the Jews in Europe, so you, Dr. Gombos, will be targeted as will all your coreligionists."

"But I'm no longer a Jew. My wife and I converted to Catholicism two years ago, so my children will be born Christian," Gombos protested. "Besides, the Germans would never move against a Nobel Laureate," he added with arrogant ignorance. "They are too civilized for that."

Rooney saw that he could not make Gombos change his mind.

With a sigh, he gave up. "You are very naïve, Doctor. At least promise me to make some arrangements so that when you will have to flee — and flee you will to survive — you will have money and a place to flee *to* when the time comes."

Arbenz arrived huffing and puffing a few minutes before the train's departure, barely in time to allow the porter to get his luggage on board.

The Swiss wasted no time in getting to the point, "I'm late because of your stubbornness." He pointed an accusatory finger at Gombos." Don't ask me how, but Rooney found out that the Nazis intend to let you into Germany but will then detain you when you try to leave for Switzerland."

"How can they do that? I have a transit visa."

"Because you're a Jew, that's how. They can do with you whatever they want once you're in Germany, and they will keep you there because *Herr* Hitler wants a Nobel physicist in his stable."

"You can't be serious!" Gombos was incensed.

"Let me tell you how serious we are. During the last forty-eight hours, Rooney and I have been working our butts off to find a solution to your problem."

Arbenz wiped his perspiring brow and went on. "This is what we want you to do. When we get to Berlin tomorrow morning, leave your ticket and luggage with me. Walk away from the train and take a taxi to the Swiss ambassador's residence. Here — I've written the address on the back of this card." The chemist gave Gombos his calling card and continued. "The ambassador is expecting to have lunch with you, so use the spare bathroom to get freshened up. Take a bath while you're at it."

"Then what?"

"After lunch, the ambassador's chauffeur will drive you back to the residence where you'll stay the night. The next day, you'll be given a so-called Swiss Service Passport and a ticket on the Basel train that departs around eleven o'clock in the morning. You'll arrive in Basel around six. I'll be there with your luggage and to help you catch the next train to Zurich, which will get you there in less than an hour.

I've booked you into the Baur-am-Ville Hotel on the *Paradeplatz* where you'll have a good night's rest. You can then deliver your lecture as scheduled, the day after, on Saturday."

Gombos was deeply touched. "How can I thank the two of you for all of this? And how much do I owe for the second ticket?"

"You owe us nothing. Rooney arranged for the U.S. State Department to pay for it. By the way, you'll be travelling in second class as befits a lowly civil servant."

"How come?"

"Your passport will be in the name of Ulrich Huber, an engineer working for the Swiss Patent Office. Remember this: the stated reason for your visit to Germany was to inspect a patent model in the design office of the *Volkswagenwerke* near Dusseldorf in connection with a patent infringement lawsuit. Memorize the personal data in the document such as birthplace and birth date."

Totally bewildered, Gombos was having difficulty adjusting to reality. "What else do I need to know?"

"Two more things. You'll be crossing into Switzerland at Basel, a town where the frontiers of France, Germany, and Switzerland meet. You're supposed to be Swiss and familiar with the layout. For God's sake, don't get off at the wrong stop. Wait until you are well and truly in Switzerland."

"What's the second thing?"

Arbenz began to laugh. "The Gestapo will be looking for you so Ulrich Huber's passport photo shows a man with a beard. I guess you'll have to grow one in the next twenty-four hours."

"But that's impossible!"

"Come on, Peter, lighten up. I'm joking. The embassy chauffeur is an amateur actor. He'll fix up your face."

"And what if he is working for the Germans and betrays me?"

"There's no chance of that. He is a German-American and works for Rooney at the U.S. Embassy in Bern."

CHAPTER 34

Gombos woke up with a start and automatically reached for his wife. Then he remembered. He was in a hotel room in Zurich, and Svetlana was in their apartment in Budapest. She had very much wanted to be at his side during his moment of glory in Stockholm, but the doctors had counseled her not to travel because she was in her ninth month of pregnancy.

Svetlana Shvedova was the daughter of Igor Shvedov, one of the last Russian Tsar's most influential Jewish bankers. When the November revolution broke out in Russia, Svetlana was visiting the Eszterházy family in Hungary. Her father and mother attempted to flee the Bolsheviks, but they were caught and executed. The Eszterházys took her in and, recognizing her considerable talent, encouraged her to become a painter. They sent her to study under Álmos Jashik, a well-known Hungarian artist and arts teacher, at his prestigious Fine Arts Academy.

Gombos had met Svetlana at an exhibition of her paintings and had fallen madly in love on the spot. After wooing her with characteristic single-mindedness, he married her a year later. He was thirty-four and she, thirty.

Their wedding was a bittersweet occasion because they were both single children, in the sense that they had no siblings, and had scant family. Svetlana's relatives were all dead, swept into oblivion by the great proletarian purges. Gombos's parents were modest, middle-class people hailing from the small town of Stomfa in Hungarian Slovakia. They had little in common with their brilliant offspring who lived in the glittering metropolis, Budapest, on generous grants from world-famous universities.

Since Peter and Svetlana were both Jewish-born but had converted to Catholicism before their marriage, their wedding was attended by only a small number of people, mainly their friends. But that's where religion ended as far as the newlyweds were concerned. They considered themselves avant-garde people with eclectic tastes and very modern acquaintances.

Gombos glanced at the clock on the night table and bounded out of bed. He was due to meet Arbenz and a banker friend of his for lunch within the hour.

While showering, he reviewed the last three days' events and concluded that he had seriously overestimated his invulnerability. He had, of course, heard about Hitler's tirades aimed at inflaming the latent and extensive anti-Semitic feelings present in just about every European country. For this reason, although not that interested in sports, he had made it a point to attend the Olympics in Berlin earlier in the year.

He had wanted to see firsthand how the so-called 1935 Nuremberg Laws, stripping Jews living in Germany of all their civil rights, were being applied in daily life. During the Olympics he could find little evidence that the Jews were being systematically victimized. This made him feel safer, especially when he realized that the laws applied only to Jews in Germany and those living in countries that might become occupied by Germany. And Hungary was not Germany nor was it about to become Germany — was it?

Then, in Sweden to claim his Nobel Prize, Gombos had learned that Hitler had suspended the enforcement of the laws for the duration of the games but that the persecution of the Jews had resumed with a vengeance as soon as the international press had gone home. This, plus the luncheon conversation with Rooney, and the warning by Arbenz on the train, had seriously eroded his composure.

After the Saturday afternoon lecture in Zurich to an enthusiastic audience that had rewarded him with a standing ovation, Gombos had attended a gala dinner hosted in his honor by the ETH faculty at which Arbenz was also present.

"I want you to do yourself a favor," the Swiss had said after the meal. "Meet me and a banker friend for lunch tomorrow. You definitely want to hear what he has to say."

"Another recruiting session, this time on behalf of a Swiss group?" Gombos could not resist giving Arbenz a dig. He was beginning to wonder whether his friend, who was very much a busy man about town, had a hidden agenda. Why else would he be wasting so much of his precious free time worrying about Gombos's safety and future?

"Far from it, Peter. I'm sure you'll find that what he has to say is no laughing matter." Arbenz was in earnest.

The atmosphere during the meal at Jackie's Staufer Stube, an elegant restaurant much frequented by tourists, was tense. The banker, Otto Graf, in his late forties and full of self-importance, was a humorless man with an encyclopedic memory and a profound knowledge of the ins and outs of Swiss private banking. He hardly touched his meal because he did not stop talking.

"In 1934," he began pompously as soon as the soup had arrived, "the Swiss Bankers Association determined that there would soon be a world war and that this event would be an opportunity for Swiss banks to make even more money. Our country would remain neutral, and all 'nervous' money would want to come to Switzerland. Such a state of affairs is, of course, *eine normale Situazion,* something that happened already during the First World War. But there is a difference this time, and this difference is Adolf Hitler's persecution of the Jews."

Arbenz and Gombos had finished their first course, and the waiter removed the soup plates, including Graf's, though it was half full. The banker did not seem to notice.

"German Jews are not allowed to have bank accounts outside their country. If caught, they are severely punished. In spite of this, many still try because they want desperately to hide their money from the Nazis. Some of these people have already disappeared as a consequence. It was, therefore, desirable for reasons of humanity, as well as for good business, to welcome 'nervous' money to our country in such a way that its owner's identity could not become known to the German authorities, or to any other unauthorized person, for that matter."

Graf began to pick at his steak."So our banking association invented the numbered account system and legalized it through federal legislation last September."

"How does the system work?" Gombos was curious.

"It is quite simple and very safe." The waiter made Graf's plate disappear with half his steak still on it.

The banker drank some wine and continued. "You pick a bank, any bank, and ask to see one of its senior officers. He'll fill out the necessary forms for opening a numbered account, and you sign them, not with your name, but with a number that you can remember. Then you deposit your money into your account, choose a password, and go home."

"Why a password?"

"The only way someone can withdraw money or give instructions about what to do with the money already in a numbered account is by giving the password."

"In other words, as long as you have the name of the bank, the account number, and the password, you can operate the account without having to tell the bank who you really are?"

Graf nodded. "Simply put, that is the case, yes. There are, of course variations and refinements."

"Such as?"

"The large banks insist that at least one senior banking official has to know the identity of the person who opened the account. So, if the client insists on absolute secrecy and anonymity, he is advised to go to a so-called private bank, such as the one I direct."

"What else?"

"Most of the clients leave a testament with the bank in which they name the heir to the account should the client die or not give sign of life for twenty years."

"Why twenty years?"

"The law governing numbered accounts stipulates that if an account lies dormant for twenty years, the balance in the account must be transferred to the Swiss National Bank."

The ambiguous answer piqued Gombos's precise, scientific mind. "And what does the law mean by 'dormant'?"

Graf had the answer. "An account is dormant if, during twenty years, nobody with proper access visits the account or gives instructions about what to do with the account or, in the absence of visits or instructions, no money flows into the account from outside sources or is paid out from it."

Gombos got the idea. "'Outside sources' presumably means money other than what the funds already in the account had internally generated."

Graf nodded.

Arbenz, who had not uttered a word during the meal, raised a finger. "I have a question, *Herr* Graf. Does one have to know the password to be able to put money into the account?"

"No, just the account number and the bank's name."

The chemist then asked the key question. "Are there many Germans opening numbered accounts in Switzerland these days?"

"We estimate that about 50,000 such accounts have been opened during this year alone, not only by Germans but by people from all over Europe — France, Austria, the Balkan countries, Poland..."

"All Jews?"

"No, not only Jews, though the majority seem to be Jewish, yes."

Gombos was flabbergasted. "Are you sure?"

"Give or take 10 percent, yes." Quite oblivious to his audience's astonishment, the banker turned to his host, Arbenz. "May I be so rude as to ask for another portion of this delicious *Sachertorte?*" Then, in a tone entirely devoid of humor, he added: "For some reason, I'm still very hungry."

Laughing, Arbenz signaled the waiter.

Gombos didn't laugh. Instead, he made an appointment with

Graf for eleven o'clock on Monday morning.

CHAPTER 35

Gombos spent Sunday afternoon in his room in a comfortable armchair, deep in thought, with no lights on, and almost without moving. At eight, he called the operator and asked to be put through to his wife in Budapest. It took an hour to get a line, but he didn't mind waiting. He needed the time to refine the plan he was in the process of formulating.

Otto Graf was the managing director of Bank Julius Odier, an institution more than one hundred years old that enjoyed such an excellent reputation that, according to Arbenz, people called it *die goldene Bank,* the Golden Bank. After opening a numbered account, Gombos deposited his Nobel Prize money — 159,850 Swedish krona — then withdrew 5,000 U.S. dollars, the equivalent of about 20,000 krona.

He instructed Graf to convert the money remaining in the account into U.S. funds because he figured that the further away his money was from Hitler, the safer it would be. In his mind, Gombos called the account at Bank Odier his "A" account. Bank Odier was to invest his dollars into a basket of gilt-edged U.S. securities, principally in science-related companies. Then on March 15, 1938, it was to transfer everything in the account at the end of the previous year, except for 5,000 U.S. dollars, to an account the number and address of which Gombos would provide in due course. (Gombos called this second account his "B" account.)

The scientist also told Graf that, on June 24, 1938, and every year thereafter on the same date, Bank Odier was to transfer into the "B" account 500 dollars. He then asked Graf for the names of five other reputable private Swiss bankers and took his leave.

The next morning, Gombos visited Moretti & Cie Banquiers, a house founded sixty years earlier that had become known for its strong reputation for making aggressive, but very shrewd, investments on behalf of its clients. He gave a false name and, with a thousand dollars, opened a numbered account (the "B" account).

After lunch, Gombos called on Monsieur Henri Lamarche, the managing director of Banque Lamarche, Lambert and, this time with 2,500 U.S. dollars, opened what he called his "C" account. He also instructed Lamarche to transfer 500 dollars to the Odier account (the "A" account) every December 21, starting in 1938. He did not use his real name at Bank Lamarche, Lambert, either.

First thing on Wednesday, Gombos was back at Moretti & Cie and told the bank's managing director about the transfer he would be receiving in March 1938. He instructed Signore Moretti to transfer to the Lamarche account (the "C" account) the sum of 700 dollars every October 17th, starting in 1938. He also outlined to Moretti the investment philosophy he wished him to follow when handling his portfolio (80 percent of holdings to be in U.S. dollar denominated gilt-edged securities and 20 percent in whatever currency Moretti wished to invest in but always with emphasis on science-related enterprises).

From Moretti, Gombos went back to see Graf and gave him the particulars of the "B" account, thereby completing what he called his "magic circle." He also handed Graf a sealed envelope.

Gombos spent Wednesday afternoon rechecking his calculations and making sure he had not overlooked anything that would render the account in which he would have the bulk of his money, his "B" account, dormant. He felt foolish spending time on trying to envisage a situation in which neither he nor members of his family nor their heirs would have access to the account during twenty years.

In any event, he was now satisfied that he had put in place

whatever was necessary to keep the accounts active indefinitely. He was particularly proud of the way in which he provided a solution to the problems that his sudden accidental death might cause.

The envelope he had given to Graf was marked "To be opened by my Legal Heir(s) on my Death or Incapacitation." Inside, there was another envelope on which he had written his wife's name and address. This second envelope contained his testament, a so called one-page holograph will in German in which he left all his possessions in Switzerland to his legal heirs, whoever they may be at the time of his death. He carefully avoided being more specific because, fearing unforeseeable complications in an uncertain future, he felt he needed to deal with the eventuality of his wife, Svetlana, and/or his children predeceasing him.

On the back of the testament, he marked the account number and password of the "A" account as well as the password of the "B" account but not the names or account numbers of the "B" and "C" banks. He was sure that his wife could figure them out from the "A" account bank statements once she had access to the "A" account. As for the disguised passwords, he intended to explain to Svetlana how to decode them.

The next day, he bought a very expensive watch for Arbenz and had it engraved *Thanks for your generous help. Always your friend, Peter Gombos. 1936.* Then he bought an equally expensive, long and heavy gold rope with acorns at each end for his wife and had it boxed beautifully.

Arbenz invited him to a farewell dinner at the Urania. They ate venison, and the Swiss had a lot to drink. He became very sentimental at the end of their meal.

"Promise me you'll keep in touch and let me know if there's anything I can do to help you." He seemed to be close to tears.

Gombos tried to put up a brave front. "I'm sure this unpleasantness with Hitler will pass, and you'll be coming to visit us soon in Budapest."

The Swiss bit his lip. "I wish I could be as optimistic as you. Anyway, here's to our friendship." He raised his glass. "May you travel safely."

"I'm sure I will, Hans. I'm booked on the Simplon Orient Express, which, as you know, passes through Austria. I won't be going near Germany."

Arbenz drove him to the *Hauptbahnhof* and helped him settle into his compartment. At 11:03 a.m. sharp, the train left, as scheduled. (The Swiss insist that their trains run dead on time.) The trip home was long and tedious. Gombos slept, then read, then slept again, but he spent most of his time thinking, fretting, and obsessing. At one point, in an effort to forget about the Nazis, he indulged in a little daydreaming about the 37,000 U.S. dollars in his secret bank account. He knew that this sum would grow to 75,000 in ten years if it kept earning 7 percent compound interest every year. Then it would double again during the next ten years, so that by 1956 he'd have 150,000 dollars to call his own — a veritable fortune.

He'd be fifty-six and Svetlana, fifty-two. Their son — he was sure the baby they were expecting would be a boy — would be nineteen and attending university, no doubt. His heart filled with joy: He would be able to afford to send the boy to the best schools in the world.

He continued his calculations. When his future grandson, his son's son, reached the tender age of forty-five in the year 2000, he'd dispose over a fortune approximating 2.5 million dollars, an amazingly large sum — real wealth.

History would show that Gombos seriously underestimated the rate at which his fortune would grow. By 1956, his "B" account would, indeed, be worth about 150,000 dollars, due to the acceleration of the post-war growth of productivity in the U.S. Thereafter, his fortune would double every five years because his money would be invested heavily in electronics (Moretti would achieve huge yields for the account through investing in the dot-com bubble) and in pharmaceuticals, plus the new science of genomics, and, of course, energy stocks.

In fact, by 2006, the "B" account would be worth over 150 million dollars.

CHAPTER 36

Budapest, March 1944

The spring weather was unseasonably warm, and the Gombos household's nursery windows were wide open. Mike, the eight-year-old, woke up first. His brother Andrew, two years his junior, was gently snoring still. The youngster stretched and listened to the noises around him. He heard the birds twittering in the trees and some sort of a murmur that emanated from the street. That's what had awoken him.

It sounded as though there were lots and lots of people outside. He could hear them chattering, but what they were saying did not sound like Hungarian. Mike placed a chair near the window and, kneeling on it, leaned out as far as he dared then looked down. There were many soldiers milling about, all dressed in gray, with an officer shouting orders at them in German.

He dashed into his parents' bedroom without knocking. "Mummy, Mummy, the Germans are here," he shouted. "I saw them in the street."

Gombos bounded out of bed and looked out the window. His son was right. He turned to Svetlana. "The endgame has begun," he said quietly. "Take the children to Kassa immediately. The three of you should be safe there. Captain Nagy will look after you." The captain, an old acquaintance, was the military commander of the city of Kassa in northern Hungary.

Gombos got dressed then rushed to the Swiss embassy. The duty officer knew him and allowed him to use the phone. He called Arbenz. "Hans," he said. "The end is near. The Germans have invaded."

"I know. It's in all the papers and on the radio. What do you need?"

"Protection for me and my family. What can be done?"

"Switzerland has foreseen the possibility of Hungary being invaded. It has an agreement in place with the Hungarian government that in the event the Germans start persecuting Hungarian nationals on the basis of race or religion, Switzerland will issue *Schutzpasses,* protective passports, to those so persecuted and will establish safe houses for them."

"What do you mean by safe houses?"

"Houses that will be declared Swiss territory and that will fly the Swiss flag. The Nazis will be forbidden to enter them."

"Do you for a moment believe that the Gestapo and the Hungarian police will respect this agreement?"

"Switzerland is not alone in this. The Swedes are doing the same thing. There's a fellow by the name of Wallenberg at their embassy who seems to be particularly effective at it."

"How does he do it?"

"The Germans know they're losing the war, and their leaders realize they'll need a place to flee when this thing is over. They can't risk antagonizing the neutral nations at this late stage." Arbenz paused then started again. "Whenever Wallenberg hears about the Nazis starting to push people around or attempt to evict them from a Swedish safe house, he rushes to the scene and starts arguing with the Nazi officer in charge." The Swiss knew he was whistling in the wind and felt very helpless.

"What happens if the Nazi officer tells him to go to hell?"

"Apparently, he whips out his pen and a notebook and asks the man his name, rank, and serial number."

"And the man gives it to him?"

"Yes. The Germans fear and respect neutral authority."

"How long will it take for the embassy here to get its act together?"

"I'd say ninety days."

"That long? What am I to do in the meantime?"

"Lay low."

Gombos laughed. That's what he had been trying to do ever since he had been awarded his Nobel Prize. But he had not been successful at it. His reputation had made him much sought after socially, and he and his family continued to live charmed lives. The Eszterházys saw to it that he was not molested and Admiral Horthy, the Regent of Hungary, invited him regularly to show that he was not biased, though he referred to Gombos behind his back as his favorite non-Jewish Jew.

Although the *Anschluss* by Germany of Austria in 1938 had made it almost impossible for Gombos to go abroad, he kept in touch with his colleagues around the world through extensive correspondence. He continued doing brilliant work — perhaps his best — at the university where he was now *Professor Emeritus*. And he did try very hard to blend in, to assimilate totally. He and his wife, having converted, attended mass regularly and observed only the Christian holidays. When their son, Mike, turned seven, they enrolled him in a special course to prepare him for his first communion.

The great event had taken place on a beautiful Sunday in May. There was a party afterward, and Svetlana decided to commemorate the occasion by painting a portrait of her little family. The picture was cleverly composed. The painter is reflected in a large mirror at her easel while her two boys, Mike and Andrew — dressed in their Sunday bests — are shown watching their famous father intently as he writes on a blackboard, apparently in the process of solving a complex mathematical problem.

The details in the picture are sharp. The four equations on the board stand out clearly: $AU = c^2m$; $P+S = OCT\ 14\ 1934$; $P = DEC\ 21\ 1900$; $S = MAR\ 3\ 1904$.

Of course, Gombos's children took all this fuss about religion for granted. They attended Catholic religious education classes and had no idea whatsoever about their Jewish origins.

Meanwhile, their relatives in Stomfa, who had also converted to Catholicism and had changed their names from Knopf ("button" in German) to Gombos ("button" in Hungarian) in a futile attempt to escape persecution, were quietly rounded up by the Hungarian *gendarmes* who had no difficulty tracking down those of Jewish origin. The good people of Stomfa, a small town where everybody knew everybody else, were only too happy to inform on them and to help them on their way east for resettlement, after which they helped themselves to the houses (and their contents) the Jews had to leave behind.

The Knopfs and their extended family were never heard from again.

Svetlana and the children were forced to return to Budapest in late June because Captain Nagy could no longer hide them from the Gestapo in Kassa. Eichmann and his henchmen, who included many members of the police and the *csendőrség*, the Hungarian *gendarmerie,* had become too well organized and effective at hunting down Jews in hiding.

While his family was away, Gombos organized their move into a Swiss safe house on their return. Although living conditions were relatively rough — the family of four lived in two rooms and had to share a bathroom and a kitchen with another family of four — Gombos did not mind. They were safe and together, and the situation would soon improve: the Russian Army was on its way to chase the Germans away.

In mid-October, the situation for Hungary's Jews took a sudden turn for the worse. Although the Germans knew that they were beaten, they were determined to slow the advance of the Red Army by all possible means. When Admiral Horthy, the Regent, denied their request for permission to mine all bridges across the Danube, they put the head of state under house arrest, Parliament was dissolved, and the pro-German Arrow Cross Party, a collection of violently anti-Semitic, right-wing hooligans, was allowed to surge to power.

Chaos ensued.

On November 4, a sunny Saturday morning, Gombos decided to go for a walk, though he knew that it was risky for a Jew to go out into the streets. But he desperately needed to get some fresh air, to be alone for a while, away from the carryings-on of his two young, rambunctious sons. Svetlana begged him not to go.

"Don't worry, dear," he told her, "I'll be careful. I'll wear my overcoat that doesn't have a yellow star sewn on it, so nobody will know that I'm a Jew."

"What if they ask you for your papers?" Spot-checks on the street by the police had become frequent.

"I'll show them my pass from the university. It says I'm a full professor and doesn't say I'm Jewish."

Feeling his acute need for solitude, she relented and made him a modest salami sandwich for lunch. Food was getting scarce.

Gombos found the streets full of people, jostling each other on the sidewalk, milling about and worriedly gossiping, eager for news. He decided to walk along the Ring then cross the bridge to Margaret Island in the middle of the river, have his sandwich in the quiet of the gardens there, and then return home. The sun was shining, there was no wind, and the weather was unseasonably mild.

It was *Feldwebel* Herman Asch's responsibility to check the mines placed under the bridges across the Danube to ensure that they could be exploded promptly when the time came. This meant a weekly inspection of the electrical cabling linking them to the detonator. He hated the job — especially when he was hung over. And hung over he was that Saturday when, after crawling under the bridge, he noticed that one of the cables was sagging. He didn't feel like climbing up the girder to take a closer look. Instead he called his corporal to fetch a pole with which he hoped he would be able to push the cable back into place.

That was Sergeant Asch's last conscious act.

The mines exploded and killed Asch, and forty of his comrades plus 600 civilians, among them Dr. Peter Gombos, Nobel Laureate, Professor Emeritus of Theoretical Physics, and perhaps the greatest living mathematician in the world except for Albert Einstein.

Like many of the other civilians, he did not die right away.

Walking along the span leading from Pest to the island when the mines detonated, Gombos was tossed high into the air. The blast ruptured both his ear drums so he never heard the bang. He felt himself falling for an eternity. Then he hit the water, landing flat on his back, but he couldn't swim.

His back was broken.

The ice-cold river carried him downstream in absolute silence, literally deaf to the world and facing the heavens. His last thoughts were about his children and his beloved wife. At peace within himself, he thanked his Maker for allowing him the privilege of knowing a woman as wonderful as Svetlana and for granting him the foresight the previous Christmas to explain the significance of the equations that he had made her paint on the blackboard in the family portrait.

When Gombos didn't return from his walk, Svetlana deduced that he was one of the victims of the accidental explosion on the Margit Bridge. Sure enough, on the Monday following, one of his graduate students called on her with Gombos's university identity card in his hand. The professor's body, he said, had washed up on the riverbank at Csepel. The police could not find the family, so they came looking for information about him at the university.

Svetlana knew what her husband would want her to do and where her duty lay. She was to make sure that their children would survive the war. In this, she counted heavily on help from the Swiss ambassador who assured her that, for the time being, she was safe where she was.

Neither he nor she counted on the savagery of the Arrow Cross in its pursuit of the annihilation of Hungary's Jews.

In the second week of December, the Red Army began its operation to encircle Budapest and started shelling the city sporadically. The streets were in chaos and public order was beginning to break down. On the night of December 17, a week before Christmas Eve, some drunken Arrow Cross goons decided to engage in a little Jew baiting. They broke into the Swiss safe house and ordered all the residents into the street at gunpoint. Then they marched them along the Ring down to the Danube where they tied them together with telephone wire in batches of three. After lining them up at the edge of the parapet, they shot every second adult person and pushed him into the river. Those who were not shot soon drowned, pulled under by the weight of the bodies to which they were attached.

Svetlana was holding Mike and Andrew by the hand when the bullet smashed into her brain. She pitched forward and dragged her terrified children down with her into the freezing, murky river below. Instinctively, they began to tread water furiously, attempting to keep themselves and their mother afloat. But they soon tired, mercifully numbed by the icy cold surrounding them.

Yisgadal, Viyiskadash, Sh'me Rabo. ('Magnified and sanctified be God's great name' – the Kaddish, the Jewish prayer for the dead).

CHAPTER 37

Buffalo, July 2008

After visiting Dr. Szilard, Elize and Jack returned to Buffalo. Bad news awaited them there. Jack's grandmother had fallen the previous day and had broken her hip. Although she was resting comfortably, the family was worried. Ninety-five-year-old ladies did not do well when forced to stay in bed. They had a tendency to catch pneumonia and die.

Initially, they dared not visit her, but she insisted, so they complied and spent an hour with her at the hospital before leaving for Europe. Neither one of them slept on the flight to Zurich. Szilard's narrative had affected them far more deeply than they had realized.

"It is our duty to put things right," Elize insisted as they lay awake side by side in the business class cabin. "Dr. Gombos's heirs are the rightful owners of SIL, and we must find them."

"What happens if there *are* no heirs?" Jack whispered back, trying not to disturb the passengers sleeping in the seats around them.

"Then we have to identify an organization that can rightfully claim the money, but under no circumstances should we just stand by while Moretti and Studer and Schmidt steal the Foundation."

"Such as?"

She looked at him, searching for options. "It has to be a charitable organization connected with Holocaust survivors."

"Not only Holocaust survivors but, in my opinion, Hungarian Holocaust survivors and their rightful heirs as well."

"Yes, and it has to be children-oriented."

"Why do you say that?"

Her eyes filled with tears. "I can't get the picture out of my mind of those two little boys drowning as they fought to keep their dead mother's head above water."

Brennan took her hand and began to stroke it. He was afraid to speak.

"Promise me something, Jack," she whispered with great intensity. "No matter what happens between the two of us, you will not rest until you've exhausted every possible way of finding the heirs and solving the equations so that they can claim what's theirs — especially their children and grandchildren."

She was not making much sense, but the thrust of her emotions was clear. He realized that he was facing a situation in which a false move might cause him bitter regret and emotional misery for the rest of his life. If, on the other hand, he gave her the answer she was seeking, he would have no choice but to keep his word, which would mean sacrificing his independence as a bachelor and his career as a successful professional.

There were no guarantees. Searching for proof of a nebulous theory for months, perhaps years, would neither ensure success nor happiness with Elize. So here it was again — the question he so dreaded. Was he ready to commit? Was she?

He heard his grandmother's voice. "This one is a keeper," she was saying. "Don't mess it up."

He took a deep breath. "I'll do it if you stand by me and help."

She kissed his hand. "I will."

"What about Kurt?"

"We'll work it out. Besides, he likes you very much, so there's no problem there."

They said goodbye at Kloten Airport, painfully aware that their relationship's character had profoundly changed. It was no longer only lust or emotional loneliness that united them but also a common and noble purpose. She took the train to Lugano, and he, a plane to Budapest. There was no time to lose: his vacation was just about over.

Moffat called Jack at his hotel mid-morning. "I've got just *the* guide for you if you want to run up to Stomfa where your man was born," He sounded eager to help.

Jack was hesitant. "Tell me about Stomfa first. Do you know anything about the town?"

"Quite a bit actually, because I keep running into members of the Jewish community in Budapest whose families originated there." Moffat sounded somewhat aloof. "Strictly a one-horse town that once was part of the Austro-Hungarian monarchy. Its significance resides in its closeness to Vienna, about fifty kilometers away. In 1670, when the Jews were expelled from the capital, many moved to Stomfa. If I remember correctly, the town boasts a rather handsome castle and a brewery that produces a reasonably good beer."

Moffat continued. "The person I have in mind for you is Tom Kárász, originally from the Slovak town of Kosice. He's about sixty, speaks English, German, Slovak, and Hungarian, and is the father of one of our local employees. I'm sure you'll find him reasonable, so I suggest you deal with him directly. By the way, Kosice used to belong to Hungary once."

Jack called Kárász, and they made a deal over the phone.

The next day, the trip to Stomfa took less than four hours, including a lineup at the border and a short stop for lunch. Jack was doing the driving in a rented car while Tom Kárász was doing the talking.

"I was born in the Hungarian town of Kassa, now called Kosice in Slovak."

"How come?"

"After World War II, Kassa reverted to Slovakia." *Here we go again,* thought Jack, *yet another frontier switcheroo — very un-American.*

"At school they taught us in both the Hungarian and the Slovak languages, but at home we also spoke German. My parents paid for me to learn English because they wanted to immigrate to Israel after the war, but that didn't work out."

"So you're Jewish."

"Not anymore. My parents converted to Catholicism to avoid being persecuted by the Nazis, but it didn't help. We had to go into hiding."

"Did everybody survive?" Jack was beginning to appreciate the enormity of the Holocaust's effect on central European society.

"No. My uncle, mother's brother, was conscripted into a labor battalion and shipped east. He perished in the Ukraine."

They stayed at the Crown Plaza in central Bratislava for the night.

Jack found that Moffat's characterization of Stomfa was not accurate. In addition to its castle, which was now a museum, Stomfa had a Roman Catholic and a Protestant church and a synagogue that was over 200 years old. The town also boasted a distillery that produced an excellent brand of plum brandy.

At city hall, they were told that birth and death registries in Stomfa had been kept in three languages: in German while the place belonged to Austria, in Hungarian when it became part of Hungary, and in Slovak after 1946.

"Peter Gombos was born in 1900," Jack told Kárász who then translated the information to the clerk.

"That would be in Hungarian times, and I'm afraid the registry has been transferred to Budapest with a copy in Vienna."

Jack was disappointed. "No copy here?"

The clerk shook his head. "You might try at the synagogue. They kept copies, and, of course, they keep their own records of Jewish births, marriages, and deaths. In fact, for a while, the regional rabbinate acted as a licensee of the registry office."

"Why?"

"There was a lot of intermarrying and conversion, and the community tried to keep the records straight, especially during and after the Nazi occupation, in 1944 to 45."

The Stomfa synagogue is maintained by a very small local Jewish community and is open to visitors on Wednesdays and Thursdays, with services on Fridays and Saturdays. The young rabbi in charge who commutes from Vienna couldn't do enough for Jack once he found out the reason for the American's visit.

"Our records up to the late 1930s are in fairly good shape," he explained in German, and Kárász had no difficulty interpreting. "Thereafter, they become sketchy, but we have been able to re-create most of the data lost during World War II."

"How did you do that?"

"Through personal interviews. But we digress." He got up and headed for the door. "Let me get the records of the Gombos family."

He was back in less than a minute with a file in his hand. "We don't have separate dossiers on each family," he explained, "but the Gombos case is special because of the prominence of the man."

He spread the papers out before him while Jack and Kárász made themselves comfortable.

"Before discussing this specific case, allow me to provide you with some background information, which I believe will be useful to you, Mr. Brennan, because, generally speaking," the rabbi gave Jack an apologetic smile, "Americans are not familiar with Central European history."

Jack nodded agreement, and the rabbi continued. "Before 1787, the Jews who lived in the Austro-Hungarian Empire had names like Jakov Ben Avram, Isaac Ben Simon, Isidor Ben Zacharias..."

"What does 'Ben' mean?"

"Son of."

"I suppose like 'poulos' at the end of a Greek name, or 'kian' at the end of an Armenian name."

"Or Jonson, Nicholson, or Jackson."

The rabbi poured them some tea and continued. "Maria Theresia's empire had hundreds of thousands of Jewish inhabitants, and she insisted on having regular and frequent censuses taken for tax purposes."

"Why?"

"To discriminate against the Jews. Being a good Catholic, she decreed that, depending on when and where a Jewish family settled in her empire, it had to pay taxes at a higher rate than the rest of the population."

"So?"

"Stop to think for a moment, Mr. Brennan," the clergyman said. "How can you distinguish one 'Isaac-son-of-Jacob' from another man with the same name if the two don't have different *family* names?"

"I take your point."

"To solve the problem, Maria-Theresia's son, Emperor Joseph II, ordered the Jews in his empire, on pain of expulsion, to apply for family names at designated census offices. They complied and bought themselves family names."

"You mean they had to pay for them?"

"Of course. The Hapsburgs were business-minded. Why should Joseph II, the son of that excellent businesswoman, Maria Theresia, be an exception?"

"I guess you're right. Tell me what happened next."

"The Jews bought German family names, and the more aristocratic the names sounded, the more they cost. For example, there was once a Jewish family who lived in the city of Frankfurt-am-Main, Germany, in an elegant apartment house with a red shield above its main entrance. They decided to call themselves Redshield or 'Rothschild' in German. Need I say more?"

"How does all this relate to Dr. Gombos?"

The rabbi then explained to Jack that Gombos was the Hungarian equivalent of the German word 'knopf', or button. He presumed that the Knopfs must have moved to Stomfa after the Jews were expelled from Vienna in 1670. Dr. Gombos's father was called Stefan Knopf, the Hungarian equivalent of which is István Gombos, a name he adopted in the mid 1890s before Dr. Peter Gombos was born. Gombos Senior was a prosperous and well-respected man who married a woman by the name of Anni Schneider, Dr. Peter Gombos's mother. István Gombos was an only child, but Anni had a sister called Irma.

"How about Dr. Peter Gombos? Was he an only child, too?"

"No. He had a younger brother, Michael, but he died at the age of fourteen in the Spanish flu pandemic of 1918. He is buried here in our cemetery."

"What about Irma, Dr. Gombos's aunt? Did she get married?"

"Yes, to a man named Jenő Preisler. They went to live in Budapest but did not Hungarianize their family name prior to leaving Stomfa shortly before the First World War."

"Hungarianize? Why?"

"To blend in more easily after Austria and Hungary separated."

"Did they have any children?"

The rabbi looked through his file then shook his head. "Difficult to say. I have no record of any children, but then they could have had some in Budapest."

While the rabbi was speaking, Jack was taking notes. He now reviewed them.

"What happened to Dr. Gombos's parents?"

The rabbi consulted his file again. "They both died of natural causes in the early 1940s and are buried here in Stomfa."

Jack was keenly disappointed. He had reached the end of the line in a manner of speaking. Dr. Gombos's wife and children, parents, and brother were all dead. Unless he could find out what had happened to the Preislers and Svetlana Shvedova's family, his chances of identifying an heir to Gombos's fortune were slim to none.

"A final question, Rabbi. If you were me, how would you go about finding out what happened to the Preislers in Budapest?"

"I'd first go to the Budapest rabbinate to see if they had any record of a Jenő Preisler married to a woman called Irma. If they do, they will be able to tell you what happened to them. If they don't, then you should visit the Ministry of the Interior to check whether they have a record of a Jenő Preisler changing his name to something that sounds more Hungarian."

As the rabbi was seeing them to the door, he turned to Kárász and began to explain something to him *sotto voce*.

"What was that all about?" Jack asked Kárász as they were driving back to Budapest.

"The rabbi asked me to try to let you down gently."

"What do you mean by that?"

The translator hesitated. "May I speak frankly?"

"Of course."

"In the early 1900s, Stomfa was a small town with about 3,500 inhabitants, of which more or less 10 percent were Hungarians and mainly Jewish, 16 percent were Germans, and the rest Slovaks, or *toths,* as they were called then. This meant that the roughly 350 Hungarian Jews were a very closely knit community." Kárász stopped talking.

Jack became impatient. "Get on with it, man," he snapped.

"Well, sir," his guide was obviously ill at ease. "The Hungarian *gendarmes* enjoyed the enthusiastic cooperation of the town's population when it came to identifying who was Jewish and who was not in a town that, by 1944, had become home to 6,000 people. It turns out that about a third, or 2,000, was Jewish. The rabbi says that very few of them managed to flee before the *gendarmes* rounded them up and sent them on their way to the camps." The man, very upset, was choking up and could not bring himself to continue. He was in tears.

After a while, he pulled himself together and cleared his throat. "It's hard to believe this, sir, but of the 2,000, less than 500 came back to Stomfa ever — even to visit."

Jack was astounded. "Which means?"

"The rabbi thinks that 100 — including the Preislers — had run away, 100 had survived and are living far away never ever to return, not even for a visit, 150 more had survived and have, in fact, come back to visit or had given sign of life, and about 300 had come back to continue to live in Stomfa. The rest died in the camps."

"Surely, he must be exaggerating."

Kárász shook his head. "No, Mr. Brennan. The synagogue has so far verified by one means or another, the deaths of over 1,200 inhabitants of Stomfa."

"Perhaps the Preislers, who had left Stomfa before World War I, may very well be among those who are still alive but don't ever want to have anything to do with Stomfa again."

"You may be right, Mr. Brennan, but the rabbi wanted me to tell you that the chances of your finding out about what happened to the

Preislers are very slim."

And there you have it, my friend, in a nutshell, Jack said to himself. He then began a silent dialogue with himself. *Are you going to give up? Not until I have visited the Budapest Rabbinate. What if there's nothing there for you? I'll go to the Ministry of the Interior. And what if there's nothing there for you, either? I'll start working on the Shvedov part of the puzzle. Will you ever stop searching? Not until Elize tells me to stop. Why? Because I love her, and I promised.*

Jack stopped his silent conversation because he suddenly realized that his commitment to Elize was complete and unequivocal and that it was time to tell Grandma about it.

CHAPTER 38

Kárász was very sorry to see Jack leave Budapest disappointed but could do nothing about it other than to promise to continue the search for information about the Preislers.

They had gone to the grand synagogue in Budapest's Dohány Utca, the second largest Jewish place of worship in the world after New York's Temple Emanu-El. Following the tour of the synagogue, they went next door and visited the Memorial Park with its Tree of Remembrance that resembles a weeping willow. It is made of anodized aluminum, and its leaves are engraved with the names of the hundreds of thousands of Hungarian Jews who died in the Holocaust.

At the Jewish Museum next door, they met its director, Mrs. Sarah Stark, an affable woman in her forties, who offered them tea and came straight to the point. "When Mr. Moffat alerted me to your visit and the nature of your mission, I told him right away that I can only help in an indirect way. By this, I mean that our records here are not suitable for the kind of search you are in the process of conducting."

"What exactly do you mean by 'not suitable'?"

The woman, though sensing that Jack was slightly put out, paid no attention to his attitude. "To start with, you must understand that more than 600,000 Hungarian Jews were killed by Hitler's thugs in the camps. That's a big number, but the Nazis were meticulous in their recordkeeping, so we were able to identify most of the victims' names. These are listed in alphabetical order on the walls of the memorial buildings that exist in each of the major concentration camps."

She poured herself some more tea. "In my opinion, your best bet of finding out quickly whether the Preislers have perished in the camps is by looking at duplicates of these lists of which there are about a dozen."

"Where are these duplicates kept?"

"We have a set here, and I will gladly give you access to them."

"Thank you." Jack was beginning to feel better. He was making progress.

"Remember two things, though. One, the Preislers may have changed their names after leaving Stomfa; and two, the absence of their names from the lists does not mean that they survived."

"Why not?"

"They may have died somewhere else other than in the camps, perhaps, on their way on foot from Budapest to Germany, for example, during one of the numerous so-called deathmarches the SS and the Arrow Cross had organized during November and Deceember of 1944, or of natural causes, or, for all I know, they may have been shot right here without having their names recorded."

A picture of the Gombos brothers struggling in the freezing, black water of the Danube flashed through Jack's mind. He felt sick.

"Then there are those who died in the ghettos. You probably don't know this, but the synagogue was part of the ghetto in 1944. Over 2,000 people died here of hunger or disease and lie buried in the yard behind the synagogue, some of them nameless."

Jack was overwhelmed. "What do you suggest I do?"

"Go through my lists first, and, if the names are not there, go to the Ministry of the Interior."

"I've been there. They're slow."

Mrs. Stark nodded. "I know, but there is no quick way. While waiting for the ministry's reply go to the passport office and check there. Then there are the various district rabbinates and other kinds of Jewish organizations that kept records of birth, deaths, Bar Mitzvahs. There are lots of alternative sources, but searching them will take time — lots of time."

Jack had heard enough to realize that finding a trace of the Preislers might take years, and he didn't have years. He put Kárász on retainer for six months and promised him a substantial bonus if he found something that would prove useful in the search for a surviving heir of Dr. Gombos. Then he hurried back to Elize and the Stapfers who also planned to attend the shareholders' meeting of the Moretti bank.

✛

The special shareholders' meeting of Moretti & Cie Banquiers was to take place on August 15th, and the only item on the agenda was the acquisition of SIL Limited by the bank. It took place in the Grand Ballroom of the Baur au Lac Hotel and was attended by close to a hundred shareholders. In spite of lively discussion, the motion to buy SIL in exchange for 230,000 preferred voting shares of the bank, each valued at a thousand Swiss francs, was passed with nary a dissension.

The good burghers of Zurich knew full well that while the shares of the bank represented "paper" of dubious value, the shares of SIL, which the bank was acquiring by issuing "paper," were backed by solid investments in "bricks and mortar," namely businesses operating at a profit.

CHAPTER 39

The Hotel Austria on Talstrasse near the Reeperbahn in Hamburg advertises itself as the ideal starting point for an evening of roaming around in the city's famous red-light district. Hans-Ruedi Schmidt knew this to be so from firsthand experience. He had stayed at the hotel on a number of occasions because the place was less than a block from the Eros Centrum, a world-famous giant bordello that he loved to visit from time to time.

Schmidt was always careful about his trips to what he called his city of sin. After a bus ride from Zurich's main railway station very early in the morning to avoid running into anyone he knew, he'd arrive at the Bale-Mulhouse airport in France within an hour and a half. From there, Hamburg was only a ninety-minute flight away.

He made it a point to take this indirect route to make it difficult for his wife to discover his ultimate destination. He could not afford a scandal that was bound to follow if she sued for divorce on the basis of adultery. Zurich's hypocritical, mainly Protestant, inhabitants were unwaveringly intolerant of senior banking executives who were caught fooling around behind their wives' backs.

Schmidt, who beat his wife on occasion — as did many of the city's male population — was into BDSM big time and needed an outlet for his definitely kinky sexual wants. Although Zurich had plenty to offer in this department, he preferred the anonymity of a pilgrimage to Hamburg, Europe's Mecca of carnal debauchery, to visiting the establishments along his hometown's Niederdorfen *Strasse* where he was bound to be recognized and, thus, subject to blackmail.

This time, his trip had to do not only with pleasure but also with business. He had an appointment with a high-class prostitute, Roza Stern, a woman he had been frequenting for two years now, who was not only a fantastic practitioner of BDSM but also Jewish, exactly what he needed under the circumstances. Her house on Schmuck *Strasse* was only a stone's throw from the Hotel Austria, which made it easy for Schmidt to arrive on time for their mid-afternoon appointment for Champagne and caviar.

The place was spacious and elegantly furnished. It was also equipped with a cellar, or dungeon, containing all the accoutrements necessary for highly successful combined S & M and B & D sessions.

By dinnertime, Schmidt had tried a number of variations of his favorite fantasies with the sex slave the woman had provided and was tiring fast. He called a halt to proceedings and suggested that they send the slave away, get cleaned up and have something to eat "to put more lead in my pencil" as he quaintly put it.

Roza suggested the Freudenhaus Restaurant on Hans-Hoyer *Strasse* where the food turned out to be excellent and the service very friendly and efficient. That the dishes on the menu had slightly naughty names added to the exciting atmosphere of the place.

Roza Stern's family was originally from Munich where her grandfather owned a bookstore, one of the first to fall victim to the Nazis on *Kristallnacht,* the night Hitler's thugs smashed countless Jewish shop windows. Hence the name: the night of broken crystal *(Kristall)*, or glass, that littered the streets of most German cities after the pogrom.

Roza's grandparents were later deported to the nearby Dachau concentration camp where they ultimately died in the typhus epidemic that ravaged the facility's population. Her parents, bookish people, survived and moved to Leipzig, a university town in what was then East Germany. Roza was born there in the early seventies.

But not for her 'academe' or the rewards of toiling in a

workers' paradise.

She ran away at fifteen and found her way to the West, where she began her hooking career as a streetwalker. A big, well-endowed girl, she found that she enjoyed BDSM, so she decided to specialize in this *branche* of prostitution and soon had her own studio.

For months now, Schmidt had been probing her background discreetly, but he needed more information, so, after their coffee had arrived, he decided on a more direct approach.

He started off with what he thought would be an innocuous question. "How is your family?"

Roza looked at him with surprise. "I thought I told you that I had no family, that I lived alone."

Schmidt was embarrassed by his gaffe and retreated as best he could. "I mean your parents. Where are they now?"

"Frankly, I have no idea. We haven't been in touch for years."

This piece of very welcome information prompted Schmidt to take the plunge.

"I have a business proposition for you," he said and took a generous sip of his after-dinner Cognac.

Her buxom bosom heaved with throaty laughter. "I love propositions," she said, "especially when it involves business."

Schmidt looked at his watch: it showed a few minutes past ten. There was no need to hurry. His time with her would not be up before dawn.

"Let's go home and first fool around some more," he proposed. "I promise to tell you what I have in mind on the stroke of midnight."

She gave his crotch a friendly squeeze under the table. "Let's go, big boy," she said, "I'm game."

She loved her job, especially when it involved horny, kinky bastards with money and imagination like Schmidt who had fat wallets and long, thick, and hard dicks.

CHAPTER 40

Back from her vacation, Elize was pleasantly surprised to see that her boss had reverted to his courteous, cooperative self.

"As far as we are concerned," he told her, "nothing has changed. The bank is the bank, and we are the Foundation. My cousin will continue to run the bank, and I will continue to direct the Foundation."

"Will your relative responsibilities not change?" Elize tried to be diplomatic.

"You mean my cousin's and mine?"

She nodded.

Studer looked away then answered with some reluctance. "I suppose they will to the extent that I will have to follow his advice more than I did in the past."

You can bet your sweet ass that you will have to — as Jack would say she thought. *For all intents and purposes, Moretti is calling the shots now. His bank owns SIL.*

Studer changed the subject. "I expect that there will be a worldwide economic slowdown as a result of the irresponsible action of Wall Street and the leaders of major U.S. and U.K. banks, but SIL is invested in solid enterprises and bonds of unquestionable stability. As you know, we also have a lot of cash on hand. In about a year, we're going to start looking for bargains to pick up." He gave her a big smile. "You should bear this in mind during your travels as auditor of the Foundation."

It was obvious that he was working hard to reestablish the relationship of mutual trust that had existed between them before the takeover.

"Meaning?"

"Keep your eyes open for acquisition opportunities, especially in the field of genomics or genetic engineering."

Elize was planning her next swing through North America to coincide with the long Labor Day weekend during which she would meet Jack in Buffalo. They wanted to have a lengthy visit with Grandma Ilona. When they got there, they found that she was still in hospital and not doing well. As expected, she had developed pneumonia, and the antibiotics she had been given to help her recover had weakened her. She perked up when she saw the two young people but tired quickly.

Jack told her about Dr. Gombos and their theory of SIL belonging to the Hungarian scientist's heirs, but at the mention of her native land, she became agitated and disoriented so they dropped the subject.

Jack flew back to Cayman to continue his work there, and Elize returned to Switzerland where she retained the services of a lawyer colleague, *Doktor Juris* Hilde Somary, whom she swore to secrecy and then instructed to write to Banque Julius Odier, Moretti & Cie, and Bank Lamarche, Lambert, using texts that Jack had prepared.

The letters were almost identical.

Dear Sirs,

We represent the heirs of the original owner of the bank account in your books designated by the number (here, the lawyer inserted the appropriate number). *Please indicate what documentation you require to enable you to turn control of the account over to them.*

Yours very truly,

All three banks replied within seven days by way of identical standard form letters developed by the Swiss Bankers Association in which they asked *Doktor* Somary for the name of the original account owner. The lawyer gave them Dr. Peter Gombos's name, whereupon Odier followed up with a request for Dr. Gombos's death certificate and for details regarding the basis of her clients' claim to being the man's legal heirs.

This was a terrific step forward for Jack's side. It proved without a doubt that their theory about Dr. Gombos being involved in the Foundation's affairs was correct!

Unfortunately, Lamarche, Lambert's and Moretti's answers were different. They both insisted that, according to their records, the original owner's name had not been Gombos and that, therefore, the lawyer was dealing with a case of mistaken identity. Dr. Somary requested that the banks recheck their records. They replied that they had done so and that, as far as they were concerned, the matter was closed.

As soon as Jack heard about these developments, he took the first available plane to Zurich to meet with Elize and Dr. Somary.

They were in Elize's dining room, breakfasting on orange juice, strong coffee, and delicious, fresh, buttered bread-rolls with jam. It was ten o'clock in the morning on a glorious September Saturday, and, in spite of having slept little on the plane, Jack was not tired. He was too excited about the situation and thrilled by having Elize near him again.

"Here's where we are," he said by way of introduction. "We should consider the Odier account to be the 'A' account, or — if you prefer — the first account that Dr. Gombos opened. There are two reasons for this. First, according to Elize, the Moretti account, which I think we should consider to be the 'B,' or second, account, receives money *from* the 'A' account and pays money *to* the Lamarche account, which I think is the 'C' account."

"And 'C' then reimburses 'A' to complete the circle," Kurt was quick to add.

"What's the second reason?" This from Karl Stapfer who was also there as was Dr. Somary, the lawyer.

"The fact that he opened the 'B' and 'C' accounts under a name that was not his own."

Elize did not accept this answer. "Explain."

"Trust, or I should say, the lack of it." Jack reasoned. "By the time

Gombos got to Switzerland, he trusted no one. He might even have concluded that Hitler would ultimately invade Switzerland, too, and that, as a result, no account belonging to a Jew would be safe. That's why he set up such an elaborate scheme."

Somary nodded. "That makes sense. What do you want me to do next?"

"Write Odier and say we're working on the documentation, but that Dr. Gombos is a victim of the Holocaust and that we might not be able to produce a proper death certificate. Ask if there might be another way to satisfy Odier's requirements."

They had their answer within days. If the presumptive heirs could provide a valid password and proof that Dr. Gombos was, indeed, a victim of the Holocaust, the bank would be willing to consider applying the rules regulating the rights of Holocaust victims in such cases.

Jack was devastated. "First, we can't decode the password. Second, Dr. Gombos is not strictly speaking a Holocaust victim. He was killed in an accident. All we can do is to obtain an affidavit from Dr. Szilard, certifying the circumstances of Dr. Gombos's death. Perhaps this would suffice instead of a proper death certificate, especially since the affidavit would come from a man of impeccable reputation, a professor emeritus at Cornell University. But even if, based on Szilard's testimony, Banque Odier accepted that Dr. Gombos was dead, it was unlikely to deal with anyone other than a legally certified heir of the man."

Elize would not give up. "There must be a way to move forward on this," she insisted.

But, unfortunately, they could think of no alternative.

Time to call the cavalry for help. Reluctantly, Jack flew to Washington. He needed to consult Uncle George. They met, as usual, for lunch at the grill of the Mayflower Hotel and started their meal with double Scotches — Saint Leger, of course.

"I'm glad you called me, Jack," the older man said, "because it's high time we cleared the air between us."

Jack was taken aback by this frontal assault. "I didn't think we had a problem," he riposted.

"Don't pretend that you are not upset with me because I know better. Things have not been the same with you and me since the Gallagher incident, and for this I'm very sorry because you're my favorite nephew and, as you know, I love you very much. So tell me what I can do for you."

Jack tried to change the subject. "I'm worried about Grandma, Uncle. She hasn't written for ages, and I can't seem to reach her by telephone."

"She's very weak and seems to have lost her will to live. Frankly, I'm worried about her, too. She's barely holding her own."

Jack felt a twinge in his heart. His grandmother was very important to him. "After I've finished here, I'll run up to Buffalo and pop in to see her. I hope that'll cheer her up a bit."

Uncle George was very pleased. "I would sure appreciate that, Jack. She's very fond of you."

"And me of her."

His uncle sighed. "Look, nephew, my mother is over ninety-five. She had a good life and has a wonderful, loving family who visits her regularly, but the quality of life she's experiencing now in the rehabilitation center is not what she's used to."

"Perhaps that's what is discouraging her."

"Maybe you're right, Jack, but, for the time being, we have no choice. She needs intensive looking after twenty-four/seven."

"Then arrange for it so that she has it at her home."

Busy with their steaks, for a while, neither spoke. Finally, Secretary Rooney broke the silence. "Out with it, nephew. You didn't come to Washington to talk about your grandmother. What's eating you?"

"I'm thirty-one, Uncle George, and my career is sliding sideways because my heart is no longer in it. I'm in love with a woman who lives 4,000 miles away and with whom I would like to spend the rest of my life, but I can't."

"Why not?"

"There's this thing in which we got involved and which is

consuming us both. We need to find a way to solve it before we can get on with our lives."

"Tell me about it."

So Jack told Uncle George all about Dr. Peter Gombos and the Foundation and the promise he had made to Elize Haemmerle. The Secretary remained silent for a couple of minutes and then pulled out his cellphone and dialed a number. He spoke into the mouthpiece for quite some time but in such low tones that Jack could not hear what was being said. When he had finished, he took a business card from his pocket, scribbled a number on its back and handed it to Jack.

"Jack," he said, "I'm a great believer in going to the best expert in the world when I need help in a matter about which I know almost nothing. What you're talking about is well beyond me, but I know of an expert who might be able to help you. Phone him and make an appointment to see him. He's expecting your call."

Jack glanced at the card. "Whom should I ask for?"

"Whom else but for the King of the Jews?"

Seeing the expression on Jack's face this answer elicited made Uncle George burst into such a loud guffaw that the waiter near their table dropped the plates he was carrying.

CHAPTER 41

Fear has a profound effect on people. It paralyzes some and incites vigorous action in others.

Enrico Moretti belonged in the first category. For days, he could not bring himself to share his dreadful secret with anyone. But since he, his family, and his bank found themselves under potential attack from not one but two directions, he had no choice.

He summoned Schmidt to his office, locked the door, and made his executive vice president swear on the Bible that he wouldn't breathe a word to anyone about what he was about to be told. Although Schmidt knew full well what was bothering Moretti, he pretended to be deeply shocked when his boss told him that the bank had received a letter from a second source, claiming possible ownership of the account controlling SIL.

"Both seem to know the account number but not the name of the account holder."

"They don't know the password either, do they?" Schmidt asked smugly.

"True, but isn't it strange that both claim to be related to the account holder?"

Schmidt shook his head. "Standard operating procedure in these wild goose chases." He had researched this point carefully before composing the letter that he had made Roza send to the Moretti bank from Hamburg. "In the first case, the lawyer, Somary, was obviously acting for the wrong client. The name he gave us had nothing to do with the account. In the case of the woman in Hamburg, we don't know yet."

"Have you written her?"

Schmidt's reply surprised Moretti. "I was thinking of going to Hamburg."

"What on earth for?"

"To short-circuit the process of qualifying her."

"I don't understand."

"I want to find a good local private detective there who could find out what her circumstances are, where she lives, what her occupation is, what sort of a family background she has, and so on. In other words, I want to establish whether she has a serious position or not."

"Couldn't a Swiss private detective do that for us?"

"Of course he could, but I don't think we should use one. Word might get out."

Moretti leaned on his desk, put his unbent fingers to his right temple, and leaned forward. "Let me think about this."

Elize found out about the letter from Hamburg by accident. Studer had asked her to lend a hand with legal matters at the Foundation. Dr. Von Tobel, the lawyer, had broken his legs in several places while high-speed water-skiing and was hospitalized. She was tidying up his office and his papers when she came across a copy of Roza Stern's letter. Its discovery had made her dizzy to the point where she had to sit down.

Why had Studer not told me about it? she asked herself. Did he trust her so little that he'd keep vital information from her? Did he not realize that she had every right to know such things if he wanted her to help protect the Foundation? Who was this woman anyway, and how could she claim to be an heir of Dr. Gombos when Jack Brennan had been unable to locate the existence of *any* heir?

Then the possibility dawned on her that Stern might know the name of the initial account holder and that she was an heir of that person. But that didn't make sense. The woman would have mentioned the name in her letter. Or would she have? Somary didn't in *her* first letter to the bank, did she?

This was bad news. It threatened Elize's and Jack's plans to make restitution to the Gombos family. Another thought welled up in her mind. Perhaps Gombos was not really the moving spirit behind the whole setup. Her heart heavy with doubt, she reached for the phone and called Jack who, she knew, was visiting his grandmother.

CHAPTER 42

An immensely likeable man, Mark Schneiderman was the grandson of a Winnipeg rabbi who narrowly escaped slaughter by marauding Cossacks in the Pale during the pogroms conducted against the Jews during the eighteenth and nineteenth centuries. The rabbi never stopped running until he got to what was then the "nowhere" of Canada, an immense piece of featureless, flat land called the Prairies. He settled in Winnipeg where he raised four children: three girls and the youngest, a boy, called Sam.

Sam had a quick wit and lots of *sechel* (street smarts). Soon after the advent of prohibition in the U.S., he figured it out that with a bit of daring, a fortune could be made from smuggling booze from Canada into the U.S. All you needed was connections. And connections could be bought.

Sam had two children, Mark and Mindy. Mark was everything his father was not: McGill- and Harvard-educated, refined and intellectually inclined, he turned his back on his father's liquor empire, became a lawyer, and started dabbling in real estate. He made a fortune and bought himself a chain of U.S. and Canadian newspapers.

When their father died, Mindy took charge of the booze business and, over a period of three decades, made it into a giant of the industry. Then *she* died, and because she was not married and had no children, she left the business to her brother.

Mark wanted to have absolutely nothing to do with distilling and selling booze so he sold the business to a French water company who paid big bucks for it, thereby making Mark even wealthier, in fact, world class.

Mark was by nature a behind-the-scenes guy. He preferred staying in the background, quietly advising men in public life from the wings. His only overt public endeavor consisted of appearing from time to time as the pinch-hitting host of an intellectually high-powered talk show aired on public television at midnight five days a week.

At one of these appearances, he met Elie Wiesel, the Jewish writer and Holocaust survivor, who told him about the shameful way the Swiss banks were refusing to return the money the Jews, killed by the Nazis during the war, had hidden from their persecutors in Switzerland. This infuriated Mark to the point where he took a leave of absence from his business and devoted five years of his life and some of his fortune to fighting the banks, using every weapon at his disposal, including the considerable clout that owning a chain of newspapers gave him.

In the end, Mark won a huge settlement for the survivors and their relatives. His grateful co-religionists began calling him affectionately "King of the Jews," and the moniker stuck.

✚

After an afternoon's visit with Grandma Ilona in Buffalo, Jack flew to New York to consult with Mark Schneiderman. The newspaper mogul, in town for the weekend, received Jack at his luxurious double-decker apartment on East 90th Street, near the park close to the Guggenheim.

After hearing him out patiently and very carefully, Schneiderman wasted no time in setting Jack straight.

"You're obviously obsessed with this thing, as is your girlfriend, Ms. Haemmerle, so your view is clouded." The Canadian was not in the habit of mincing his words. "Step back for a moment and take stock."

"What are you driving at?"

"You're in a reactive rather than a proactive situation. SIL has been sold to this Moretti bank in exchange for a substantial ownership in the bank. Therefore, all that the numbered bank account that used to own the Foundation is now left with is 230,000 shares of the damned bank, right?

"I suppose so."

"Very well then. You should do three things." Schneiderman ticked them off on the fingers of his right hand. "Investigate the financial position of this Moretti bank in depth, that's one."

"Why?"

"To make sure there's no danger of the bank being taken over by its depositors, in which case the shareholders might lose everything."

Schneiderman continued. "The second thing is to find out all you can about Roza Stern."

Jack nodded. "And the third thing?"

"You should get a top-notch Swiss lawyer to prepare two interlocutory injunctions that you could spring on the directors of the bank at a moment's notice in case they try to do something cute at their next meeting."

Jack was lost. "I need you to explain what you mean."

"The word 'injunction' is legalese for forbidding people to do something. An interlocutory injunction is an order not to do something before their case is heard in court. In your particular instance, the first injunction should forbid Moretti to vote the bank shares held by the numbered account until either a legal heir of the original owner is found or a certain amount of time has passed, say a year."

"And the second injunction?"

"It should prohibit the directors from paying a dividend on the 45,000 shares held by the general public. This would give these so-called public shares ten votes per share rather than only one."

"Why would we want to do that?"

"It's a question of simple arithmetic. With nobody voting, the 230,000 shares belonging either to the Stern woman or to your group, the total number of votes that could be cast would be limited to 1 million."

Schneiderman took a sip of the seltzer water in his glass and carried on. "Of these, the Morettis would have 400,000, the general public, 450,000, and your friend, Karl Stapfer, 150,000."

"Which would make Uncle Karl the key man, the kingmaker," Brennan whispered, shaking his head in disbelief.

"You got it." The Canadian sounded pleased.

Jack tried to control his incipient euphoria. "I suppose it's difficult to obtain such injunctions."

"Very, especially against a Swiss bank in Switzerland unless you have a really solid, well-reasoned case."

"On a scale of one to ten, what would you say my chances are?"

"Slightly better than fifty-fifty."

"That high? How come?"

"Don't forget, you'd have overwhelming world opinion on your side."

"I don't see how I could obtain that."

Schneiderman was smiling broadly. "I know just the right investigative reporter who could make this story sing." He looked at Jack hard, and the smile disappeared. "Of course, you'd have to cooperate, and you and your friends would also have to give up your anonymity."

"Thank you, Uncle George, for standing by me once more," Jack whispered on his way out, deeply moved and overwhelmed by his good fortune. "All is forgiven."

CHAPTER 43

Hamburg is an old city. It was founded in the ninth century and quickly became an important port because of its strategic location. Today, it is Germany's second largest city after Berlin, and its port is the second busiest port in Europe after Rotterdam in Holland.

Because of its commercial importance, the city merits special attention from the U.S. Department of the Treasury, not to mention the DEA, since the huge quantity of goods passing through the city's port contains at times merchandise of a questionable nature. In other words, like at all large ports, smuggling activity cannot be eliminated completely.

Law enforcement agencies live by the motto of "follow the money" to lead them to the guilty. That is why the U.S. Treasury has a special agent at the Consulate in Hamburg who works closely with Germany's financial intelligence unit that monitors suspicious monetary transactions.

The agent, Robert Schiller, aware that Jack was related to the Secretary of the Treasury, received his visitor with open arms. After Jack explained his problem, Schiller requested a confidential report on Roza Stern from the Hamburg police, which he obtained within twenty-four hours.

"Where do we go from here?" Jack asked and poured them more coffee. They were having breakfast at his hotel, the *Vier Jahreszeiten*.

"Allow me to set the record straight," Schiller replied. "Whoring

is a perfectly respectable profession in Hamburg, just like in the
Barrio Chino in Barcelona, at the Chicken Ranch in Nevada, and
in the famous red-light district of Amsterdam, not to mention Bugis
Street in Singapore and the sex bars in Bangkok."

"You don't say." Schiller sounded like a man of some worldliness.

"Even more so if you run a specialized studio like Roza
Stern does."

"You mean this domina business."

"Yes. Here they are considered to be therapists." Schiller glanced
at the police report. "Don't condemn her on appearances. Just
because she is a sex-worker, her claim to be related to someone who
had money in a Swiss bank before World War II may be perfectly
legitimate." He was fluent in Goethe's language; his parents hailed
from Frankfurt before emigrating to the States. "The woman
is Jewish."

"How do you know?"

"It says so in the report. Besides, the name, Stern, meaning 'star'
in English, is typically Jewish."

"What are you getting at?"

"Simply this: She may have easily had some relative who died in
the Holocaust and whose papers have only recently surfaced."

After debating the matter, they decided to visit Ms. Stern.

Schiller did all the talking. He told her they were U.S. Treasury
Agents investigating international money laundering rings and
asked her to help them. She was polite, but cool. After a fifteen-
minute chat, she reluctantly admitted that she had recently written
to a Swiss bank because she suspected her grandfather, who died
in Dachau during the war, may have had a little money hidden
in Switzerland.

Jack asked Schiller to ask if the bank had answered.

She shook her head. And that was that.

After the Americans left, Ms. Stern made two telephone calls:
the first to a number given her by her good client, whom she knew as
Freddy Keller, a sales rep. for *Oerlikon Waffen Fabrik*. As instructed,
she left him an innocuous message and waited for him to call back.

Her second call was to an unlisted number at the Israeli Embassy in Berlin.

"Freddy" called back a week later. He asked her to repeat every detail of the interview with the Americans and then thanked her for her help and promised to be back in touch within a couple of weeks.

"Freddy," alias Schmidt, was very pleased with the efficiency and promptness of the private detective agency that he had retained in Hamburg because, before providing him with an in-depth report on Roza Stern (that substantially confirmed what he already knew about his domina mistress), they had taken the initiative to double check, with a personal visit, what was said about the woman in their written report.

At least that's what Schmidt thought. In fact, the agency had simply obtained the same confidential police report that Schiller had gotten from Hamburg's finest, then recopied it, and sent it on to Banque Moretti with a bill for services for a thousand Swiss francs.

Schmidt only found out much later that the men who had visited Roza were not employees of the detective agency pretending to be Americans, but, in fact, *bona fide* U.S. citizens and Treasury agents.

CHAPTER 44

The Swiss call the Monday after the third Sunday in September the Day of Federal Fasting. It is a public holiday across the land, and nobody works, except those who live in the Canton of Geneva.

Of course, no self-respecting Swiss would face such privation — a whole day of staying away from work without eating — unless he fortified himself with a *very* substantial meal the day before. Hence the tradition of preparing a special pea soup on the eve of the feast that contains leaks, potatoes, vegetables, spices, an entire smoked ham and, of course, a large quantity of peas.

Hans-Ruedi Schmidt chose that particular Monday to start working on the implementation of the *coup d'état* he had been preparing for months. For starters, he planned to give Morettti more bad news: The bank's investment portfolio was to take yet another huge hit.

The office was deserted except for a lone security guard seated behind the reception desk at the head of the magnificent staircase that swept upward from the *rez-de-chaussée* to the main entrance of Banque Moretti's elegantly furnished offices on the building's first floor. He scrambled to attention when Schmidt arrived.

"*Herr Direktor* Morretti is already here," he reported obsequiously as he unlocked the door leading to the bank's inner sanctum. "He is waiting for you in your office."

Schmidt was taken aback. "My office?"

"Yes, sir. He forgot his key at home, and my master key does not open his door. I was able to open yours so he made himself at home there."

Irritated, the banker nodded curtly. "Very well. Please bring us some coffee."

"I can't, *Herr* Schmidt. Our kitchenette is locked, and I can't leave my post for the time it would take to get it from across the street."

Schmidt barged through the door cursing and headed for his office where he found Moretti looking through the papers on Schmidt's desk. This infuriated him, but he bit his tongue and waited for Moretti to finish rifling through his correspondence.

Moretti looked up and, by way of greeting, waved a piece of paper in Schmidt's direction. "I see we'll have to write down some more of our investment portfolio." He was holding a letter the bank's auditors had written to Schmidt demanding a write-down of the bank's reserves.

"That's right," Schmidt said curtly, "By the end of December, all our reserves will have disappeared so, in the next quarter, the authorities will not allow us to pay the dividend on the shares held by the public or on the 230,000 shares we issued to pay for SIL. All these shares would then become entitled to ten votes each."

"How does this impact our position?"

"Our bank's annual general meeting is scheduled for next March 15 at which we have to elect directors for the coming year. We might not be able to get our own people elected. This might lead to us losing control over the bank's and SIL's operations."

Stunned, Moretti sat down behind Schmidt's desk. Schmidt remained standing. "How come?"

"Including Stapfer, we'd have 550,000 votes, plus the votes of the so-called SIL shares, while the public would have 450,000."

"So? We'd still have control."

"Yes, but what if we were not allowed to vote the SIL shares and Stapfer voted with the public?"

Moretti checked his figures before replying. "If we were not allowed to vote the SIL shares, nobody else would, either. I'd see to that."

"How?"

"By going to court."

"Doing that would not guarantee that we would retain control. If Stapfer simply abstained, the public could still outvote us."

Moretti looked puzzled. Then he rechecked his figure and turned pale. "You're right," he whispered. "We'd have 400,000 votes, and the public 450,000." He was beginning to sweat, and his empty stomach was churning. He hadn't eaten breakfast.

Schmidt felt the time was ripe to deliver yet another blow below Moretti's belt. "I've looked at the situation from all angles, and I've concluded that there's only one way out of this mess."

"Which is?"

"To make sure we retain the right to vote the SIL shares."

"But how?"

"By making a deal with the legitimate heir of the account that owns 230,000 bank shares with 2.3 million votes."

Moretti laughed derisively and headed for the door. "I suppose you will now tell me how to do this, even though we don't even know who the shares' owner is."

Schmidt moved in for the kill. "I know who it is," he said very quietly, "and so do you."

Moretti stopped in his tracks and then spun around. "I do?"

"It's Roza Stern, of course. All she needs to enable her to prove her rights is a little help from you."

"You mean I should tell her the password," he looked at Schmidt in amazement.

His underling met his gaze without flinching. "Yes, I do. And I assure you that I can make it happen."

"What would it cost?"

"We'd buy Roza Stern's share certificate evidencing her ownership of SIL for a 100,000 dollars, that's all."

"Who is 'we'?"

"You and me, of course, fifty-fifty."

Moretti was so surprised that he had to sit back down again.

His head was spinning. For the first time, he saw Schmidt for what he really was, a dangerous, small-time crook with big ambitions. He had to distance himself from the man as quickly as possible.

"Your idea is bold and very intriguing," he said playing for time. "Let me sleep on it."

Schmidt thought he had won his point and followed up on his perceived advantage. "Believe me, my way is the only way to make sure that nobody can wrest control of your bank from you."

Except you, Moretti said to himself, but nodded, as if in agreement. But he knew better. He'd make a pact with that miserable curmudgeon Stapfer before getting involved further with Hans-Ruedi Schmidt.

CHAPTER 45

For Jack, Christmas in the tropics was an incongruous affair. There was no snow, most of the sweating Santas in the shopping malls were wearing ill-fitting semi-transparent red mesh tunics, and their black plastic boots looked ridiculous.

The music wasn't appropriate, either. The incessant rendition of "Jingle Bells" blaring out of loudspeakers hanging from every conceivable nook and cranny had an irritating Caribbean beat, and the lyrics were totally inappropriate.

"...oh what fun is to run in an open sleigh..."

Oh paleeese...! Jack was thoroughly fed up. Nothing was going his way. Citing vague rules under the Companies' Bankruptcy Act, Pinsky had refused — at least for the time being — to release the moneys owing to *post partum* account holders, which had unnecessarily upset a number of people, including Elize, who owned the largest such account. Everybody needed extra money for the holidays, especially during times of world-wide financial difficulties.

Then there was the matter of Pinsky wanting Jack to stay on in Cayman for another six months. Jack had kept refusing to agree, though he knew that his bargaining position was weak. On the one hand, he needed the generously high salary the liquidation was paying; the costs of flying around the world chasing phantoms and retaining a guide in Budapest and a lawyer in Zurich were depleting his savings at an alarming rate. On the other hand, he wanted to resume his career in Toronto — and to be near his family in Buffalo, especially Grandma Ilona who was still in hospital and very weak. On top of it all, there was the fate of the two interlocutory injunctions that Somary had served on Moretti & Cie. Banquiers.

Both had been approved by the courts. The first, forbidding the bank from voting the SIL shares at the annual general meeting of the bank's shareholders on March 15 had been granted for a period of one year or until the rightful owner of the SIL account was identified and confirmed by the courts. In the latter case, the owner would then be able to vote the shares as he pleased.

The second injunction, prohibiting the bank from paying the annual dividend on the bank' shares held by the public and SIL, was approved to remain in effect until the bank returned to profitability. This meant that, at the meeting, the Morettis were going to have 400,000 votes and the public 450,000 and that everything depended on how Karl Stapfer would vote — or *not* vote.

A week before the Christmas break, Jack invited Pinsky to dinner at Papagallo's, an exotic restaurant started by Montrealers in West Bay, some distance from George Town. Both men knew it was crunch time.

Pinsky, not a man to mince words started his attack as soon as the pre-lunch double gins and tonic had arrived.

"Jack, your work at the liquidation was at times inspired and on the whole eminently satisfactory, but lately, you've not been paying attention to detail."

Jack had expected the criticism. "You're right, Albert, and that's just the point. I have lost interest. I've been on the island too long."

"So what are you going to do about it?"

"Frankly, nothing. I want out."

Pinsky was taken aback. He had not expected such a countermove, so he attacked again. "Has it ever occurred to you that if you pulled out of here now you'd kind of blot your copybook with the firm, so to speak?"

Jack laughed. He had foreseen that his boss would ultimately start pressing him hard but had expected the veiled threats to begin with the coffee at the end of the meal rather than at the start of it with the gins and tonic. He took a big gulp of his drink, set his glass down carefully and leaned across the table. "Albert, you're forgetting that I've been working with you closely for over a year and that I know most of your tricks, so please don't threaten me. Fact is, you and I need each other, but I suspect you need me more than I need you."

"Says who?" Pinsky was always ready to give as good as he got. "I know that you're spending money like a drunken sailor on shore leave on this crazy project of yours and that I'm your only source of revenue. Stay, and I'll make it worth your while."

Jack shook his head. "From you, such an offer is very tempting, but I can't. I must see my project through, and I can't do it from here."

Pinsky ordered lobster tails for two and a bottle of Ladoucette, a dry white French wine, then switched into conciliatory mode. "Suppose you tell me about what's going on, and we'll see how I can help you."

That was precisely the opening Jack had been waiting for. He brought Pinsky up-to-date on how the Gombos situation stood, told him about his grandmother not being well, and explained his concern about his career.

"You see," he said, summing up, "I need to spend Christmas in Buffalo and the first week of the New Year in Toronto to look around a bit. I can be back here by mid-January, but only for six weeks."

"Why?"

"Because I have to be in Zurich to prepare for the Moretti bank's annual meeting."

"For God's sake, what for?"

"To make sure Karl Stapfer doesn't cave in to the Moretti clan."

Pinsky thought about all this for a while. "I see your point. But he's not the only potential threat."

"What do you mean?"

"What you call the public shares is not a monolithic bloc. Some of the public shareholders might be persuaded to side with the Morettis."

Jack was quick to agree. That problem had occurred to him, too.

"The more reason for me having to spend time in Zurich, perhaps even a full month."

Pinsky laughed. "To spend time with your Swiss girlfriend, I bet."

"That, too, but I'll see her in Buffalo at Christmas anyway. She's coming over with her brother to stay with my family for a week."

"I see things are getting to be pretty serious between the two of you."

Jack blushed and told him about his promise to Elize. "You may be right."

"When are you bringing her to Cayman?"

Jack gave in with a smile. "Okay, Albert, here's what I am willing to promise. Easter is early this year, the last week of March. I'll come back to Cayman with Elize for Easter, and I'll stay here until June 30. Then I'm outa here. But it'll cost you."

"How much?"

"A return ticket from Switzerland to Cayman in business class for Elize and her brother."

"Done deal," said Pinsky. They shook hands.

And that's how they left it. But man proposes, and God disposes...

CHAPTER 46

Jack's family was very happy. They were hosting Elize and Kurt for the holidays, *and* it turned out that Grandma Ilona was strong enough to return to her home in time for the Yuletide season.

On Christmas Eve, the clan gathered at her house for a festive dinner. The next day, it was Uncle George's turn to play host. He had arranged for all the youngsters' unopened presents to be placed under the gigantic Christmas tree in his palatial family room to where he had invited their intended recipients to open them starting at the ungodly hour of eight o'clock in the morning.

This they did with delighted squeals and lots of excited running about under the bemused eyes of their sleepy progenitors, most of whom had attended midnight mass the night before.

Christmas Day dinner started at six and lasted well into the night. Elize and Karl had a ball, reveling in the warmth of a very large family's festive gathering.

New Year's Eve was celebrated at Grandma Ilona's house. She was remarkably chipper during the day but retired shortly after midnight with a slight headache.

On Boxing Day, Elize, Karl, and Jack drove to Toronto where they spent a couple of days sightseeing, and then the Haemmerles took a Swiss flight back to Zurich.

✚

The call came just as Jack was leaving his senior partner's office in downtown Toronto.

Grandma Ilona was in the hospital again, this time as the result of a mild stroke. She was drifting in and out of consciousness, and the doctors were worried.

Jack tried to get a flight to Buffalo, but the January weather was so blustery that all flights were grounded for the time being. He rented a car again and fought rush hour traffic and sleet and wet snow for four hours before reaching her bedside at Mercy Hospital in Buffalo around ten o'clock at night.

His mother and sister, Mary, were already there. Uncle George and his wife were on their way back from Washington, and Uncle Patrick, the archbishop, walked in a few minutes after Jack got there.

Grandma Ilona was in a restless state, drifting in and out of consciousness, periodically calling out for Jack. He bent over, kissed her on the cheek, and squeezed her hand to let her know that he had arrived. When she heard his voice, she came to for a few moments and gave him a big smile. Then she started muttering something that he did not understand.

He tried to withdraw his hand, but she would not let go. Instead, she switched to German and began to repeat over and over again *"Auf Deutsch, auf Ungarish, auf Deutsch, auf Ungarisch."*

Jack tried to calm her by chanting the words with her, but she astonished him by translating them into Hungarian: *"Magyarul, németül, magyarul, németül."* After a while, he began to understand what she was saying because the words were two of the few she had taught him when he was a little boy. They meant "in Hungarian, in German."

He squeezed her hand and replied in Hungarian, *"Értem."* (I understand.)

This seemed to have a magically calming effect on her. She released his hand and fell asleep. Grandma Ilona died at 4:14 a.m. without ever regaining consciousness.

✚

It seemed that half the planet came to attend Grandma Ilona's funeral. Elize was there, of course, and so was, surprisingly, the 103-year-old Professor Arbenz, as were many other dignitaries and friends from all over the world.

Ilona Rooney-Pasztor had been a very popular person in her day.

The eulogy was pronounced by her son, the archbishop of Buffalo, in the Basilica of Our Lady of Victory, and Grandma Ilona was buried in the Rooney family tomb beside her beloved husband in the Holy Cross Catholic Cemetery on South Park Avenue in Lackawanna.

At the wake, held at Grandma's house, Archbishop Rooney approached his nephew with a strange question. "In what language was my mother speaking to you just before she died?"

"In German and in Hungarian," Jack replied.

"That I could figure out. But before that."

"You mean while she was muttering and making strange sounds?"

"Yes."

"No idea, Uncle Patrick. Why do you ask?"

"Simple curiosity my boy, simple curiosity."

CHAPTER 47

Jack Brennan flew to Zurich in a state of great bewilderment. Grandma had left him her house in Buffalo. She had also left him all her possessions that were situated outside the United States. The problem was that she had no such possessions, having repatriated everything she had owned in Switzerland many, many years ago.

What was he, a bachelor, to do with the Rooney family mansion? Why did Grandma not leave it to Mary, his sister, who had a young and growing family?

Was Granma trying to tell him to move back to the U.S. with Elize, get married, and have kids with her? Did she not realize that his career lay in Toronto with his partners there?

Sooner, rather than later, he would have to empty the house and sell it, probably over the vehement objections of his entire family. He couldn't blame them. The place represented everything that the Rooneys were to Buffalo: tradition, elegance, massive financial solidity, dependability, and influence.

He couldn't afford to keep the house, even if he had need for it. Most of his savings were gone, spent on the chase after the Gombos fortune. Thank God for the 50,000 dollars of "spending money" Grandma had left to each of her grandchildren, including Jack. He needed every penny he could lay his hands on. The battle for control of the Moretti Board of Directors was imminent.

Jack had been pleased when the injunctions Dr. Somary had

served on the Morettis were granted because now everything depended on what the kingmaker, Karl Stapfer, would do. Would he abstain from voting, or would he vote with the opposition? Jack wondered whether there really was a united opposition and who led it. On the other hand, Stapfer was unlikely to vote against the Morettis. He was too political for that. Besides, at his age, he would not want to make new enemies. Too risky.

Stapfer was only one problem among many and not the biggest. Dr. Arbenz had told Jack about rumors in Zurich to the effect that Banque Moretti and Banque Julius Odier, the Golden Bank, were thinking of quietly forming some sort of an alliance to buy shares on the open market in an effort to bolster the Morettis' position. Very worrisome.

The purchase of 30,000 more shares would allow the Morettis to keep control of their bank, even if Stapfer abstained. Jack suspected that speculation in the stock was already taking place: The share price was slowly but steadily rising. He figured that it would reach about 1,300 Swiss francs by the time the alliance had finished buying up the number of shares it required. The cost? About 30 million francs.

Was it worth taking such a risk without knowing what Stapfer intended to do? Was it not cheaper simply to bribe Stapfer with, say, a couple of million to make sure he "did the right thing."

Jack made a mental note to speak to Elize about this. Perhaps she could shed light on the subject, thereby enabling them to recover some of the expenses they had incurred in trying to prove the Gombos theory.

Of course, their biggest worry was Roza Stern. Was she really Dr. Gombos' legal heir? How did she propose to prove her right to the fortune? Did she know the password to the Gombos account?

Ever since they began seeing each other on a regular basis, Jack started staying with Elize Haemmerle every time he visited Zurich. It was in her dining room that they'd confer with Stapfer and Dr. Somary to plot their progress and coordinate their search for the Gombos heir. Jack was greatly relieved when Stapfer, who had come up from Lugano to meet him, announced that he had good news.

"Enrico Moretti asked me to meet him, so I took the train to Zurich yesterday. We had dinner, and he asked me how I intended to vote at the annual meeting. I told him I hadn't made up my mind."

Greatly relieved, Jack began to laugh. "What did he say to that?"

"He made me an offer I couldn't refuse."

"Which was?"

"If I voted with the Morettis, he would give me a seat on the board of directors again."

"And what did you say to that, Uncle Karl?" Elize asked, frowning. She was still hoping that, somehow, the Gombos fortune would remain intact and ultimately revert to its rightful owner. But the board that controlled the bank would also have control of the fortune for the time being, and this could be bad for SIL. Elize was sure that the Morettis would somehow siphon off some of the money.

"I told him I'd accept if he got Schmidt off the Moretti board and named you in his stead."

Elize was flabbergasted. "Me?" She hated the idea of having to work even more closely with Studer. The man was a cold, disloyal fish, and Moretti, the sly quiet one, who never told anyone what he was thinking, was even less inspiring. Surely, they would quietly, insidiously change her — squeeze all the gentleness and love from her soul and turn her into a tough, ruthless, businesswoman.

"Yes, you. Why not? You have all the qualifications." Stapfer was insistent.

Jack cut in. "Moretti would never agree to such a thing."

"That's where you're wrong, Jack." Stapfer grinned. "He was quite taken aback to start with, but in the end, he said he'll sleep on it and let me have his decision this morning." He chuckled. "You see Moretti is very worried, almost desperate."

Kurt was shaking his head; he couldn't believe what he was hearing. "When did he say he'd call?"

"He didn't, but he already called, early this morning." Stapfer paused for effect. Then he let out a hearty yell. "We're in! He accepted."

The group was ecstatic. With Schmidt gone, there would be only five directors left: Moretti, Studer, Stapfer, Elize, and an independent, who would be named as a sop to the public vote. Moretti would still have a tie-breaking vote in case the directors were evenly split, but this was unlikely to happen — only if a director would fall ill, die, or fail to attend a meeting. So the presence on the board of Stapfer and Elize would ensure that, at least for the time being, nothing too damaging would befall the Gombos inheritance so long as the independent director would side with them.

But this was not a given.

CHAPTER 48

Hans-Ruedi Schmidt was beside himself with rage and fear. His boss had double-crossed him! Two years of planning, scheming, and maneuvering down the drain and just when he got within reach of the brass ring. Twenty-four months of eating shit, working long hours, and being at the beck and call to satisfy every whim of a little effeminate Napoleon — and now this: demoted and disgraced.

Life was just not fair. God damn Stapfer and that bitch Haemmerle. And shame on him for having underestimated the pair: the doddering old fool of a has-been banker and the uppity smartass female ball-breaker who thought she could rule the world with what she had between her legs.

There was only one thing to do: He had somehow to obtain the password for Roza Stern to enable her to claim ownership of the SIL account. But there was too little time left for that. With the annual meeting only two months away, he had no choice but to play for time. But how?

Then it came to him: neutralize the Stapfer vote. Make Stapfer disappear — kill him. With Stapfer out of the picture, nobody could vote his shares. First, his estate would have to be probated and that would take months. In the meantime, Schmidt could emerge as the leader of the opposition to the Morettis' rule. He'd ally himself with Banque Odier, thereby getting *them* off his back, and obtain a sufficient number of proxies to outvote the bank's present controlling shareholders.

Schmidt knew he had no choice. He needed the money and needed it *now;* he was running out of time. *Admit it,* he said to himself ruefully, *for a small-town boy, you have more balls in the air than you can keep track of.*

He had been born in Regensberg, a small, tidy, typically Swiss municipality with cobblestoned streets, neat gardens, and beautiful flowers in the summer. In addition to the reconstructed ruins of a medieval castle, the place also boasted the deepest sod cistern for catch-water in Switzerland — fifty-seven meters. Boring.

Mercifully, the town would come to life on weekends in winter when the Buck, a popular hill nearby, would be overrun by skiers from Zurich, fifteen kilometers away.

Young Hans-Ruedi had waited on tables at the *Gasthaus zum Löwen* in the summer. In winter, he worked as a ski assistant at the Buck and perfected his English by practicing it with the Brits and Americans visiting the region. It was an excruciatingly boring existence for a teenager constantly thirsting for excitement that never came his way.

His parents sent him to university in Zurich and forced him, through financial pressure, to choose a career in accountancy and business management. This left Schmidt with only one way to taste the adrenaline of adventure that he craved. Gambling. But the gaming tables of roulette and poker weren't for him. No, he wanted more — beating the odds in the commodity and stock markets.

After graduating, he went to work for McKinsey Switzerland and became a specialist in business systems and methods. He concentrated on consulting for medium-sized private banks where his talents were sorely needed since their systems of internal control were generally inadequate.

The clients liked his work. Although he was abrasive, he was effective and his reputation kept growing — that is, until he got to the Golden Bank, Odier.

While working on an assignment for the bank some years earlier, he opened a modest trading account through which he funneled a number of stock market transactions that resulted in a profit of about a 100,000 francs by the end of the year. The following year, he began to trade in copper futures quite recklessly and was showing a paper profit of over 2 million francs by Christmas. It seemed to him that he really did have the Midas touch.

Unfortunately, nobody was monitoring his account because — using the access codes he had been given to do his work — he had marked it as having "no limit."

Then the copper market crashed. Schmidt was not only wiped out but also ended up owing Odier over a million francs because he had been trading on razor-thin margins. He was called on the carpet by no lesser a personage than Jacques Odier, the great grandson of the bank's founder.

To his surprise, Odier insisted on conducting the interview with no one else present.

"You owe me 1 million francs, and you don't have a centime to your name." The banker wasted no time in coming to the point. "How do you propose to pay me back?"

Schmidt blushed in anger and shame. "The same way I got myself into the hole I'm in," he replied defiantly.

"Meaning?"

"Allow me to continue operating. Grant me a small line of credit, and I'll make the money back by continuing to trade in commodities."

"How much?"

"Ten thousand francs."

Odier thought the proposal over for a few minutes. "Too risky," he finally said. "Ten thousand is not enough, and giving you more is out of the question. You are bound to lose it all."

"What makes you think that?" Schmidt refused to back down and show remorse.

"Face it, your luck has run out, and desperation will cloud your judgment." The older man's voice was matter of fact, his demeanor cold, neutral. "You're finished in this town, my friend. In fact, you're finished in the financial community worldwide...unless..."

Odier paused.

Schmidt held his breath.

"Four things. One, you will sign a full confession describing in detail the way in which you defrauded the bank. Two, you will sign a promissory note in our favor for 2 million francs, payable on demand. Three, you will carefully complete your assignment here as quickly as possible at which time I will give you a first-class reference for a job well done. Four, you will apply for the position of controller and systems and methods manager at my main competitor's bank."

The lights went on in Schmidt's brain. "Banque Moretti?"

Odier nodded. "You're a bright man, Schmidt. I'm betting that within a few years, you'll be senior vice president at Moretti's. Use those years to find a way to redeem your promissory note."

"And when I do, what then?"

"I'll tear up your confession and sign whatever paper you want saying that you've done nothing wrong."

"So I'll be completely off the hook?"

"The moment you redeem the note."

"And if I can't?"

"As long as the note is outstanding, I expect you to keep me informed about all that is going on at Moretti's that may be of interest to me."

"I understand. You want me to spy for you. For how long?"

"I give you five years at the end of which I will feel free to make your confession public and press criminal charges against you if I'm so inclined. It goes without saying that as long as you provide me with useful information, I will not be so inclined."

CHAPTER 49

By the time Schmidt got home that night, he could hardly control his fury. When his wife saw him heading for the Pflümli bottle, she scampered away, well aware of what was coming.

Schmidt hit the booze hard and was fairly drunk by the time his wife placed his supper before him. He lost control, picked up the soup bowl, and threw the hot liquid at her. Then he dragged her into the bedroom and beat her savagely before raping her.

Spent, he fell flat on his belly and passed out.

The next morning, his head throbbing with a colossal hangover, he pretended that he couldn't remember what had happened the night before, though he couldn't help wincing when he saw how badly he had bruised his wife's face, even though she had tried desperately to ward off his blows. Her arms had paid the price: they were black and blue from wrist to shoulder.

During the following week Schmidt's hatred of Stapfer grew exponentially, fuelled by an unreasonable thirst for revenge. He gradually talked himself into blaming Stapfer for everything that had gone wrong with his plans. But licking his wounds was not his style. He was a man of action.

On Saturday night, after having beaten up his wife again, he sat down to plan how he would neutralize Stapfer, his nemesis. Killing him was one way, but, after careful reflection, Schmidt rejected the idea, although he wished Stapfer dead with all his heart. He did not have time to plan and execute the perfect crime, so murder was out. This left the money side of the situation, and for this he needed Jacques Odier.

He and Odier did not meet regularly and never in public. Whenever either of them had something to communicate to the other, he would call a certain voicemail number and leave a message. Both of them monitored the number twice a week — on Mondays and Thursdays — and acted accordingly.

This time, they met on Tuesday and, as usual, in a hotel room at Forch, twenty kilometers outside Zurich in an area where neither of them was known. After outlining the latest changes at Banque Moretti, Schmidt ended up by confessing that he had been demoted.

"Enrico Moretti has invited that bastard Stapfer to a meeting at which, to solidify his position, he asked the old man to promise he'd vote for a board of directors at the annual meeting that would ensure continued control over the bank's activities by the Moretti clan. Stapfer declined saying that unless he and that bitch Haemmerle became Moretti directors and she was elected a director of the *Pro Nobis* Foundation, he would not serve and that, to make sure this would happen, he'd even align himself with the opposition. Moretti panicked and caved in. He insisted I resign from the Moretti and Foundation boards."

Odier interrupted. "I suppose in return for a generous retirement bonus."

Schmidt shook his head. "No. Just 200,000 francs for the two resignations. I have been a director for less than five years."

Odier let out a low whistle. "That's still pretty damned generous."

"Not really. Not after all the extra effort I was forced to put in. Anyway, Moretti has made up his mind and has told Stapfer and Haemmerle that I am out and that they're in."

"Effective when?"

"Immediately after the annual meeting, which is on March 15."

"That's in less than six weeks."

"I know." Schmidt fought hard not to show that he was beginning to panic. "Frankly, I'm stuck for new ideas. The key to this situation is the *Pro Nobis* Foundation and its control over 230,000 'B' shares. If I could somehow get to vote these shares, we'd be in the pink."

"Who owns the Foundation?"

"An account in the Moretti bank. And no one knows who owns the account."

Odier was puzzled. "No recent news from the owner?"

"None."

"For more than twenty years?"

"I believe that is indeed the case."

"So why was the account not transferred to the Swiss National Bank?"

Schmidt then explained to Odier that the account was not dormant and that, in fact, it received an annual remittance from Banque Odier.

Odier turned pale. It took him all the self-control he was capable of not to betray his shock of discovery. He suddenly remembered the letter he had received from *Doctor Juris* Somary inquiring about an account in the name of a person called Gombos. He had asked his secretary to look into the matter, which she had done, and had then typed up the standard answer to all such inquiries.

Odier recalled signing the letter in which he asked Somary to provide proof that her client was, indeed, an heir of this Gombos fellow. He also recalled his secretary apologizing for bothering him with such a *bagatelle,* such a trivial thing. The size of the account was very small, a few hundred francs, and the movement in it insignificant: one or two entries per year.

But then, she was only following standing orders established when the Holocaust scandal had come to light making Swiss bankers look cheap and heartless in the eyes of international Jewry. The rule at Banque Odier stipulated that all correspondence relating to inquiries about the identity of clients who had opened accounts prior to World War II were to be handled by Odier himself. Furthermore, all such correspondence and documentation was to be photocopied and kept in a special file by the managing director's secretary.

"Let me think about this," Odier said to Schmidt, seemingly losing interest in the subject. "Perhaps I can come up with something by the weekend."

He left the room before the disappointed Schmidt had a chance to say anything.

CHAPTER 50

As soon as he got back to his office, Jacques Odier asked his secretary for the entire Gombos file. "I mean the works, *Frau* Fischer," he added. "Starting with the documents that opened the account, plus all the ledger cards since its inception, all items in our custody that relate to the account, correspondence — everything!"

It took three clerks three full days under Frau Fischer's supervision to locate the material sought because it had been warehoused off-site. Of course, the most sensitive part of the documentation was in the managing director's special safe where the records relating to numbered accounts were being kept.

Other than the seventy-odd ledger cards (one for each year) that reflected, with monotonous regularity, the same entries year after year plus some insignificant internal correspondence having to do with routine 'housekeeping', the material contained a document opening account number 35220 and signed by Dr. Peter Gombos and a heavy, high-quality manila envelope that was, in addition to its flap being carefully sealed, also protected from tampering by string wound around it, bonded to the paper in ten places by red sealing wax. There was no way anyone could open the packet without leaving a trace.

In addition to the name of the person opening the account, the document also showed the account owner's address: Bulyovsky Utca 2, Második emelet 2, Budapest VI ker.

Odier was the scion of an old banking family. The institution bearing his name had survived Napoleon, two world wars and numerous assaults on it by its competitors. He and his ancestors had learned that to prosper in their industry they had to do onto others before they did it onto them. The success of the Swiss banking network, and similar organizations worldwide, was based on greed. Morality came into play only if and when it coincided with expediency and profitability.

Borderline legality was common practice — hence Odier's arrangement with Schmidt.

The first thing Odier did was to Google Dr. Peter Gombos. To his amazement, he found that he was dealing with the affairs of a world-famous scientist, who became a Nobel Laureate in 1936 and who died in 1944.

Next, he examined the account cards and identified the initial deposit of 159,850 Swedish krona, which he presumed was the value of the Nobel Prize in 1936. After confirming his suspicion via Google, he traced the transfer of the bulk of the money to Banque Moretti. He also noted that the transactions in the account that took place year after year were always the same every year. From this, he deduced that Gombos had set up a triangular cash flow, using three banks to keep his accounts perpetually alive — his, Moretti's, and Lamarche's.

Obviously, the man knew what he was doing, he mused, *and someone in the bank must have been advising him.*

Odier then determined that the managing director of the bank in 1936 was Otto Graf. Armed with this knowledge, it took Odier no time at all to locate the highly confidential correspondence between Graf, Dr. Arbenz, and William Rooney, Roosevelt's famous American ambassador. The correspondence also referred to Graf having recommended Moretti and Lamarche to Gombos.

I must tread carefully, Odier cautioned himself. *There's more to this than first meets the eye.*

He spent a couple of days digesting the information and finally concluded that since Banque Moretti was still the account's custodian bank and, according to Schmidt, had had two inquiries about Gombos, (Dr. *Juris* Somary and Roza Stern), the account at the Moretti bank had *not* been opened in Gombos's name. Therefore, he, Jacques Odier, was the only living person who knew that the *true* owners of the *Pro Nobis* Foundation were the heirs of the Hungarian Jew, Dr. Peter Gombos, the Nobel Laureate.

This knowledge was worth a fortune to him if he could find a way to use it to become the custodian of the Gombos account. Unfortunately, the obstacles he'd have to overcome before this objective could be reached were enormous. He would have to deal with Holocaust survivors, senior American government officials, crooks like Roza Stern and Schmidt, adverse public opinion, not to mention all the directors, present and future, of Banque Moretti.

And, of course, there was the question of the account password.

Odier was pretty certain that the manila envelope in his possession, bearing the inscription "To be opened by my legal heir(s) on my death or incapacitation," held the solution to this problem, but he could not be sure without opening it. And once opened by an expert (and, if necessary, resealed by same), the knowledge thus gained could not be used by Banque Odier directly in any way to gain control legally of the account, which meant that the exercise would have been undertaken in vain.

Having sorted out all the options that were available to him, Odier came to the conclusion that, in this instance, greed and morality might coincide, so he decided first to reduce communications with Schmidt to a minimum and, second, to write to Enrico Moretti.

CHAPTER 51

The parcel, addressed to Jack Brennan, was delivered by TNT to Elize Haemmerle's home address ten days before the Moretti annual meeting. It was from Monsignor Emery Kohn, his uncle Patrick's secretary and a curiosity in the Catholic Church, a high-ranking priest, born a Jew in Hungary who converted to Catholicism at the age of eighteen. The parcel contained a packet of documents and a letter from Jack's grandmother.

My most beloved grandson, I am an old woman and my hand trembles, which makes my writing illegible, so I am dictating these lines to Father Emery with instructions that he send their typed version to you sixty days after my death, which, I know, is not far off.

I'm afraid I'm getting weaker by the day.

It was wonderful to see you and Elize so happy together at Christmas time. She is a lovely woman and definitely a keeper. I hope you will ask her to marry you and that she will say yes and that you then settle into my house, which, as you know by now, I have bequeathed to you.

I have also bequeathed to you all my earthly possessions outside the United States of America, a disposition that must have raised many eyebrows when my last will and testament was read to my heirs.

I can just imagine how they must have carried on. "She obviously lost it in the end," they must have muttered. "Everybody knows she repatriated her foreign investments years ago."

This was and still is true, but the situation will, I am sure, change the moment you find out who the rightful owner of the Pro Nobis Foundation is.

And that moment is now.

You see, my dearest and most beloved grandson, the owner of the Foundation is me, your grandmother, and you will become its owner once my will is probated because I am bequeathing the Foundation to you.

Let me explain.

Your grandmother is not what you think she is. Other than my husband Bill (who knew from the very beginning about it) only Father Emery and now you know that my parents' name was Preisler. Originally from Stomfa, a small town that was at times Hungarian and at other times Slovakian, they moved to Budapest and converted from Judaism to Catholicism in the early 1930s because they foresaw what was in store for European Jewry and hoped to escape the horror by changing their religion. For the same reason, they also changed their names to Pásztor so as to blend into Hungarian society even more. As we all know now, to no avail.

To protect me as much as possible, in 1938, my parents sent me to Barcelona to study when Hitler started to persecute the Jews in earnest. From there, I had to flee to Switzerland, where I met your grandfather who eventually got me a U.S. passport in which my religion was shown as being Roman Catholic. I lived as a Catholic ever since (in constant fear of discovery because anti-Semitism is not the exclusive prerogative of the Nazis), and everybody in the Rooney family assumed that I was born a gentile.

But that was not the case. My mother — Irma Schneider was her maiden name — was Jewish, and I was born a full-blooded Jewess whose children are Jewish by definition. (It used to amuse me to think that your uncle Patrick, the archbishop of Buffalo, is a Jew.) By the way, so are you Jack, since your mother, my daughter May, was born from a Jewish mother, as were you.

Such concepts would have had no significance at all had Herr Adolf Hitler not made it his life's work to exterminate Jews everywhere. As you know, he managed to assassinate over 6 million of them, including my father and mother who died of typhus in January 1945 on the long march from where they were hiding in Budapest toward Germany, organized by the Nazis under the direction of Adolf Eichmann.

Father Emery will attest to this; his father was with them when they died.

You used to press me for information about my family every time the Rooneys trotted out their fine Irish lineage at family gatherings. You must have noticed that I was always evasive about answering. Now you know why.

I had a bad time of it when you came back from Stomfa and reported finding out about the existence of the Preisler family. This, coupled with what you had told me about your decision to turn the world upside down in an effort to identify the owner of the Pro Nobis Foundation, convinced me that sooner rather than later, you'll stumble onto my secret and expose me as being the liar that I am — a pretend-Christian who had succeeded in worming her way into the core of one of America's most distinguished gentile families.

Forgive me for deceiving you all these years, but fear of persecution is hard to overcome. Ask any black man in America.

After my wedding to Bill, I was all for telling the world about my situation, but your grand-father said he couldn't give a damn about what people thought, so I went along with his advice and said nothing. Of course, the longer I said nothing, the harder it became to say anything without hurting an awful lot of people.

May God forgive me for lying about myself to you all for sixty years.

As I said before, my death is imminent, I feel it. I have, therefore, decided to make a clean breast of things and help you in your and Elize's noble quest. All I ask is that, should you succeed in gaining control of the Foundation, you make sure that you do what Elize has told you should be done: distribute the annual profits of the Foundation among the Hungarian survivors of the Holocaust and their descendants who need help.

The enclosed package contains the documentation you need to prove substantively that you are the owner of the Foundation. It consists of

> *My birth certificate, showing who my parents were and where they lived when I was born,*

> *My original Hungarian passport that shows my name is Pásztor, née Preisler,*

> *A certified copy of a family tree prepared by the rabbi of Stomfa (now Stupava), showing that I am Dr. Peter Gombos's cousin. My mother Irma Schneider was the sister of Dr. Peter Gombos's mother, Anni. I am Dr. Gombos's closest living relative because his parents, brothers, sisters, aunts, and uncles are all dead, except for me. Therefore, I am his heiress, and I have bequeathed the Foundation to you. (You have a copy of my will, I am sure.)*

As for Peter and Svetlana Gombos's deaths and the deaths of their two boys, you already have Dr. Szilard's testimony about these events.

This leaves you with two problems: proving that Svetlana has no living direct descendants left and working out the name and password for the account in the Moretti bank.

I am afraid I cannot help you with these two problems, but you and Elize are dynamic and ingenious young people with powerful friends. I am sure you'll succeed if you really are determined to see justice done.

God bless you both. May you have a long, happy, and healthy life together with lots of beautiful children.

I will do my very best to watch over you from wherever I am going because I love you and will always go on loving you.

Grandma Ilona

Deathly pale, Brennan sat quietly at the breakfast table, unable to speak for a long time. Then he handed the letter to Elize and left the room. He needed time alone.

Curiously, the greatest impact the letter had on him was not the discovery that he was potentially the heir to a fortune worth over 200 million dollars. No. What moved him was the thought of how extraordinarily painful it must have been for his grandmother to live her life after her husband's death. With Bill Rooney gone, she would not only have lost her beloved husband but also the only person with whom she could openly share her past.

He shuddered when he recalled the many anti-Semitic jokes members of his family had recounted in her presence and felt very ashamed. He bled for her having had to give up her native land, her home, her friends at the young age of twenty, and having had to fend for herself for years while fleeing persecution. He wondered when and how she had found out about her parents' death and suspected Grandpa Bill's fine Italian hand in the conversion of Emery Kohn and his appointment to the post of secretary of his Uncle Patrick.

Profoundly saddened, he sat on his bed, not moving, just staring into empty space until Elize knocked gently and came in to embrace him wordlessly, her eyes red from crying.

"Pull yourself together, my love," she whispered into his ear, brandishing the letter at him. "We have work to do."

CHAPTER 52

The effect of Ilona's letter on Jack's crew was euphoric. They wanted to rush into battle against the Moretti forces, but Dr. Somary vehemently opposed doing anything before the bank's annual meeting.

"Let's just get Elize and *Herr* Stapfer elected on the board first," he counseled. "With them on it, we'll have an easier time controlling things."

The Banque Moretti annual shareholders meeting ultimately became a nonevent. With Stapfer and Moretti voting together, there could be no effective opposition to the composition of the board proposed by Chairman Moretti. There was one surprise, though, as far as Jack was concerned: when the votes were counted, it became apparent that Banque Odier had bought up almost 22,000 Moretti shares on the open market.

A week after the meeting, Odier sent a written invitation to Moretti for lunch at a little Trattoria just off the Stadthaus Quai. He liked eating there because he was fond of Italian food. Besides, there he could always count on a quiet table in the corner alcove where he could discuss sensitive business without being overheard.

Moretti, who dared not ignore or decline the invitation of a dangerous competitor and was very interested in finding out what his opponent had in mind, made sure he'd arrive exactly seven minutes late, thereby hoping to signal that he was not particularly anxious to meet Odier.

Odier, who knew the game well, made absolutely no reference to the other man's tardiness. On the contrary, he welcomed Moretti effusively and refused to start talking business until the cognacs and cigars arrived with the excellent espressos after a delicious meal — Vitello Marsala for Moretti and Osso Buco for Odier — which they washed down, as a concession to the meal being eaten in Switzerland, with a very fine and expensive bottle of Dole.

"We should do this more often, Enrico," said his host with an expansive wave of his cigar. "Although we're competitors, as were our ancestors, we have been in the business long enough to know that there's room for both of us in the marketplace."

"True, but the marketplace is shrinking, and there are more and more of us in it."

"Not for long. I hear Julius Baer, as well as Sarrazin, is selling out."

"To the big boys?" Moretti was shocked. This was news to him. "Are you sure?"

Odier nodded, pleased to have one-upped his guest. "Pretty sure. And I'm happy about it. Leaves more room for us."

"About time, too. Margins are getting thinner and thinner."

This was the opening Odier had been waiting for. "I've noticed so. I saw from your financial statements that you took a terrible hit when your investment in the ABCP deals went sour. I presume you started buying into them because they were a way to increase margins. I'm sorry it didn't work out," Odier went on, "but I see that you were able to recapitalize through acquiring the solid assets of the *Pro Nobis* Foundation for paper."

Moretti was beginning to worry. *Where was this conversation leading to?* he asked himself. Time to fight back. "Yes, that was an excellent deal for us."

"At a price per share of Moretti stock that was highly inflated," Odier couldn't resist the dig. "Still don't understand how the Stock Exchange allowed you to get away with it." He shook his head in disbelief and mock admiration. "Anyway, the main thing is that you managed to pull the wool over everyone's eyes, including mine." Jacques Odier threw the last remark in for effect. He had known all along what was going on at Moretti's. Schmidt had kept him thoroughly informed.

Moretti took offence at the observation. "I cannot see any reason why you should feel so. Everything was quite above board, everything."

It was time for Odier to move in for the kill. Like all good tacticians, he started off with a compliment. "I assure you, I'm full of admiration for the way you managed to right the ship of state, so to speak. I thought you noticed that I indirectly supported you all the way."

"How so?" Moretti asked, fuming but somewhat mollified.

"Do you think I would have bought into your bank to the extent I have, without being confident of your managerial capabilities. Have you not noticed that my bank has bought close to 22,000 shares of yours? Hell, we own about 7 percent of Banque Moretti."

"How do you figure that?" Moretti was taken aback.

"Easy. There are a total of 330,000 shares outstanding."

"You mean the total of 'A' and 'B' shares together?"

"Correct. My bank owns about 22,000, which is about 7 percent of the total. The big shareholder, the *Pro Nobis* Foundation — or I should say, the owners of SIL — owns 230,000, so it owns two-thirds of the bank."

"Yes, but not the votes."

"True, but once the injunction prohibiting the voting of the shares expires, unless you maintain control over the right to vote them, Stapfer will become the kingmaker."

"How so?"

"Without Stapfer, you have 400,000 votes. I and the general public will have 45,000 votes, and the Foundation and Stapfer will have 380,000 votes. If everybody, including Stapfer and me, votes against you, the Morettis will lose control over the bank." Odier grinned wolfishly. "Four hundred thousand for you and 420,000-odd for the opposition."

"But if some of the general public vote for me, or abstain, I can still hang in there." Moretti knew that the public was never monolithic. Besides, he still had time to buy up some of the shares held by the public.

"Granted, but why take the risk?"

Moretti sensed that this was the crux of the matter, the reason for Odier's invitation.

"What do you have in mind?"

"I think I can find a way in which we can make sure the Foundation's shares will always be voted by you, Enrico."

I wonder how much he'll charge me to do this. Moretti thought to himself. Aloud he said, "I'm listening."

CHAPTER 53

Jack Brennan struggled hard for weeks to absorb the emotional shock caused by his grandmother's post-humous letter. It had impacted his outlook on life profoundly and also made him realize that he needed to be exceptionally careful about how his side interacted with the Moretti camp.

The Sunday after the shareholders' meeting, he met with Kurt and Elize to review his plan and obtain their consent to it. On Monday afternoon, he called his sister, Mary, in Boston and asked her to arrange a family Easter luncheon at his late grandmother's (now his) house. He asked her to enlist the services of Vali and Lani for the occasion whom he had retained to look after the house while he was away in Europe.

"Ask Vali to cook something Hungarian in memory of Grandma Ilona, and tell the family that after the meal I would appreciate having a family council to be attended only by her direct descendants."

"You mean only Mom, Uncle George, and Uncle Patrick?"

"No. You and Uncle George's boys as well."

"No spouses?"

"That's correct. No wives or husbands."

"This sounds serious, Jack." His sister's voice betrayed her preoccupation. "What's up?"

He made himself sound nonchalant. "Oh, I just want to bring everybody up-to-date on what I have been doing these last few months and ask for advice about some of the things I'm planning to do in the near future."

Mary chuckled, relieved. She figured her brother wanted to announce his formal engagement — or perhaps his marriage — to the beautiful and so very smart Elize.

After a sumptuous meal of liver-dumpling soup, Holsteiner Schnitzel with mashed potatoes, a fantastic green salad with sweet Magyar dressing, and an Esterhazy torte for dessert, the family retired to the library while the spouses, accompanied by Kurt and Elize, shepherded the children into the huge living room next to the solarium. It took a few minutes for everyone to settle in, which Jack used to sort out the papers he had brought with him.

Having been discreetly forewarned by Mary to expect great good news, the gathering of Rooneys couldn't understand why Jack was so nervous and pale. He looked positively ill.

"Nervous future groom," whispered his mother, May. "He'll be a wreck by the time his wedding day arrives."

"And what's he doing with those envelopes he's fiddling with?" asked the archbishop who was sitting next to her.

Jack began in a soft, low voice. "I asked you here because I need the help and advice of everyone present." He looked into his relatives' eyes one by one then took a deep breath. "I was going to tell you myself what has befallen me, but I now see I had better let Grandmother Ilona explain what this meeting is about.

"I have here a manila envelope for each one of you," He handed them out. "Please make sure you open them at the same time," he added, sat down without another word and waited while his audience finished reading — seven long minutes — at the end of which Mary and May were crying, and the men were choking back tears. It was Patrick Rooney, the archbishop of Buffalo, who broke the silence that followed. He turned to Jack.

"I had an inkling of Mother being Jewish. Remember the night she died I asked you what language she was using when she said something to you? To me it had seemed that she had been reciting the Kaddish."

Jack nodded. He remembered very well. "Question is: what do we do now and more specifically, what do I do?"

"What do you *want* to do?"

"I want to marry Elize and do my best to win my inheritance so that I can create a Foundation in accordance with Grandma's wishes."

"Then do so, my son," the archbishop said, and everybody stood up and began clapping.

Jack looked around the room. "Will you all help me?"

After a resounding yes, George Rooney's younger son, Liam, had a question. "I have now discovered that I am Jewish by definition but Catholic by religion. Is Judaism a race or a religion?"

"Both."

"How does that work?"

"Don't ask me," answered Buffalo's first Jewish Roman Catholic archbishop. "We'll just have to wing it."

CHAPTER 54

Dr. Somary's letter to Jacques Odier, head of Banque Odier, was succinct.

Sehr Geehrter Herr Direktor,

I refer to your letter dated November 15 of the last year in which you inquire about my client's family relationship with Dr. Peter Gombos, the owner of the account in your bank, the number of which is 35220.

My client is the grandson of Ilona Pasztor (née Preisler). The late Ms. Pasztor was Dr. Peter Gombos's cousin (Dr. Gombos's mother's sister's daughter).

My client is Ms. Pasztor's legal heir.

My client has now provided you with the name of the person who opened the account and the account number. This is sufficient under Swiss banking law to claim ownership of the account by a victim of the Holocaust or his/her descendants. What remains now is for my client to prove his kinship with the late Dr. Peter Gombos and the circumstances of his death in the Holocaust.

I would welcome the opportunity of meeting you personally to discuss this matter further and to provide you with Prima Facie evidence of said kinship.

Hochachtungsvoll.

Doktor Juris Hilde Somary

Jacques Odier burst out laughing. The letter meant, he saw in a flash, that he now found himself in an absolute win-win situation. He would first receive Somary and listen to what he had to say. If the claim appeared serious, he'd meet with the supposed heir and ask him for the account's password. If he had it, Odier would give him the envelope Dr. Gombos left behind, but only after all formalities were properly completed and the heir could prove that Dr. Gombos died in the Holocaust — not any easy thing to do!

He estimated that obtaining the scientist's and Ms. Pasztor's death certificates in proper form as well as Ms. Pasztor's probated will (original, or copy certified by a notary recognized by the Swiss authorities, notarized translations thereof into German) — here Odier permitted himself a discreet chuckle — would take at least a year, and a lot of things could happen in a year. "I could arrange a takeover of Moretti by my bank then spin the Moretti-Odier package off to a major U.S. player with deep pockets," he mused. "The American would stonewall the heir forever. Having exhausted his finances on litigation, the heir would settle for a fraction of the value of the Foundation."

Conversely, if the heir could not prove that Gombos died in the Holocaust and did not know the password, he would just tell him to get lost. In such an event, he would, after a decent interval (two years perhaps) take over the Moretti bank and, a couple of more years later, open the envelope the contents of which he was sure would enable him to take over the Foundation — with Moretti's help of course.

"I could even let Moretti do the dirty work for me. Or Schmidt — let him open the envelope, let him break the seals."

CHAPTER 55

"Don't get your hopes up too high." Dr. Somary admonished Jack and Elize in his office. "*Herr* Odier is obviously curious but far from convinced. He has agreed to see me and asked that I show him whatever documentation I have to prove our case, but I'm sure he won't be alone when he receives me."

"What does that mean?" Jack was puzzled.

"His lawyer will be present, and they will proceed with the usual routine. Odier will be cool but seemingly very cooperative and sympathetic. Then the lawyer will take over and outline the legal requirements that will have to be met before the bank could proceed further."

"Such as?"

"The account's password to start with."

"We don't know it."

"I know that, but I will say that the case involves a Holocaust victim and that special rules apply in such situations and that, therefore, the requirement for knowing the password may not apply."

"Strictly speaking, Dr. Gombos was not killed in the Holocaust. He was the victim of an accidental explosion."

"I know that, too, but the *heirs* of Dr. Gombos were killed in the Holocaust. To a degree, we can prove that in the case of at least three potential heirs. Unfortunately we only have hearsay evidence of what happened but no eyewitness's account."

"You mean Dr. Szilard's story."

"It sounds tragically convincing, but an eyewitness's account would be far, far better."

Jack shook his head. "They're probably all dead, and those that are still alive would be unlikely to want to testify."

"So where do we go from here?" Elize was bitterly disappointed. "Is there no justice? Can we not appeal to a court somewhere to get a fair hearing? Is it not obvious that everything that we are saying is true?"

"We are far from being able to claim even that." Dr. Somary then listed all the requirements that needed to be met, such as the probation of Grandma Ilona's will, the notarization of all documents and their translation into German, and so on. "Let me be frank. Odier can stonewall us for a long time and bleed you dry financially. You should also bear in mind that success with the Odier bank is just part of the story. Our main goal has to be to get into the records of the Moretti bank." Somary shook his head. "We're talking about years of work and hundreds of thousands of francs in expenses and legal fees."

"So what do we do?"

"Solve the password puzzle, or at least find an eyewitness to testify to what happened to the Gombos family."

CHAPTER 56

Roza Stern was very pleased with the physical appearance of her newest client but also somewhat apprehensive. He did not appear to be the type that liked being dominated. On the contrary, he seemed like someone who would be the dominator rather than the dominated. But then one never knew, did one? Besides, it didn't matter; she had a string of Sapphos at her disposal amongst whom she could easily find one that would be available within fifteen minutes of her call.

The man, who moved with the grace of a gigantic, muscular Siamese cat, said he was from Lebanon and that his name was Georges. He headed toward the living room. "And where did you hear about my establishment?" Roza asked in French, one of three languages that she spoke fluently.

"You are most kind, Roza," he replied, and made himself comfortable on the sofa. "My mother tongue is French, so, naturally, I operate the best in it."

They both laughed at the obvious *sousentendu*.

"Drink?" she asked.

"Perhaps a glass of rosé."

"Rosé for Roza," she poured them some wine from an already open, ice-cold bottle she kept in her refrigerator and, with a glass in each hand, walked over to him.

They laughed again. She sat down beside him and watched him

take a sip.

"Excellent Rosée. Where is it from?"

"Ah, *un connaisseur*," she exclaimed and dropped her free hand casually on his thigh. "From Provence, in France, of course." Roza Stern was a high-class dominatrix who treated her customers to first-class service in every respect, and charged accordingly.

"The concierge at the *Vier Jahreszeiten* suggested that I contact you. Has he not called?" Georges inquired.

Roza smiled and her hand shifted ever so slightly toward her customer's crotch. "Just checking."

To her surprise, he gently removed her hand. "Rest assured, Roza, that I shall pay the usual fee for a one-night stand — that is to say for eight hours of your precious time — so allow me to ask a few questions before we get too seriously involved." He gave her a charming wink and stood up.

"Fire away; there's no rush."

"Do you remember calling the Israeli Consulate some time ago about one of your clients called Keller?"

"*Scheisse!*" said Roza in German with feeling and also stood up. "You're from the Mossad."

Georges smiled down at her. He was at least a head taller than she. "I'm not actually. I am just an outside contractor who helps the Simon Wiesenthal Institute occasionally."

CHAPTER 57

The warm evening breeze gently caressed the faces of the people seated around the dinner table on Karl Stapfer's terrace as they watched Elize serve the strudel she had bought that afternoon at the Patisserie Viennoise, one of Lugano's best pastry shops specializing in Austro-Hungarian desserts.

She was having trouble; the phyllo pastry was so light that it crumbled at the slightest touch. Laughing, she gave up and allowed the guests to serve themselves to the delicious portions of apple-filled dessert that they would then top with a dash of *schlag* — whipped cream.

It was a bittersweet moment — the last evening of the summer vacation season, the night before what the French called *la grande rentrée,* the annual mass migration of hundreds of thousands of holiday makers back to the slavery of their dreary daily existence.

They were drinking Champagne with the dessert, Crystal no less, and Elize, proposed a toast. "To us, the privileged few who are allowed the luxury of a few more days of rest before having to head back to work." She looked lovingly at Jack. He reciprocated. "Thank *you* all for helping me survive this tough summer, especially you, Uncle Karl, such a steadfast supporter." Turning to Dr. Somary, he added, "and to you, my most respected attorney, for having fought so tenaciously for my rights."

"You have all put up a good fight." Mrs. Stapfer chimed in, "It's just that you have run out of time."

"And ideas." Kurt Haemmerle reached for a sheet of paper in his pocket. "Allow me to summarize because I don't want us to leave here tomorrow, after two wonderful weeks of good wine, good food, and great companionship, with the impression that we are defeated. Admittedly, our case is hard to prove, but we haven't lost yet; the paperwork we need is in the works, and our financial position is protected by Uncle Karl's and Elize's presence on the Moretti and Foundation boards. Patience my friends, have patience.... There's still time to act."

Jack bit his upper lip, a habit of his when he was worried. "I'm afraid we have less time than you think, Kurt. I have this premonition that Odier is planning a nasty surprise for us."

"What makes you think that?" This from Elize.

"He was much too smooth, much too self-confident by half when Dr. Somary and I met him last. Maybe it's my imagination, but the way his lawyer kept emphasizing that the process of authenticating my claim, even if legitimate, will take lots of time and lots of money, gave me the impression that they are planning something nasty."

"Such as?"

"Some sort of a major stonewalling tactic to gain time."

"What for?"

"I have no idea. Perhaps to get to the next annual shareholders' meeting of the Moretti bank by which time the injunction we served on the bank and the Foundation will have expired..."

Kurt was curious. "What, if anything, would that change?"

"Suppose for the moment that Moretti's bank could somehow, perhaps through an alliance with Odier, show enough profit by then to pay the 4 percent dividend on the 275,000 shares the public and the Foundation control."

"That's about 11 million francs," cut in Stapfer, forever the banker, "not exactly small change."

"Granted, but achievable," this from Elize.

"In such an event, the Moretti side would have 630,000 votes, and the opposition 195,000 maximum, including your votes,

Uncle Karl."

Elize finished for Jack, "And the shareholders would elect new boards for the bank and the Foundation that would not include either you, Uncle Karl, or me."

Jack continued. "Once Moretti regains control of his bank and the Foundation, he can direct how the Foundation is to operate SIL. Then he can start double dealing and ripping off SIL with impunity."

"How much time do we have to get our ducks in a row?"

"If we're lucky, six months. Until the next year's Moretti AGM which, as you know, usually takes place in mid-March."

CHAPTER 58

Karl Stapfer died on Three Kings' Day, January 6. He fell down the stairs leading from his terrace to the garden. Apparently, he had gone outside to look for his cat, had slipped, and had tumbled down twenty-one steps. His wife, who was watching the ten o'clock news, had heard him yell out and had gone to investigate, but by the time she had reached him, he had died from a broken neck.

The Brennan team was in shock. Not only had they lost a beloved friend and colleague, but his demise destroyed any opportunity for the Brennan side to limit the extent to which the Morettis would be able to rape SIL.

Stapfer's obituary in the *Winnipeg Clarion* and immediately picked up by every major financial paper in the Western Hemisphere, including the *Neue Zürcher Zeitung,* was a testimonial to his having been well liked and highly respected.

A LEGEND DIES

Karl Stapfer, the model of what a Swiss banker should be, died at his home in Lugano, Switzerland, last night in his beloved garden of which he was so proud.

Stapfer started his banking career at Zurich's Banque Moretti & Cie in the late 1920s and worked his way up from mail clerk to Executive Vice President and Principal. He witnessed the creation of the Swiss numbered bank accounts system, designed to offer a safe financial haven to those who were forced to flee persecution during the Second World War.

Always courteous, helpful, understanding and, above all, discreet, Uncle Karl (as his good clients permitted themselves to call him) was a staunch supporter and advocate of the secret bank account system, convinced that there was a moral obligation on the part of private banks to offer such a service.

Karl Stapfer was one of the few Swiss bankers who, when World War II ended, immediately commenced the repatriation of the funds Jews fleeing persecution left in his care. Last year, he was recalled to Banque Moretti's board of directors to help that well-known private bank, which has recently weathered difficult times, to resolve a delicate dispute between it and a client, the heir of a Holocaust victim.

The obit was authored by Josh Friedland, an investigative reporter for the Schneiderman Newspaper Group. It provoked in Enrico Moretti a near apoplectic fit.

"How did they get hold of this story?" he screamed at Schmidt, one of whose duties was to monitor media relations for the bank. "I demand to know immediately who is responsible for this leak." Trembling with rage, he groped for the carafe on his desk and poured himself a glass of water that splashed all over his papers. This infuriated him more still. "Get out, get out, and don't come back until you have an answer to my question."

Schmidt didn't move. He decided to add fuel to the fire, to stir the muck some more. "Who else but that Haemmerle bitch?" he asked. "She's stirring the shit because that's all she can do to help her boyfriend's case now that Stapfer's dead."

That stopped Moretti cold. "What do you mean by that?"

"Don't tell me you don't know what all of Zurich knows. Her boyfriend is that *Amerikanischer* Brennan who says he's the heir to the SIL account."

CHAPTER 59

The memorial service for Karl Stapfer was held at the Grossmünster Church one week after his death so as to give the many people from around the world who wished to attend a chance to do so. They came from all over: colleagues from every Canton in Switzerland, bankers from Germany and France and Britain, and clients from as far as Australia and Argentina and Mexico and Poland who remembered that Karl had helped when there were very few people around who were prepared to help.

To accommodate the needs of this international gathering, church officials went the extra mile — in addition to printing the program and the prayers in Switzerland's three official languages (German, French, and Italian) they added a fourth, English.

Jack, Kurt, and Elize sat in the third row behind the family, close enough to lend moral support to Clara, Karl's widow. Elize's offer to help with the funeral arrangements had been gratefully accepted by Clara, so, to reduce unnecessary running around, Elize had invited her to stay at the Haemmerles until the funeral. This had given Jack the opportunity to act as Clara's chauffeur and factotum thereby affording her some modicum of physical comfort. Jack was happy to help. He felt he owed Stapfer a great deal.

The service began with the recitation of the Lord's Prayer in as many languages as there were nationalities present. As Jack listened to the cacophony swelling around him while his eyes darted from language to language in the printed programme, he suddenly and most vividly recalled with extraordinary clarity the image of his sick, feverish grandmother clutching his hand on her deathbed, insistently repeating *auf Deutsch, auf Ungarisch, in German, in Hungarian.* The realization of having totally misunderstood her dawned on him with such a force that he almost fainted. He fell to his knees and began to cry.

Dr. Peter Gombos, the brilliant Nobel Laureate spoke, Hungarian and German like a native. And also English, very well. Which alphabet would he have used when coding the passwords to his three numbered accounts?

Maybe all three!

CHAPTER 60

Immediately after the wake, which took place in the Haemmerle home, Jack Brennan sat Kurt down in the man's office and revealed his epiphany to him.

"We've run out of time. Unless we can produce the passwords to the Odier and Moretti accounts and thereby lay our hands on the 230,000 shares I am supposed to be the heirs of, our goose is cooked."

"How much time do we have left?"

"With luck, maybe a month, but we must be on guard. Roza Stern and Schmidt might conspire with Moretti to beat us to the punch."

"What on earth do you mean?"

"These men are desperate. Moretti has access to the most important of the passwords, the password for the 'B' account."

"And you think he'll give it to Schmidt who'd use Roza Stern as a beard to gain control of the account?"

"Precisely."

"But that's preposterous. They'd never get away with it. We could show that you, and not Stern, are Gombos's heir."

"Maybe yes, maybe not. Moretti might draw a red herring out of his hat and demand an investigation of whether there were any survivors on Svetlana Gombos's side. Besides, the Moretti account was not opened in the name of Dr. Gombos — we know that."

"And meanwhile the password would rule supreme."

"Yes, and we would not have it." Jack looked his future

brother-in-law in the eyes. "Here is what I want you to do, and I want you to start doing it now, this very minute! Assume that equations two, three, and four in the painting represent passwords to the Odier, Moretti, and Lamarche accounts respectively and in that order. Further assume that four languages were used in creating the codes for the passwords: Hungarian and German, for sure, then probably English and maybe French."

Kurt had no experience in cryptography, but he was bright and determined to contribute to the almost crusade-like passion that his sister and Jack were dedicating to ensure that the Gombos inheritance would not be stolen.

It was clear that any code to hide information put together in the 1930s would be relatively simple, as the crude visual analogies in the painting had already illustrated. The equations had to be a symmetrical encryption, using the same key for encryption as decryption. If the code had been created by using the Hungarian alphabets, it should not be too hard to decipher. The clues in the painting were all very short, and therefore unlikely to contain "padding" to confuse the decipherer.

The first problem was which of the several alternative Hungarian alphabets did Gombos use? Kurt settled on what he could find on Google as being the current one. This got him nowhere. By the time he figured out that every language evolves continuously — and its alphabet with it — almost a week went by. Jack solved his problem by calling Dr. Szilard and obtaining the answer in ten minutes: thirty-eight letters.

Kurt already knew the number of the account at Banque Odier (35220) and, by applying Szilard's alphabet, discovered that Dr. Gombos had used it by assigning the number 38 to the letter A and the number 1 to the letter ZS (the last letter in the Hungarian alphabet in use in 1936).

Then he tried to solve the second equation (S+P = OCT 14 1934) by using the same method and got S+P = 17359141934. This looked too long to him, so he settled on 17359, a pure guess. An alternative, should Gombos have reversed the process and assigned the number 1 to A and the number 38 to ZS, would be 223530.

Yet another alternative, so Kurt reasoned, would be to include the letters S and P in the mix, but such a move, he realized, would produce serious complications: a large number of permutations and combinations.

"Let's assume that Gombos tried to keep things as simple as possible under the circumstances," Kurt said to his colleagues as they reviewed the progress, or lack of it, toward developing a meaningful-looking series of numbers. "Hopefully, he did not mix numbers with letters."

"Why would he have?" Jack asked. "Isn't the whole system based on numbered accounts?"

"That only applies to the name of the account, not the password."

"Then we're stymied. We need an expert in cryptography."

Elize cut in. "Not really. Gombos would not have made the decoding process too difficult. Probably, he simply gave his wife a paper on which he marked the pertinent numbers."

"Then why did she bother with the painting?"

Dr. Somary had a flash of inspiration. "Maybe Gombos was trying to wear belt and braces."

"Meaning?"

"To be sure that the information would not get lost, he had his wife paint the picture in case she or her heirs could not get to the paper on which he had marked the information. During a war, papers get mislaid, stolen, destroyed."

Clara Stapfer slapped her forehead "Of course, of course. Why did I not think of this earlier? I'm sure Dr. Gombos left a testament at the bank and a letter to his wife; I've seen this done before. It was the thing people usually did in those days. The question is: in which bank?"

Jack was quick to answer. "Odier, of course."

"Why?"

"Dr. Arbenz took Dr. Gombos to Odier's, remember? He was friends with the managing director there. That's where, as we know, the triangulation of the money starts. I'm sure Gombos would not put all his eggs in one basket. He'd have his testament in one bank and his money in another."

Nobody argued the point.

CHAPTER 61

To Moretti, Karl Stapfer's death was a God-sent reprieve. Nobody could vote Stapfer's shares until his will was probated and a legal heir was approved by the courts, a matter that would take at least six months. Thus, the Moretti Group could elect its own slate of directors at the March AGM and prevent Brennan's side from stopping the systematic rape of SIL that Moretti needed to undertake to make the bank's operations look profitable.

Without profit, there could be no dividends, and without dividends, the shares held by the public would have ten votes and could outvote Moretti.

Schmidt, like Moretti, was also happy about Stapfer's demise. He figured he would be asked to rejoin the board. When he found out that another independent — a friend of Moretti's who would act as a Moretti puppet — had been co-opted instead of him, his rage assumed spectacular proportions.

He tried to contact Odier who refused to see him. Thirsting for some kind of revenge, Schmidt decided to reactivate Roza Stern and traveled to Hamburg to speak with her personally — and to have a "go" at her, naturally.

After making the required arrangements, Schmidt took his usual route to Hamburg, arriving at Roza's apartment in mid-afternoon. Inspired by anticipation, Schmidt performed magnificently, leaving the woman literally breathless.

After a light dinner at their usual haunt, they returned to the studio where, true to form, the banker, exhausted by his sexual travails, asked the domina to make him a strong espresso.

"I have a big surprise for you," he said. They were sitting side by side on the sofa. "My informant tells me that the letter you wrote to the Moretti bank has begun producing results."

"Oh, really?" She took a sip of her coffee. All of a sudden she was wide awake. "How so?"

"Apparently, the bank checked up on the account holder's antecedents and found that he did, indeed, have relatives in Munich."

Roza pretended to be very pleased but became very wary, knowing full well that "Freddy" was making the story up as he went along. "What's the next step?"

"You already have the account number. All that remains is for me to get the password, which I expect to have within a couple of weeks."

"You don't say! That calls for a celebratory drink. She headed for the bar and poured cognac into two snifters."

Schmidt gave her a dazzling smile and took a sheet of paper from his pocket."There's just another detail we have to take care of..."

"And what would that be?"

"An agreement that protects both you and me."

"That sounds fair. Did you prepare one?"

Schmidt handed her a very simple, innocuous-looking document:

LETTER OF AGREEMENT

Any time during the next ninety (90) days hereof I will sell, on demand, all my rights, title and interest in Account Number _____ on the books of Banque Moretti & Cie, Zurich, Switzerland, to Reinfeld AG of Vaduz, Lichtenstein, for the sum of fifty thousand United States dollars ($50,000).

Signed, in Hamburg, on January ____ 20____

Roza Stern

Witness: _____   _____

"Why did you leave the account number blank?" Roza was no fool.

"Because I don't know it yet." He slid his hand up her thigh to her crotch. "We'll fill it in when I come back to give you the password as well."

Roza started to haggle. "We said I'd get a hundred thousand, Freddy," she whined. "I'm signing blindly here and may be giving away a fortune."

"I have to make a few dollars, too," Schmidt riposted smartly, "and if I gave you a hundred, I'd make no money on the deal."

They continued bargaining until they finally settled on 75,000 dollars. Next morning, Roza called the concierge to come up to witness her signature while Schmidt hid in the bathroom.

Roza made a photocopy of the document and handed the original to her client before he left for home — after yet another spectacular *auf wiedersehn* fuck, of course.

"Take care of yourself, Freddy. Let me hear from you as soon as possible about the password, *Ja?*"

To Schmidt, she seemed genuinely excited about the chance of making enough extra money to buy herself a small apartment in Benidorm on the Costa Brava.

CHAPTER 62

Josh Friedland's second article about Karl Stapfer and the bank he had worked for so long, published a week after the funeral, turned out to be a humdinger. He had secured an exclusive interview with Jack Brennan who, having consulted his Uncle George and Mark Schneiderman (both of whom counselled him not to hold back), had been surprisingly forthcoming about the position in which he found himself.

The first half of Friedland's article was devoted to Jack's background and a brief summary of how and why he had gotten to interact with Karl Stapfer.

"I worked with him for just over a year, but he impressed me from the very start with his fabulous memory and his ability to get to the bottom of a problem."

"Such as?"

"I was initially skeptical about the connection between the picture of The Four Equations and the fortune of which I am the presumptive heir. It was Uncle Karl who insisted that I assume that there was such a connection."

Friedland then summarized the steps Jack had taken to claim his inheritance and the obstacles he had to overcome. The article ended with a lament from Jack. "We were almost there. We had gained control of the Moretti board and were going to make sure that the interests of the rightful owner of SIL were protected while the purely bureaucratic fumbles preventing me from claiming my inheritance were sorted out when Uncle Karl died."

"Could you be more specific?" Friedland asked.

"Sure. My side needed Uncle Karl's vote at the next Moretti AGM to maintain control of the board and prevent biased dealings in the assets of SIL."

"What exactly do you mean by 'biased'?"

"It's all a question of conflict of interest. SIL is run by a board, the head of which is a director of the Moretti bank. Moretti himself is on the board of SIL so all decisions affecting SIL tend automatically to be biased in favor of the bank's interests. The majority of the ownership of the bank is in the hands of a numbered account of which I am the presumptive heir. But I cannot protect my eventual interests because, due to multitiered voting arrangements, the numbered account's votes — even if I had the right to vote them — would always be outnumbered as long as Karl Stapfer's estate is not properly wound up, and his heirs get the right to vote his Moretti shares. And that will take months."

"What makes you think they'd vote in your cause's favor?"

"Good question. Karl Stapfer's presumptive successor is his wife, Carla, who is eighty-five years old and very frail."

The article created a *cause celebre* in which Swiss banking cronyism became the villain. Translated into many languages and reproduced in just about every significant financial publication in the world, it went viral on Twitter, YouTube, and Facebook and showed Swiss banking in the worst light possible. This caused the Swiss Bankers Association, already under pressure for having caved in to demands by the U.S. government to lift the veil of secrecy surrounding private banking in the land of the Cuckoo clock, to launch an immediate and full-scale investigation of Banque Moretti's dealings.

This gave *Dr. Juris* Somary the opportunity to apply for an interlocutory injunction to suspend the holding of the Moretti AGM until the investigation's findings were tabled but, in any event for at least six months, and to allow the Brennan interests to name a director *pro tem* to replace Stapfer on the Moretti board.

The injunction was not granted. Instead, in typically hypocritical manner —mindful of the high profile of the case in the international press — the court suggested, through informal channels, that Dr. Somary make an application for allowing the widow Stapfer to vote her late husband's shares at the upcoming AGM, without having to wait for a formal probate of her husband's will.

Of course, Dr. Somary did so, though she knew that this "act of kindness" by the court in the name of common justice, changed nothing other than making Switzerland look less inhuman in the international press.

CHAPTER 63

Schmidt bypassed Moretti's secretary and walked into his boss's office unannounced. Moretti did not hide his displeasure. "What do you want?" he snapped irritably. "Make it short; I'm busy."

Schmidt stared him down. "I have the solution to our problems if you'll cooperate." He brandished a couple of legal-sized envelopes in the banker's face. "I went to Hamburg and got Roza Stern to sign an agreement with us."

"Us?"

"Yes, us. I have incorporated a bearer-share company in Vaduz, which we'll own fifty-fifty. It's called Reinfeld AG, and your bearer shares are in here." He handed Moretti the thicker of the two envelopes.

"And where is the Stern agreement?"

"The original is in here." Schmidt handed over the second envelope. "I've kept a copy."

Moretti was flabbergasted. In spite of having promised himself not to get involved further with his smarmy employee, he could not resist the temptation to examine the papers the man had brought him. He looked at Schmidt and tried to hide his distaste as best he could. "And what would be the next step if I went along with this farce?"

"It's not a farce, Enrico, it's a necessity." Schmidt thought he had convinced the man. "I understand the Brennan faction is working feverishly at trying to break the password code, and once they succeed our goose is cooked."

Moretti decided to prevaricate. "Let's just back up a little. Even if we give Roza Stern the password, how will she convince the powers that be that she's Dr. Gombos's heir?"

"She won't have to. Knowing the account number and the password is all that's needed to take possession of the account."

"Brennan will challenge that, and his lawyer is good at producing injunctions. The public is riled up, the Banking Federation is watching us like a hawk and so is that damned reporter...that Friedland fellow..." Moretti made up his mind. "No, Schmidt. I prefer to wait for a while."

"Perhaps you've forgotten that, as far as Moretti & Cie are concerned, we have no account opened under the name of this Peter Gombos, the man mentioned by Friedland in his article. The SIL account was opened under another name, and that person may well be related to Roza Stern as far as we know."

In fact, Moretti had indeed forgotten. He continued to temporize. "Leave the papers with me. We'll meet in a couple of weeks and make a decision then."

"Why not now?"

"Let things calm down. Let the public brouhaha settle."

Schmidt stormed out of the room before he lost his cool and strangled the son-of-a-bitch who thought of himself as a decisive executive.

CHAPTER 64

Moretti had a very good reason not to accede to Schmidt's proposal. He was in advanced merger discussions with Jacques Odier.

To keep things simple, they proposed that Banque Moretti buy Banque Odier by issuing 80,000 "A" shares for 100 percent of Banque Odier's stock, thereby valuing Banque Odier as being worth twice the Morettis' holdings in their own bank. This meant that the shareholders of the expanded Moretti & Cie bank would be:

The account owning the SIL shares	230,000	*("B" Shares)*
The Odier group	80,000	*("A" Shares)*
The Moretti family	40,000	*("A" Shares)*
The Public	45,000	*("B" Shares)*
The Stapfer Estate	15,000	*("A" Shares)*
TOTAL	410,000	

Since the "A" shares had ten votes each, control of the expanded bank would rest firmly in the hands of Odier and Moretti as long as the dividends on the "B" shares were paid. This dividend would amount to 11 million Swiss francs (4 percent of 275,000 shares at 1,000 francs each) per year, which the expanded bank could easily afford to pay from its accumulated earned surplus.

Should this dividend not be paid, control of the bank would pass into the hands of the account owning the SIL shares.

So Moretti had nothing to worry about. Even if Clara Stapfer's and all the public's shares voted against him, the Morettis had 400,000 votes, comfortably enough to carry the day at the upcoming AGM.

Thus, getting the proposed merger plan accepted by the shareholders at their annual general meeting would not be a problem.

CHAPTER 65

"We had better be very careful when we visit Jacques Odier the next time. We don't have the best of cases and he is bound to use every misstep on our part ruthlessly against us." Dr. Somary mused in a somber mood. "I think we should write to him, rather than visit him, and say we believe we have the password to account number 35220."

"What would we say?" Jack Brennan was pretty desperate. The Moretti meeting was only a month away, the Moretti board was again controlled by Enrico Moretti (he had the deciding vote even if the votes split into two against two, an unlikely event), the papers he needed to prove that he was the Gombos heir were still not legally perfected, the upkeep of the house he owned in Buffalo and in which he did not live was costing him a fortune, there was hardly any of the cash left of the money Grandma Ilona had left him, his relationship with Elize had put her employment with the Foundation in danger, he needed to go back to Toronto to reintegrate into the office there because the liquidation was winding down...

There was no end to his troubles, the most heart-wrenching of which was the realization that he could not make enough money to support Elize and her brother in Canada, nor could he move to Switzerland because he could not work there.

It was a Sunday morning, and, as usual, they were all having brunch in Elize's kitchen: Kurt, Jack, Elize, Clara Stapfer, and Hilde Somary. It was cold and raining outside — a typical somber early spring day in Zurich — and everyone was feeling depressed.

"We have to take a shot and submit the two passwords Kurt has developed for the Odier account and see whether one of them works. We'd send a copy of the letter to the Swiss Bankers Association to make sure there's no hanky-panky." Somary sounded tentative.

"And what would that accomplish?" Jack wanted to know. "There is probably not much money in the Odier account. We need to access the one at Moretti's."

"I feel strongly that Dr. Gombos must have given the Odier bank some sort of a written paper, a letter or testament, or such-like, for his wife or heirs." Clara Stapfer was insistent. She was still staying with the Haemmerles. Remarkably resilient for her age, she was in Zurich to attend to the business of winding up her late husband's affairs with determination.

On Monday, Dr. Somary wrote Odier, with a copy to the Banking Federation, and a week later, they had their answer: yes, one of the numbers submitted was, in fact, the correct password and would Dr. Somary arrange an appointment with the bank's legal counsel so that the client may be given access to the account.

Four days later, Jack and Dr. Somary met with the Odier attorney who handed Jack a large box that contained almost 1000 statements of the account, one for each month since inception, that the bank had held for pick-up by the owner as per instructions clearly penned on the first — the opening — statement.

The statements were monotonously identical. Each showed an annual receipt of funds from Banque Lamarche, Lambert of 500 dollars and an annual payment to the Moretti bank of a like amount, all as per a standing order marked on each statement.

The first statement also showed the original deposit in Swedish Krone that Gombos had made when he opened the account. The transfer of most of the money to the Moretti bank was reflected in a 1938 statement.

The balance in the account stood at less than a thousand dollars after 150-odd transaction charges had been debited against it.

No letter, no testament, no correspondence. It seemed that the bank had followed Gombos's instructions to the letter: no communication with the owner whatsoever.

A crushing, bitter, soul-destroying disappointment for Jack Brennan and his friends! It was the end of the road to their quest.

CHAPTER 66

After working for the Swiss Bankers Association for over twenty years, Wolfgang Graf knew instantly that he was being handed a very hot potato indeed when his boss, SBA's Chairman, put him in charge of the Moretti investigation. He was sure that at least one of the parties involved (the Morettis, the international press, the general public, the SBA, not to mention that damnable fellow Brennan he had read about in the papers) would find his report's conclusions unacceptable.

Graf's gut told him that whatever his findings, he had better come up with a report that would do two things: appease the international press (which would mean having to deal with the wronged-Holocaust-heir problem sympathetically) and show the world that Swiss private banking principles and practices were humane as befits a society, the Swiss, that prides itself on always extending a haven to those who were being persecuted. He also realized that the latter required a serious distortion of reality.

So he went back to his chairman and requested that he be assigned two full-time assistants and a senior secretary and given six months to complete his findings by the end of which, he was sure, the world would have turned its attention to more weighty things than the Moretti-Brennan affair.

He found that though the purchase by Moretti of SIL in exchange for bank paper (Moretti shares), albeit strictly legal, with all *i*'s dotted and *t*'s crossed impeccably, was unassailable, the valuations used were predatory and smacked of conflict of interest.

Then he turned his attention to the way Moretti was handling the two claims, Roza Stern's and Jack Brennan's, for ownership of the account that held the SIL shares and concluded that, again, the proceedings were unnecessarily intolerant and punctilious.

Graf, an essentially decent man, was troubled by this, especially in light of the fact that, by the time he had gotten to review the situation, all the documentation needed for establishing that Jack Brennan was Dr. Gombos's legal heir had been submitted in proper form, acceptable under Swiss law. But this did not matter in any event because the account in the Moretti bank had not been opened in Dr. Gombos's name and Jack Brennan did not have the relevant password.

It was all water under the bridge. The Moretti annual meeting was long over, the Odier-Moretti fusion had been consummated, a new board, that did not include any representative of SIL, had been elected, and the Roza Stern claim shelved.

Graf felt that he could submit a report in which he would conclude that the rights of everybody had been respected and that legalities had been scrupulously observed.

As for morality — that was not a matter on which he was required to report.

One thing did bother him, though. Why did Roza Stern not follow up on her claim?

CHAPTER 67

Jack and Elize found themselves under unbearable stress. Having had to face the destruction of their cherished dream, they now had to cope with reality: the consequences of having chased a rainbow for almost two years.

For Elize, the consequences were enormous. As expected, she was given the gate six months after the Moretti AGM. Since she could not be dismissed for cause because she had kept a careful record of the praise her boss had heaped on her work during the last ten years, the Foundation had to pay her a separation allowance of one year's salary.

So she had one year to find a job that paid what she earned at the Foundation. Or should she pack it in, marry Jack, sell her house in Zurich, move to Buffalo, and take Kurt with her? This would mean that Jack would also have to make his home in Buffalo — and that would be a wonderful thing. They would be a real family and may be even have a child.

Jack was all for it. He was sure his family would rally around them. Uncle George would find him a well-paying job at the Treasury; he would also make sure that Elize and Kurt would get green cards in short order so they could start earning money almost immediately. Or could they really?

Kurt certainly couldn't. He would no longer have access to his sister's marvelous information network, and his newsletter would lose readership. So he'd have to try for a job as a university professor. But who would want to employ a paralyzed German-speaking professor in Buffalo, New York, however fluent his English may be?

Elize was sick with worry. She feared that she may have to give up her happiness with Jack in exchange for being able to look after Kurt properly by staying behind in Switzerland. A gut-wrenching choice.

CHAPTER 68

Unlike most Swiss men, Wolfgang Graf was a bit of a romantic and, as such, fancied himself as being somewhat like James Bond: a crusading secret agent fighting the bad guys, the rotten apples that gave Swiss banking a bad name. And like most Swiss men, Graf also had a salacious side to his mind.

No way was he going to pass up the opportunity to meet a professional domina, especially since he could charge all the expenses of the meeting to his employer. So he went to Hamburg to interview Roza Stern on a rainy Wednesday afternoon.

He was very impressed by the unexpected elegance of the woman's apartment and beguiled by her voluptuous sexuality.

"A *schluck* of *schnapps*?" she inquired and held up a chilled bottle of Pflümli. Roza, who was under the impression that Graf was some sort of a Swiss financial detective, firmly believed that a person in her position should always be as ingratiating as possible with minions of the law, whatever their nationality may be.

"Don't mind if I do," replied Graf and made himself at home on the sofa.

Roza came around with two thimbles full of the stuff. "*Prosit*," she said. They lifted their glasses in unison and swallowed their drinks in one gulp.

"That's better," sighed Roza as the liquid fire spreading in her gut brought tears to her eyes. "Now tell me," she asked coquettishly, "what can I do for you? Is your visit one of free enterprise or one of professional interest?"

Graf roared with laughter. "I hope both," he said good-naturedly and relaxed. He began to like the woman in spite of himself and the prejudices he had dragged along in his Calvinistic mind.

He began by telling her about the SBA and his job as its chief investigator. Then he talked about the battle for control over the Moretti bank and the bad publicity the SIL case was creating for Swiss banking.

"You may not know this, but the international journalistic crowd is again up in arms about how we Swiss have treated and are continuing to treat Holocaust heirs and their money we are supposed to be holding for them in trust."

"*Die alte Geschichte* — the same old story."

"That's right, the same old story. There are exceptions, of course." He held out his glass for more Pflümli, and Roza obliged.

They drank.

"Such as?"

"You, Roza Stern, you. How come you never followed up on your claim?"

"Because I sold it."

"You what?"

"I sold my claim." Roza Stern then had another *schluck,* poured one for Graf and told him all about her client called Freddy. She also gave him a copy of the agreement she had signed.

At the end of her story, Graf asked her for yet another *schluck* and, beginning to feel pretty mellow, put a question to her for which he didn't really expect an answer. "You wouldn't, by any chance, have a photo of this Freddy, would you?"

"Yes, I would. Last time he was here, we went out for dinner to celebrate the deal, and I asked the waiter to take a picture of us with the camera in my telephone. Let me show you." She handed him her iPhone. The picture was sharp. Graf instantly recognized the man sitting next to her in a garish-looking restaurant.

He was looking at Hans-Ruedi Schmidt, the Moretti executive

vice president and architect of the SIL acquisition by Banque Moretti, whom Graf had come to dislike intensely during his investigation of the transaction.

While she went to make them coffee, he fiddled around with the phone and managed to email himself the picture.

After Graf had left, Roza called Georges, the man from the Wiesenthal Institute and told him all about the SBA investigator's visit.

CHAPTER 69

Graf did not bother to chase down the owner of Reinfeld AG because he knew that his efforts would lead him nowhere. Even if he got the incorporating lawyer to tell him who had arranged for its formation (probably another attorney in the Cayman Islands or the Isle of Man), the company's real ownership would be veiled through the use of bearer shares.

He was pondering about whether to confront Schmidt with what Roza Stern had told him now or wait and dig deeper. Was Schmidt acting alone or in collusion with Moretti? Were the two trying to rip off the legitimate owner of the account? Graf feared that Moretti was certainly in a position to do so — he could produce the required password any time he wished. All he needed was some sort of a likely intermediary, a "beard", who would be willing to help him walk away with a fortune.

Roza, with Schmidt acting as the cut-out, would certainly fit the bill. And hadn't Moretti's bank been in financial difficulties before acquiring SIL for paper? Was Schmidt not following up on the deal with Roza Stern because Moretti felt that the merger with Banque Odier had consolidated his bank's financial position to the point where there was no need to take the risk of committing a crime and getting caught doing so?

Graf put the Schmidt matter on the back burner of his mind and made an appointment to see Jacques Odier. He intended to find out how Odier was handling the bad publicity created by his bank being involved in the Gombos-Brennan Holocaust case.

Odier was effusive. He offered Graf excellent espresso and delicious biscotti, and then he called in his in-house legal counsel.

"All this is a tempest in a teapot," the lawyer started off. "The facts are clear. Dr. Peter Gombos, a Hungarian Jew, opened an account at Odier's and deposited most of his Nobel winnings. Two years later, the bulk of the money was transferred to Banque Moretti to an account, which, we understand, was not opened in Dr. Gombos's name. Odier does not know the name of the account and has nothing to do with it."

"Except that it transfers 500 dollars to it every year," interjected Graf.

"Pursuant to a standing order by Dr. Gombos."

"Have you asked yourselves what the connection between the two accounts was?"

The lawyer gave Graf a dazzling smile. "Come now, *Herr* Graf. You know as well as I that we are not in the speculating business. We have strict rules of conduct. As soon as Mr. Brennan, who, we understand, is Dr. Gombos's legal heir, produced a valid password, we turned over control of the account to him, together with all pertinent documents."

"This took some time." Graf was getting annoyed.

The lawyer sensed it. "Yes, *Herr* Graf it did, mainly because Mr. Brennan took his time about producing a valid password."

"Have you kept copies of the relevant documents and statements, or should I contact Mr. Brennan so that I can inspect them?"

"We anticipated your request and have made copies of the relevant correspondence for you." The lawyer, sounding ingratiating, handed Graf a manila envelope. "After examining it, please do not hesitate to contact me with further questions, if any. As for the account statements, Mr. Brennan has copies, and we, here, have the originals. You are welcome to inspect them at any time."

Odier looked at his watch and got up. "Is there anything else we can do for you, *Herr* Graf?"

"Not for the moment." He got up as well. "Whom do I contact if I felt I needed to see the statements?"

"Call my secretary, *Frau* Fischer. She'll arrange everything for you." Odier's manner was dismissive. "Allow me to excuse myself. I have another meeting scheduled shortly, and I must get ready for it."

CHAPTER 70

In hindsight, Graf reflected as he sat in his office fingering the Gombos file, he had not liked the way the meeting had gone. Here was a situation the centerpiece of which was the Gombos inheritance, about which the international press had raised a huge hue and cry that had, in the end, forced the SBA to open an official inquiry. To characterize the matter as a tempest in a teapot was too facile, almost insulting.

His gut said that something was missing, something was wrong, something was being hidden.

The file in his hand was very thin. It contained only three sheets of paper. The first was a letter from Dr. Hans Arbenz, the Nobel Laureate, to his friend, Otto Graf, Managing Director of Banque Odier, introducing Dr. Gombos to the bank. Wolfgang Graf smiled; Otto Graf had been his paternal granduncle.

The second sheet was a letter from William Brennan, President Roosevelt's special representative in Bern and a friend of Dr. Arbenz. It vouchsafed for Dr. Gombos's character.

The third piece of paper was an account opening form signed by Dr. Gombos.

"How odd," said Wolfgang Graf to himself. "These men were obviously trusted by Gombos and respected by him for their savvy. How come none of them told him to leave some personal note with the bank, such as, perhaps, a letter to his wife in case of his death?"

In most similar cases that Graf had come across, the bank would insist that at least a testament of some kind be lodged with it.

Graf remembered Dr. Arbenz vaguely, having met him but once and only briefly at his own lavish twenty-fifth birthday party. In those long-gone days, a Swiss male became a legally major person and mature enough to vote only after he had reached the age of twenty-five. So a twenty-fifth birthday was a big deal.

He asked his secretary to find out discreetly whether Dr. Arbenz was still alive and well enough to receive him.

The 104-year-old Arbenz was delighted to see him. Although very frail and only able to move about with the help of a walker, he seemed to be alert and very much in control of his faculties.

His opening salvo to Graf was "I suppose you came here because you want to discuss the Odier-Brennan file with me."

Graf was taken aback. "Yes, but how did you know, Professor."

"Don't be obtuse, Wolfgang. I can't see very well, but I have one of my minders read the papers out loud to me every day, and I also watch television. I know where you work and that you're in charge of the Moretti investigation."

"But how do you know about Brennan?"

"I follow the boy's activities closely. His family and I go back a long time. He is the grandson of a very good friend of mine. Besides, his girlfriend drops me a line every now and then. I think she likes me."

"And who would that be?"

"Elize Haemmerle. She used to work at the *Pro Nobis* Foundation and was also a director of the Moretti bank, but she got booted out."

One of Arbenz's minders helped the old man to an armchair and gave him a glass of water. "Out with it, Wolfgang, what do you want to know? Get to the point before I get too tired."

"How is your memory, Professor?" Graf shot back.

"Can't remember what I had for breakfast today, boy, but I remember the war years very well and the good times I spent with Brennan's grandfather and grandmother. Those were memorable days, with us Swiss surrounded by Hitler's hordes."

"Have you ever met a Dr. Gombos?'

"Of course I have. We were colleagues. He and I got the Nobel the same year: 1936."

Graf let out a deep sigh. The old man was right on the ball. "Do you remember recommending to Dr. Gombos that he open an account at Odier?"

"Yes. Your granduncle was the managing director of the bank, and he was my friend, so, naturally, when Dr. Gombos needed to do business with a Swiss bank, I took him to your granduncle. Surely, the bank's files must show that."

"Yes, they do."

"Well, then, why are you asking me about things that you already know? I have no time to waste on idle chatter."

Graf felt badly. The old man had reason to be angry. "You're right, Professor, and I'm sorry." He had to make amends so he took the plunge, but, in his nervousness, he made a mess of how he expressed himself. "One last question: Would you know by any chance if Dr. Gombos left with my granduncle a letter or some sort of writing with instructions for his wife in case he died and could not come back to claim his money personally?"

Professor Arbenz looked at Graf in amazement. "What a stupid question. It was a standard requirement in those dangerous days to leave a testament behind at the bank. Peter Gombos certainly did. He confirmed this to me during our last meal together at the Urania."

Graf went rigid. Nobody at Odier had said anything about a testament, nor had there been a notation on the file about it.

"Are you sure?"

"Don't be dense, Wolfgang, of course I am sure. Remember, I was saying goodbye to a dear and respected friend and colleague whom I knew I would never see again. A sad, almost traumatic occasion, and you're asking me if I remember it. I remember every word that we spoke that day." He held up his wrist. "He gave me this gold watch. I wear it almost every day."

CHAPTER 71

The second Christmas without Grandma Ilona was even tougher on the Rooney family than the first. As always, they had gathered in her cavernous house, now Jack Brennan's, even though Jack's mother had tried to persuade them to hold the Yuletide festivities in *her* home.

They all had said 'no'. They were a proud, fiercely loyal, and stubborn lot who wanted to show Jack and Elize that they were 100 percent behind them and that they would help him in whatever way they could.

In anticipation of selling the house, Jack had applied for a mortgage on it to give him "walkin' around money," as he put it, but he had been turned down. No bank would take the risk, given the economic conditions existing in the United States, to lend money to a virtually unemployed young man, however fine a family he could claim as his own.

Uncle George had solved the problem by arranging for Jack to be awarded a one-year consulting job at the Treasury and by guaranteeing a quarter-million-dollar mortgage loan personally. The plan was to downsize the contents — an enormous job because Ilona, an inveterate hoarder, had accumulated many *objets d'art* and bric-a-brac during a lifetime in her house — and put the property up for sale at a realistic price.

Unfortunately, *realistic* was the key word. The house, in its heyday, had been worth close to 2 million dollars. Jack figured that he'd be lucky to get half that if he wanted to get rid of the place within a year.

As for the SIL situation, Jack had given up hope and watched in silent, impotent fury as the Odier-Moretti cabal commenced the dismemberment of a once proud and humane charitable Foundation.

Matters were also getting to be complicated for Elize. She had not been able to secure an acceptable job in Zurich that met her financial requirements and ambitions as a legal professional, and she, too, needed to start thinking about selling the family home.

Her brother, Kurt, though he tried to hide it, was extremely worried and had developed a nervous tic in his left eye as a result of stress.

It was against this sorry background of travail that the Rooney-Brennan family attempted to bring Christmas joy into the hearts of its members.

CHAPTER 72

Graf had an uneasy Christmas holiday. He kept worrying about the Moretti investigation. A seasoned bureaucrat, he knew that to make accusations, even by innuendo, would spell *finis* to his career at SBA, and he did not want to lose his pension to which he had been contributing for over thirty years.

"I'm going to end up either a bum or a hero," he whispered, an expression he had learned when he had visited Canada and had attended a few hockey games, his favorite team sport.

His problems were certainly not due to a vivid imagination. They were real. Obviously, Schmidt — and, perhaps, Moretti — was a crook. But what proof did he have? There was no provable trail that led from the bent banker to Reinfeld AG, the Lichtenstein company, only the word of a Hamburg prostitute.

Then there was the question of the missing testament. Did it get mislaid accidentally, or was it "lost" on purpose? Jacques Odier was a respected and powerful man in banking circles. When accusing him of misfeasance, one had better be on very solid ground; otherwise, *kaput,* bye-bye job and pension. Arbenz's testimony, even if he survived long enough to attend at court, could be easy to discredit as the mistaken recollections by a 104-year-old man of a conversation that had taken place eighty years ago.

Graf needed something, anything, tangible to hang his hat on if he really cared for justice to be done.

And, funnily enough, he did care. He came from solid Calvinistic stock with a deep sense of values. To him, lying and dissembling were definitely unpardonable sins.

Back at his office the day after Epiphany, Graf was idly leafing through his messages when the phone rang.

"Am I speaking to Wolfgang Graf, the SBA's chief investigator?" The man was speaking passable German, not Schwitzerdeutch, with a distinctly French accent.

"Yes, you are."

"Happy New Year. My name is Georges Riscalla, and I work for the Simon Wiesenthal Institute. I, like you, am an investigator."

"*Ach ein Kollege.*" Graf was pleased. "Happy New Year to you, too. How can I be of help?"

"I happen to be in Zurich for the day, and I would like to meet you, if you're not too busy."

"May I inquire what the subject of our meeting would be?" Graf knew all about the Institute, not exactly a friend of Swiss bankers.

"It concerns the so-called Gombos-Brennan inheritance. I might have some information that may be of interest to you."

Graf's heart skipped a beat, but he decided to watch his step. "Where are you calling from?"

"From the lobby of your building."

The answer pleased Graf no end. "Well, then, come up. I presume you know we are on the sixth floor."

Riscalla wasted no time coming to the point. "One of our informants in Hamburg reported that a man named Freddy was trying to mount a fraudulent scheme to steal the Gombos inheritance. Do you know about this?"

"I do."

"Do you know who Freddy is?"

"I do."

"And do you know that this Freddy, who is the executive vice president of Banque Moretti has, for at least the last three years, been meeting regularly and in secret with Jacques Odier, Moretti's competitor, at a small hotel in Forch?"

"You mean a restaurant."

"No, *Herr* Graf, I mean in a hotel room where they stay for about an hour every time they meet."

"You mean they are lovers?"

Riscalla burst out laughing. "No, *Herr* Graf, they're not."

Graf was, to say the least, puzzled. "What do you think they were doing then?"

"I think — no, I know — that Hans-Ruedi Schmidt has been spying on Moretti on behalf of Jacques Odier for at least three years, telling Odier what his fiercest competitor was planning to do."

"How do you know this, Monsieur Riscalla?"

"My people have been keeping an eye on Herr Schmidt for some time now and have interviewed the hotel's staff. They have also managed to record snippets of the conversations these two gentlemen were having."

This was a shock to Graf. He had not expected to have to deal with yet another case of breach of trust in his investigation. His shoulders sagged. He lifted his hands to his cheeks and began to shake his head. "What a mess, what an awful mess."

CHAPTER 73

Jack was getting ready to take Elize and Kurt to the airport when the telephone rang. Mary Rooney picked it up.

"It's for you, Jack. Sounds like long distance." She held out the receiver for her brother.

"Sorry to disturb you, Mr. Brennan, during your holidays, but I need some information somewhat urgently so I took the liberty of tracking you down. My name is Wolfgang Graf, and I am the SBA investigator in charge of the Odier-Moretti file, a file in which you are indirectly implicated."

Jack was immediately on his guard. The call was totally unexpected and probably meant bad news. He took a deep breath, "How did you find me?"

"I called *Freulein* Haemmerle's house, and her housekeeper gave me this number. I presume you are in Buffalo."

"You presume correctly. Now please tell me what you would like to know because I'm in a bit of a hurry."

"Sorry, Mr. Brennan I will just take a minute. Tell me, when you met Jacques Odier to take control of the account your relative, Dr. Peter Gombos, opened in Odier's bank in 1936, you were given the relevant bank statements and some correspondence relating to the account. Am I right?"

"Very little correspondence."

"Yes, I know, just a couple of letters." Graf was quick to agree.

"And a copy of the form opening the account."

"Right. What about a testament or a letter from Dr. Gombos that he may have left behind for his wife or heirs? Were you given any such documents?"

"I have received no such documents." Brennan was beginning to get angry. What a waste of time.

"Thank you, Mr. Brennan, for your help. Will you be visiting Zurich again soon?"

"Not before Easter, I think."

"Let me know if you do, and we'll have a chat. I would very much like to meet you personally one of these days."

Jack lost it. He slammed down the receiver.

"More bad news?" his sister inquired. She, like all the others, was seriously worried about her brother's state of mental health. Gone was the carefree, charming handsome Irishman, replaced by a perpetually frowning, morose and taciturn individual. She missed the spring in his step, the smile on his face, the twinkle in his eyes.

Mary looked at Elize who was watching Jack. She bit her lip, and tears sprang into her eyes.

CHAPTER 74

Graf spent the weekend brooding about his work. He had never expected to come across such blatant indications of incompetence and impropriety when he had been handed the file, though, for him, the Moretti acquisition had always had a strong whiff of self-serving dealings about it. However, his examination of the details had shown that the transaction was legally *korrekt,* so he was willing to let it pass.

But not the behavior of Schmidt: fabricating false claims in collusion with a German whore, betraying his employer — all that was just too much.

And Jacques Odier, that pillar of rectitude among Swiss bankers! Was he guilty of just a simple administrative oversight, or was Dr. Arbenz wrong? And did it matter? Nobody was getting hurt. Except perhaps the non-existent heirs of a Hungarian Jew.

Graf corrected himself. An heir did exist: Brennan, that objectionable, rude American, but with a powerful family behind him *and* the international press.

What if there really had been a testament, and the bloody journalists found out about it? Turning in a report whitewashing Swiss banking and then being found out later about overlooking blatant evidence of improper behavior would do more harm than good.

There would have to be a scapegoat, and Graf would be it.

These thoughts were rattling around in Graf's head on Monday

morning when, arriving late at the office and out of sorts, he picked
up the Brennan file and stared mindlessly at the copies of the three
documents in it.

Copies, copies, copies. Copies everywhere.

The copies — that was it! The copies of everything that the banks
did, the copies, the copies, the copies. Who made the copies? The
clerks, the secretaries, the office boys, the tellers...everybody.

And where did this mass of paper end up? In the archives? What
archives? Active and passive. Those that were over twenty years
old, were purged — EXCEPT FOR THOSE RELATING TO
ACTIVE NUMBERED ACCOUNTS.

It was a shot in the dark, but worth trying. Graf decided that
he'd go on a fishing expedition and spend some more time question-
ing *Frau* Fischer.

Odier's secretary for over two decades, *Frau* Fischer was a fifty-
five-year-old divorcee with a very strong libido who had developed a
more than passing interest in Wolfgang Graf. This was understandable. Graf, also a divorcee with no children, was tall, intelligent,
had a full head of silver-gray hair, startlingly blue eyes, and a fit look
about him. He was a captain in the Swiss Army Reserve, an organization that had very few commissioned officers, picked not only for
ability but also for reliability. Most of them were, therefore, scions of
old, established families of which the Grafs were certainly one.

When she got Graf's call asking for her help, Fischer put him off
for the following Friday mid-afternoon because she knew that her
boss would not return after lunch. She was intending to drag out the
conversation until six o'clock, the end of the working day, hoping
that she could then talk Graf into taking her to dinner, and if not, at
least for a drink.

On Friday she put on a form-fitting but conservative black dress
that showed off her ample bosom to advantage without looking
vulgar, on top of which she wore a white cardigan because the office
was not particularly well heated. Swiss miserliness. She intended
to discard the cardigan at dinner, thereby putting her charms even
more in evidence.

Graf, who had had occasion to interact with her previously while he was conducting a review of Odier's involvement with the Morettis had to admit that the woman was very attractive and had sensed her interest in him. In fact, he was intending to exploit it.

Things got off to a splendid start with an excellent espresso that they shared sitting in Odier's office. After some inconsequential small talk during which both signaled that, at the moment, neither had any close personal attachments, he gently steered her toward the purpose of his visit.

"Could I please see the originals of the correspondence and the documents relating to the Gombos file?"

She gave him an inviting smile. "I assumed that you would be asking for them, so I had them pulled. You are welcome to look them over at a table I cleared for you near my desk. You do understand, though, that you cannot take any of them with you because they are the originals and the property of the bank."

"But you will make copies for me if I need them, *Ja?*"

"Of course."

Graf leafed through the material and noticed that the woman had also provided him with a certified copy of a Judgment by the *Kantonal Regierung* attesting to Jack Brennan being a legal heir of Ilona Rooney, nee Preisler, as well as copies of the monthly statements right from the very start of the account. He held one up. "These are originals. I presume Mr. Brennan has copies."

"Not quite, *Herr* Graf. We make two so-called originals of each statement. One we keep, the other we send to the client. In the Gombos case, we had been instructed not to send copies of statements to Hungary, so we kept his copies here, to be collected when he came to visit."

"But he never did visit, did he?"

"*Jawohl.* That is so."

"And what did you do with them?"

"We gave them to Mr. Brennan when he took over the account after he gave the correct password and showed *Herr* Odier documentation that he was Dr. Gombos's legal heir."

Graf pretended to make a note. Then he continued leafing through the file and saw that, in addition to the papers he had been given during his previous visit, there were also internal memos in the file — instructions regarding transfers and charges. The early ones bore the initials OG.

He laughed out loud and looked at the woman. "This certainly brings back memories of my youth."

"How so?"

"Look at this. You see these initials?" She came over and stood beside him in such a way that he could not escape noticing both her ample bosom and attractive derriere. She smelled of *Angele,* his favorite perfume for women.

He looked up at her and commented on it. She smiled at him warmly.

"Do you know what they stand for?"

"Of course. Otto Graf. He was the *General Direktor* in Dr.Gombos's time"

"My granduncle."

She pretended delighted surprise. "My goodness me. What a coincidence." Of course, she had known this all along, having carefully researched Graf's antecedents while checking on his marital status.

Graf continued his examination of the documents, this time slowly and thoroughly, and noticed that, in the space for "general remarks" on the account opening form, his grand uncle's initials were preceded by the letters GDT.

He walked over to the secretary. "Who is GDT?"

"Funny you should ask because I asked the same question of my boss. He didn't know, either, so I researched it. Apparently, these were the initials of your granduncle's head clerk. His name was Gerhardt Dietrich Tonelli. He was from the Tessin."

"The Italian part of Switzerland. Lake Lugano is very beautiful."

" *Jawohl.* Unfortunately, I have never been there."

"Then you must go there. It's worthwhile."

She looked at him coquettishly. "With you?"

He laughed. "Perhaps one day," he said and began putting his papers into his briefcase. Then he suddenly stopped. "You know what? I will not take you to Lake Lugano tonight, but if you have time, I'll buy you a drink and dinner. Will you come?"

She was thrilled. "I'll be delighted."

CHAPTER 75

Graf took *Frau* Fischer to the Café Schlauch on Munstergasse. They had a couple of drinks before ordering dinner and wine with their meal so that by the time the main course arrived they were feeling quite mellow and were laughing a lot.

"You know, I almost didn't ask you out tonight." Graf sounded pensive.

"How come? Did you not feel that I wanted you to?"

"I did, I did, but I got distracted with this Signor Tonelli thing. I presume he has retired."

"No, he died."

He winked at her and lifted his glass. "May he rest in peace. For a moment there I thought that GDT stood for *General Direktor, Testament.*"

"It did also. The managing director keeps the testaments of numbered account holders in his office safe. That's why it's *so* big." She laughed suggestively

"Did Dr. Gombos leave a testament behind?" Graf made his question sound very offhand, very casual.

"Of course he did."

Graf addressed his veal chop with gusto and asked, his mouth full of meat, "How can you be so sure?"

Frau Fischer hiccoughed and wiped her mouth. "We had a hell-of-a time finding it six months ago when my boss asked for all

Gombos-related documents. We finally located the whole file in our off-premises storage vault. It contained everything except the letter Gombos left behind for his wife. Then we had to start looking for it."

"How come you knew that you had to?"

"Come on, Wolfgang, use your head. You yourself said that GDT meant 'Testament with Managing Director.' That was the code. Anyway, the envelope was in my boss's safe."

"But you said a letter."

"Letter-shmetter, it's a thick manila envelope with a million red seals all over it. I'm sure it must contain a testament, too. I made a color copy just for the fun of it. It was so retro, string and all."

"Where is it now, Greta?"

"What? The envelope or the copy?"

"Both."

"I suppose my boss gave the envelope to Mr. Brennan when he came to pick up his account, and I kept the photocopy as a souvenir."

"A souvenir?"

"Yes, I am a romantic and sentimental woman, Wolfgang. Imagine, sealing an envelope with hot red wax and pressing your seal into it to stop people from peeking. The smell of melting wax on paper. How cute, how sensuous." She took another gulp of the wine in her glass. "The copy came out beautifully. I'm going to have it framed."

Graf willed himself to sober up while pretending to be tipsy. Slurring his words he asked the waiter for coffee and cognac for two.

His companion agreed enthusiastically. "Good idea, Wolfgang. Let's sober up a bit. We still have lots of work to do tonight." She squeezed Graf's thigh playfully under the table.

CHAPTER 76

At eight o'clock on the dot on Monday morning, Wolfgang Graf and his boss, Andreas Rilke, CEO of the Swiss Bankers Association, met with a subdued, ill-at-ease Greta Fischer at her office to plan how they would confront Jacques Odier when he returned to work after the weekend. They were fortunate in that the man usually arrived no earlier than ten on Mondays so they had time to set things up properly.

For Graf, the weekend had been a whirlwind of activities punctuated by unusual emotional highs and lows.

He had awoken on Saturday morning in *Frau* Fischer's bed, totally disoriented and with a screaming headache. He remembered taking her home at midnight — a respectable hour — and standing in front of the building in which she lived, watching the taxi disappear into the night. She had insisted that he come up to her apartment and had told the driver that they'd call him later.

From there on, matters became hazy in his memory.

They had a few more cognacs and then — well, as far as he could remember — she raped him and he submitted only too willingly. Which he should not have done. It was a breach of professionalism that impacted his objectivity, and he said so to his boss, Andreas Rilke, when they met at an emergency meeting that Graf had called after he had gotten over his hangover on Saturday afternoon.

At first, Rilke would not believe him, but when he saw the color

322   ROBERT LANDORI

photocopy that Greta Fischer had given Graf under protest, he realized that Swiss banking would take yet another major public relations setback if they did not act with speedy decisiveness.

Graf had felt like a cad. Not only had he breached the rules of
professional conduct, but he had also dragged Greta Fischer into the
mess. Remarkably, Fischer did not see things the way Graf did. She
had been incensed when Graf told her that Jack had not been given
the envelope and had urged that the oversight, as she called it, be
remedied immediately, though she did ask that it should be done
without involving her.

Logical.

If she would be found to have committed the greatest sin under
the unwritten rules of employer-employee relationship, blabbing, she
would lose her job. Rilke offered to protect her as long as she cooperated. Which she agreed to do.

Odier arrived a few minutes after ten and had no choice but to
receive Rilke and Graf, though he wasn't shy about showing his
displeasure at having to see unscheduled visitors. As planned, *Frau*
Fischer quickly brought in espresso and biscotti, which eased the
tension somewhat.

Rilke was the first to speak. "*Herr* Odier, we've come to a point in
our investigations where it is impossible for us to continue to forge
ahead without your assistance. Since we knew that you would be
ready to help us, we took the liberty of calling on you unannounced
for which we ask for your forbearance."

Odier, mollified, turned to Graf. "I told you last week that if you
needed help, you should contact my secretary. Could she not provide
the information you're after?"

"Actually, no."

"So what is it?"

Graf leaned across the coffee table toward the banker and showed
him the account opening form. "Just a little formality. Whose are
these initials?" He pointed to GDTOG. The question was intended
to give Odier a chance to redeem himself, but he chose not to.

"My predecessor's. Otto Graf was the managing director, the

General Direktor, of the bank when the account was opened."

"That accounts for the OG, but what about the GDT?"

Stubbornly refusing to realize where he was being led, Odier shook his head. *"Keine ahnung.* No idea." He was getting irritated again.

"Frau Fischer seems to think that those are the initials of the then chief clerk, Gerhardt Dietrich Tonelli."

"So then, that's what they are," Odier said to Rilke and continued haughtily, "How do you expect me to remember every trivial detail of our operations? And this is a pretty trivial matter." He looked at Graf with open hostility. "Certainly not something that deserves barging in here on a Monday morning without an appointment."

"Agreed," intervened Rilke quietly, "but what if GDT meant *General Direktor Testament?"*

Odier turned pale. He suddenly realized what the real reason for Rilke's visit was, but he had already gone too far down the road of pretended ignorance to be able to back out of his predicament. Besides, Rilke had no proof, Odier was sure. The Gombos envelope was safely locked away in the strongbox sunk discreetly into the wall opposite his desk.

He decided to tough it out. "Are you implying that there was a testament in the Gombos case?"

"I'm implying nothing, *Herr Direktor,* just asking."

"What exactly?"

"Was there or was there not a testament or some sort of document left behind by Dr. Gombos for his heirs?"

Instead of striking his head and saying something like "Oh my God, I forgot to give the man the envelope," thereby making it sound like an oversight, Odier walked right into the trap Rilke had laid for him. He said: "I don't really remember, but I don't think so. I would have to check."

Rilke continued to press. "Last week, *Herr* Graf spent considerable time looking over the Gombos file very carefully and found no such envelope. I must, therefore, presume that, if there is one, it must be where such documentation is usually kept for numbered accounts, namely in the safe that you have in this room."

Odier looked very ill at ease. "I'll check." The tone of his voice was tentative.

Rilke took a folded sheet of paper from his breast pocket and laid it on the coffee table. "May I respectfully suggest that, in order to save time and avoid unnecessary publicity, you open your safe here and now and ask your secretary to locate the Gombos envelope, if, of course, there is one."

He unfolded the sheet but did not hand it to Odier.

There was no need to do so.

Odier instantly recognized the photocopy for what it was and realized that he had lost just about everything he had worked for all his life.

CHAPTER 77

In the weeks that followed the confrontation with Odier, Graf had been busier than at any other time during his career. Rilke had given him the Gombos envelope with orders to transmit it to Jack as soon as possible. Graf telephoned Jack who flew to Zurich immediately.

Before giving him the envelope, Graf made Jack sign an agreement in which, for consideration to be mutually determined subsequently, he undertook to assist the Swiss Bankers Association in protecting the good name of Swiss private banking.

Jack opened the envelope and looked through its contents. On the back of the testament he found two penciled lines: Név: Petőfi Sándor; Jelszó: 12247141934 (Gombos had employed the reverse of the English alphabet as the key to the password's code). The name he used for opening the account was that of Hungary's most famous lyrical poet.

Armed with this information, Jack, accompanied by Dr. Somary and Graf, marched down to Moretti's office and took possession of the SIL account. He was then asked to attend a meeting with the SBA's CEO, Andreas Rilke, at which he was formally informed of Roza Stern's identity and her initiative to prevent the miscarriage of justice through involving the Simon Wiesenthal Institute. Georges Riscalla was also present to recount the shameful activities of one Hans-Ruedi Schmidt.

"We now come to a delicate point in our discussions." Rilke

paused and looked at Jack. "Legally, we cannot stop you from revealing the improper behavior of Odier, Moretti, and Schmidt, and you would probably be able to sell your sensational story to this Friedland fellow's employer, the Schneiderman Group, but, perhaps, we could come to some agreement as gentlemen and businessmen...?" His voice trailed off.

Jack was not in a charitable mood. After all, these men had made him suffer, spend money, lots of money, not to mention the emotional strain they had inflicted on Elize, Kurt, and his own family. There was also the irreversible financial damage that they had caused by transferring ownership of an independent Foundation, which he considered to be a sacred trust to be used to help victims of the Holacaust, to Banque Moretti for shares of a bank that was now a small part of a large enterprise.

He shook his head. He insisted on securing a direct say in how this money was to be used. "These men have to be made to pay for what they have done. Somehow I must be allowed to have control of how *my* funds are used in the future."

Then it came to him. Before Rilke could start protesting, he continued with an intensity that surprised all those present. "Here is what I want. First, Odier and Moretti must agree not to pay the dividend on the 'B' shares, which will mean that these shares will have ten votes each at the upcoming shareholders' meeting. This will allow me to name directors of *my* choosing to the board. Second, immediately after the meeting, Odier and Moretti, as well as the Stapfer estate, will voluntarily convert their 'A' shares into 'B' shares, thereby giving up forever their privilege of having ten votes each."

"That's impossible, quite impossible!" Rilke was adamant.

Graf was smiling. He admired the way Jack had seized the moment. "I cannot see why," he interjected. "In fact, this solution is quite elegant. It saves face for Swiss banking and protects everybody's financial interests while penalizing the guilty ones. The non-payment of the 'B' dividend can be justified by claiming that this is being done to preserve capital."

"But it gives control of the bank to Mr. Brennan." Rilke was not buying.

"I am entitled to that," Jack retorted. "Moretti and Odier are not financially impacted. Their penalty is only loss of control since they will continue to have the same equity position as before." He looked Rilke straight in the eyes. "Besides, these conditions are not negotiable."

"Meaning?"

"You either acquiesce, or I go to court, start getting injunctions, and commence criminal proceedings, which will entail far-reaching publicity. Not good for Swiss banking."

Rilke would not back down. "I simply can't see how I can get all this done."

Jack thought fast. "Why not blame everything on Schmidt? I'm sure Odier will want to cooperate."

Rilke understood. He had no way out.

EPILOGUE

With pressure from the SBA's board and realizing that by cooperating they could avoid public opprobrium, Odier and Moretti agreed to all of Jack Brennan's demands.

Of course, Clara Stapfer was glad to help out and was the first to convert her late husband's holdings from "A" to "B" shares.

In a *pique*, Jacques Odier produced Schmidt's defalcation confession and insisted that he be prosecuted. This move backfired badly because at his trial Schmidt spilled the beans about everything: the Roza Stern affair, Odier blackmailing him into spying on Moretti, and his role in buying SIL for overvalued bank paper by hiding Banque Moretti's true financial position at the time of the acquisistion.

As a consequence, both Odier and Moretti had to resign from the board and were barred from serving as directors of any public corporation. Schmidt was condemned to five years of hard labour but was murdered in prison under very suspicious circumstances during the third year of his sentence, the first time in half a century that a prisoner was assassinated while serving time in a Swiss prison.

Jack appointed his uncle George, who by then had retired from his post as Treasury Secretary, to be chairman of Odier, Moretti, & Cie Banquiers and named Wolfgang Graf as its CEO.

Elize sold her house in Zurich. After Jack married her, she and Kurt moved to Buffalo to live in Grandmother Ilona's house. The wedding ceremony was conducted by Jack's uncle, the archbishop of Buffalo, at Our Lady of Victory Basilica. All the men attending were asked to wear kipas.

Elize, Jack, and Kurt became directors of both the bank and the *Pro Nobis* Foundation that runs the affairs of SIL under the capable direction of Helmut Studer. Elize and Jack kept their promise they had made to each other after their visit to Dr. Szilard. Elize is in charge of supervising how the profits of SIL are spent: half is reinvested into the companies that SIL controls; the other half is distributed, in accordance with the terms of a perpetual trust, among needy Hungarian descendants of Holocaust survivors and their families.

Kurt continued to publish his monthly newsletter, which is still in great demand.

Jack Brennan became a frequent special consultant to the U.S. Treasury Department.

ACKNOWLEDGEMENT

I owe a huge "thank you" to my friend, Andre Link, for inspiring me to write a book about banking chicanery involving Holocaust money. The general outline of this book's plot was created by him.

Keith and Claire Norman labored hard to turn the first manuscript of Four Equations into a smoothly flowing and highly readable text.

A panel of friendly enthusiasts lead by Ivan Smith helped perfect the design of the cover.

The folks at FriesenPress, headed by Dana Mills, combined all these elements to create a book that I hope will please the reader.

As for the research required to create a credible background for this very topical and timely tale ... I simply described what I saw as a young boy in Budapest, Hungary during 1944 and 1945, what I experienced in Grand Cayman as a Bankruptcy Trustee in the period from 1974 until 1982 and what I learned about Swiss Private Banking from a distant cousin whose family owned a private bank in Zurich in the 1930's and 1940's.